"Bridget _____ ander and her dating es_ _____ eaves together faith, hun _____ omeone could only after having survived the ordeal herself."

— TRACEY BUMPUS, editor, Salem Publishing

"If you've ever navigated the highways and byways of dating, then you will appreciate *Around the World in 80 Dates*. With realistic characters, witty dialogue, and believable scenarios, it's a novel that accurately reflects the twists and turns a Christian single might take along the path to finding true love. I recognized myself in many of Sydney Alexander's dating predicaments and life choices, and I have no doubt other readers will too! I'd love to take another trip with Sydney and am ready to go wherever her next adventure may lead."

— LAURA MacCORKLE, senior editor, Crosswalk.com

D0669421

AROUND THE WORLD IN 80 DATES

CONFESSIONS OF A CHRISTIAN SERIAL DATER

CHRISTA ANN BANISTER

OUR GUARANTEE TO YOU

We believe so strongly in the message of our books that we are making this quality guarantee to you. If for any reason you are disappointed with the content of this book, return the title page to us with your name and address and we will refund to you the list price of the book. To help us serve you better, please briefly describe why you were disappointed. Mail your refund request to: NavPress, P.O. Box 35002, Colorado Springs, CO 80935.

NavPress
P.O. Box 35001
Colorado Springs, Colorado 80935

ISBN-13: 978-1-60006-177-6
ISBN-10: 1-60006-177-X

Cover design by The DesignWorks Group, Tim Green, www.thedesignworksgroup.com
Cover image by Getty Images
Author photo by Jessica Folkins

Creative Team: Kate Epperson, Jamie Chavez, Kathy Mosier, Arvid Wallen, Pat Reinheimer

This novel is a work of fiction. Names, characters, places, and incidents are either the product of the author's imagination or are used fictitiously. Any resemblance to actual events, locales, organizations, or persons, living or dead, is entirely coincidental and beyond the intent of either the author or publisher.

Banister, Christa Ann, 1976-
  Around the world in 80 dates : confessions of a Christian serial dater
/ Christa Ann Banister.
    p. cm.
  ISBN-13: 978-1-60006-177-6
  ISBN-10: 1-60006-177-X
  1. Single women--Religious life. 2. Christian women--Religious life.
3. Single women--Conduct of life. 4. Single women--Sexual behavior. 5.
Mate selection--Religious aspects--Christianity. 6. Dating (Social
custom)--Religious aspects--Christianity. I. Title.
  BV4596.S5B36 2007
  241'.6765--dc22
                                        2007021513

Printed in the United States of America

1 2 3 4 5 6 7 8 9 10 / 11 10 09 08 07

To Will, my husband, my heart, my forever peaches.
I love walking through life with you.

ACKNOWLEDGMENTS

I would like to thank:

- My mom, who has been such an encouragement to me all these years. I hope this new chapter in Colorado Springs is everything you've dreamed of—and so much more.
- Casey, the coolest brother a girl could have. It's been so much fun hanging out with you since we've been back in St. Paul.
- My sister, Lindsey, the inspiration for Samantha. Here's to success in love and life. I've enjoyed every one of our crazy adventures together.
- Jesse Butterworth, who listened to all my crazy stories in Nashville and encouraged me to write this book. I'm forever grateful.
- Krista Bergstorm, one of my favorite people on the planet. Thanks for your friendship and your servant's heart. I'm so excited about what you're doing in Africa.
- Wendy Lee Nentwig and Melissa Riddle for taking a chance when I was the new kid in town. Thanks for all your encouragement and opportunities in pursuing writing.

- The kind folks at NavPress: Kate, Kris, and Arvid. Thank you for loving this story and for making my dream of having a novel published come true.
- Jamie, my oh-so-patient editor. You rock!
- All my friends and family. Thank you for your thoughts, prayers, e-mails, and phone calls. I love you so much.
- Last but certainly not least (we always save the best for last, right?), I'd like to thank God, the author of life. You've blessed me in more ways than I deserve, and I'm eternally grateful.

CHAPTER 1

IN SERIOUS NEED OF THERAPY

My darling girl, when are you going to realize that being normal is not necessarily a virtue? It rather denotes a lack of courage!

> —AUNT FRANCES OWENS (STOCKARD CHANNING)
> IN *PRACTICAL MAGIC*, 1998

WHEN DANIEL TOLD ME he was in between jobs, I believed him.

And when Michael told me that I was the only girl for him, I believed him too. Well, until I found out he was also dating Jenn, Allison, and Jordyn. Then there was Taylor, who was more in love with his own reflection and his favorite Diesel jeans than he could ever be with me. And Tyler, who didn't have much self-esteem and always wondered if he was good enough. With Ben I was the girl friend, never the girlfriend. See, he was dating Lauren, and while they had almost nothing in common, he wanted to go out with her and have me as a confidante on the side. Now, isn't that a nice arrangement?

Yeah, nice for everyone except me.

After I got over Ben, there was Travis. Tall Travis. He was six foot eight, impossibly sweet, and a medical missionary in training. For once, it wasn't him—it was me, in fact. Or rather, my ambitions. He told me when I was done with "my little writing thing" he'd consider dating me for the long haul. I guess I could see his point: If I was going to have that family of ten he'd dreamt about ever since he was a kid, I was going to have to start as soon as possible. Trouble is, I really loved writing. And I still do.

So good-bye, Travis; hello, Daniel.

Confused yet? Yeah, so am I, and it's *my* story. As we speak, it's six days after my twenty-seventh birthday, and as I was polishing off the rest of the delicious marble cake my friend Kristin made, I realized that after more than ten years of dating, I'm *still* a serial dater. I don't know how this keeps happening, but frankly, it's getting old. Really, why isn't there some kind of support group for my condition? Why are there weekly meetings for Weight Watchers, mystery novel fans, and even knitting enthusiasts (believe it or not, there's a Thursday night knitting club that meets in my church's basement), but not for excessive daters?

In fact, I can just picture it now. *I'm sitting in a circle in a small, sweat-soaked room at a nearby YMCA with other guys and girls just like me: "Hi, my name is Sydney Alexander, and I'm a serial dater." "Hi, Sydney!" they chime back enthusiastically, their sympathetic eyes fastened on my brown ones, wondering how it all went wrong for me. Then one by one, we tell our traumatic tales of love gone wrong.*

And even as difficult as it would be to do that in front of complete strangers, it would be strangely comforting to know I'm not alone.

Now, if you knew me well, which you will very soon, you'd understand that the serial dating route wasn't exactly the plan I'd envisioned. And since we're in the process of becoming such good friends, I'll go the full disclosure route and tell you that I once devised what I thought was a pretty amazing future for myself. Unlike the majority of my Christian college friends, I decided I could forgo the husband for the first couple of years after graduation. Instead, I'd date casually, concentrate on my career, get more involved in church, and pay off that pesky student loan. And since I was being so responsible, maybe I'd save up for a down payment on a renovated downtown loft. And maybe the latest Prada bag. Or a trendy Fendi clutch, depending on my mood.

Of course, after all that was accomplished and I'd traveled to some of Europe's best sights, I'd consider settling down and getting married. Now, of course, there's nothing wrong with having goals. But mine were a bit presumptuous, even if I didn't believe it at the time.

And like most man-made plans (or in this case, woman-made!), things didn't exactly go the way I'd hoped. Quite the opposite, actually. Even if I'd wanted to get married right after graduation, I probably wouldn't have had time. After all, I barely had time to sleep. See, it took me a little longer than I'd scheduled to land a respectable job in journalism, and I was forced to work three not-so-glamorous jobs to make ends meet. So when I wasn't sporting a hideous smock while working the late shift at Walgreens or serving as the requisite errand girl at an upstart music magazine, I was trolling the temp agency circuit to see if I could pick up a gig or two to supplement my less-than-stellar income.

So as you can probably guess, I didn't spring for the loft, a designer purse, or a trip to Paris. But somehow, each month God provided enough funds to pay the rent and stock up on Lean Cuisines, luxuries I learned to appreciate in a hurry.

Three years later, even though I drive a responsible, fuel-efficient Toyota Prius instead of the Lexus SUV I really wanted, proudly own my first condo in the warehouse district of downtown Minneapolis, and have managed to pay off the majority of my student loan, I can't seem to break the casual-dating cycle I once thought was perfect. It's just date after date without any hope of a future. And frankly, I'm beginning to think that prearranged marriages aren't such a bad idea. Seriously.

My mom even suggested as much when she drove over from Wisconsin one Friday afternoon recently. "You know, there was a time when relationships weren't so complicated, Syd," she'd said as we browsed around the juniors department at Macy's in search of a gift for my sister, Samantha, who was about to celebrate her twenty-first birthday. "Before you were born, I could've just arranged for you to marry . . . oh, I don't know . . . Jeff Carson, and that would've been—"

"What? You mean the Jeff Carson who hated me so much that he threw rocks at me so I'd fall off my bike?"

"Maybe that was his way of showing he cared," she'd said with a laugh as she held up a pale pink cardigan. "Think she'd like this?"

"Yeah, I think that color would look really nice on her," I said. "Too bad I can't find a man as easy as we can find the right sweater for Samantha."

"Well, it wouldn't have to be if you just weren't so—"

"Weren't so what, Mom? Picky?"

"To be honest, honey, you are a little picky," she said. "I mean, it's important to have standards, but I think yours are a little out of whack sometimes. It's like you think Prince Charming is the only option."

"So, what sounds good for lunch?" I asked. My mom and I

didn't see each other that often, so an argument didn't really seem worth the trouble.

Okay, before you assume that I'm just another whiny drama queen who likes to complain about men, that's not my modus operandi. But have you ever noticed how men are truly puzzling creatures? Just when you think you *almost* have them figured out, they sprout a new anomaly you never knew existed.

Take my most recent boyfriend, Daniel, for example.

Everything started off perfectly. Okay, maybe not perfectly, but work with me here. I was visiting a friend in Chicago right before Christmas when I met him. I desperately needed a break from the excess of deadlines I had at *Get Away*, the monthly travel magazine I've worked at since I officially turned in my smock at Walgreens. So I decided to do just that—get away—and Chicago is always a great escape. Even if it's just for the shopping on Michigan Avenue, a casual lunch in Greektown, the unbelievable deep dish pizza at Gino's East, or a Cubs game at Wrigley Field, you can always count on having a good time in Chi-town.

And my good friend Drew (he's a writer too) insists on nothing less whenever I am in town. With him, it's go, go, go. After we hit about fifteen thrift shops (his favorite places to pick up odd eighties memorabilia that I *still* can't figure out why he collects) in the course of five hours, I was exhausted. My feet hurt, and I really needed some Starbucks. And after I sighed for probably the fifteenth time in fifteen minutes, Drew decided we'd had enough thrift shop therapy, and we made our way back to his house.

"There's someone you *have* to meet," Drew said as he put away the Bananarama, Bangles, and Pat Benatar records (yes, records) he'd bought. "His name is Daniel. I met him at this battle of the bands thing I was judging the other night for the *Trib*, and I

13

think you'll have lots to talk about. He plays guitar. You know, trying to do the band thing."

That should've been my first clue that things weren't going to work out. Even though there's something unbelievably attractive about a man who plays guitar and sings (and I have plenty of experience with *that*), there's usually a whole slew of problems and psychoses that go right along with it. And most times the guy's desire to land that elusive record deal interferes with all reason and responsibility. That description fit Daniel perfectly, although I didn't realize it at the time.

I ended up meeting Daniel later that evening just as Drew promised, and we did have a lot to talk about. We chatted about movies we liked. Music. Our faith and how we arrived at believing what we did. It was all pretty surface-level conversation, but there wasn't a lull. And before I had a chance to analyze things too much, he asked me to dinner. As I debated whether or not to go, I glanced over at Drew, who had the biggest grin on his face. Clearly, his mission was accomplished.

The next night Daniel and I headed downtown to his favorite Italian bistro. After a basket of bread drowning in olive oil and asiago cheese, a bowl of pasta, and two forks for tiramisu, things were going fine. Nicely, even. I could tell that Daniel was enjoying himself too because he asked a lot of questions and listened intently whenever I spoke. Basically we chatted about nearly every subject two people could talk about. He has a huge, loud Italian family, while mine's relatively small, since my dad passed away when I was a freshman in high school, leaving just my mom, my sister, and me. He likes to read historical fiction; I prefer the classics, chick-lit, and my guiltiest of all guilty pleasures: *Us Weekly* magazine. *Shhh*, don't tell anyone, but I've always been fascinated by how they make the biggest deal about the most trivial matters, like when Paris Hilton went clubbing and got in a fight with her "rival" Lindsay Lohan (but wait — are they friends this week?) or how Renée Zellweger is "just like us" because she doesn't wear makeup when she takes out her trash. It's fluffy reading, for sure, but I've bought one almost every week for years — for its sheer entertainment value.

But what really seemed to be on Daniel's mind more than reading was his band, Mission Space, and his plans for making it big commercially while maintaining his indie artist credibility. Thank goodness I've worked as a music critic, otherwise the debate on whether to get signed or stay a little more underground would have seemed a little esoteric.

"Don't get me wrong, I wouldn't mind having a few mil in the bank and touring with someone like U2," Daniel said. "But I have to stick to my principles. That's why I'm not sure if a record label is right for Mission Space. They'd want to make us a Top Forty pop act, and I hate writing pop hooks with a passion."

"What's wrong with a good pop song?" I asked. "They make people happy."

"Well, that's the trouble," he said. "I'm not happy enough myself to make other people happy."

This also might have been a clue that Daniel wasn't exactly relationship ready — if I'd been paying more attention to what he was saying and less to his quirky sense of humor and cute smile.

As we left the restaurant a couple of hours later, it couldn't have been more beautiful outside. There was a light snow falling and the twinkle of Christmas lights in the distance. Couples walked by arm in arm as they glanced in the decorated store windows. And as I watched them hug, laugh, and hold hands,

I felt that familiar pang of how much I wanted a love to call my own, especially during a time of year when you're very aware of your singleness. I longed to share this incredible Chicago moment with someone, and Daniel just happened to be there. As we made our way to Starbucks for gingerbread lattes to warm us up, he seemed to have read my mind and grabbed my hand.

After a few more hours of sipping coffee and telling stories, Daniel drove me back to Drew's place. As he turned off the key, I got the nervous, slightly nauseous feeling in the pit of my stomach that I always get as a date comes to a close. Just for the record, I've never particularly enjoyed the end of a date (unless the night was truly rotten and I'm finally free of my suffering). You're never quite sure of what will happen or how you'll say good-bye. And for me, a slight control freak, the unknown is a scary, scary thing.

In fact, as Daniel thanked me for a fun evening, I was having a flashback. Last summer I went on a blind date, and after a relatively fun day of hanging out in parks and coffee shops, my date leaned in to say good-bye. While I'm still not sure why, I got so nervous (and not the good kind of nervous, just to clarify) that I said, "It was really nice to meet you; take care" — and I opened the car door at record speed and bolted to the front door faster than I'd make my way through a mall to a shoe sale. In fact, it was such an awful good-bye that Samantha *still* teases me about it. "It's like Hugh Grant's 'surreal but nice' comment to Julia Roberts in *Notting Hill*," she said at the time. "I can't believe you told him to take care. Who says 'take care' anymore? You're never going to hear from him again." And she was right: I didn't. But I was actually sort of relieved, because when it came right down to it, I hadn't really felt any sparks. And how does one recover from a scenario like that, anyway? It wasn't one of my more shining dating moments, to say the least.

Anyway, I didn't tell Daniel that it was nice to meet him. Or to take care. In fact, before I could say anything at all, he pushed my hair away from my face and kissed me. And so began our relationship . . . just like that.

CHAPTER 2

GUESS I'LL MAKE IT A
BLOCKBUSTER NIGHT

A relationship, I think, is like a shark. . . . It has to constantly move forward or it dies. And I think what we got on our hands is a dead shark.

—ALVY SINGER (WOODY ALLEN) IN *ANNIE HALL*, 1977

LIKE MOST PEOPLE IN relationships, however, Daniel and I began ours in the thick fog of denial. For the unacquainted, that's the phase where you both believe the best about how things are going, even if, deep down, you know they aren't right. Or even close. My time with Daniel lasted only about two months, but it felt like a year. And not in that good, nostalgic way. Now, before you think I'm mean or far too melodramatic, let me provide a little context. Remember the part where I told you that he wanted to be a rock star? Well, I thought that meant he worked some other piddly, part-time job to pay the bills while he pursued his dreams. But I was wrong. He didn't work at all.

Like I said in the beginning, when Daniel told me he was in between jobs, I believed him. We've all been there one time or another, right? So while he looked for "steady employment," I happily picked up the tab for dinners, movies, concerts, and everything else that cost money whenever he came to visit. It was the least I could do while he found something, right? Come to think of it, I did the same whenever I visited him in Chicago. And if everything wasn't already awkward enough, I found out that he'd borrowed ten dollars from Drew to get me a Blockbuster gift card for Valentine's Day. After all, nothing says love like free movie rentals.

Hmmm . . . red flags were everywhere. But I was temporarily color-blind.

Basically, no matter when and where I saw Daniel, he was between jobs. And he always provided what he thought were perfectly rational excuses for why this was. One day it was a brilliant new song that required his immediate (read: nonworking) attention. Another day he had just received a "once-in-a-lifetime" opportunity (pro bono, of course) to go on tour and sell T-shirts for an up-and-coming artist, which allowed him more time to network. On yet another occasion, he was offered the opportunity to be an extra in an upcoming Jennifer Aniston movie that was filmed in Chicago. With so much on his plate, he *clearly* didn't have time to work. And I was naive enough not only to go along with it, but to finance it. Call me old-fashioned if you want, but a girl should never have to fund her own dating relationship.

However, it wasn't money—or his lack thereof—that was the last hurrah, as far as I was concerned. See, I'd picked up tickets for a John Mayer concert that I was looking forward to going to with him. We hadn't seen each other in nearly two weeks—since Valentine's Day—and we both agreed it would be a fun night out. But instead of watching the show with me, he tracked down John's road manager and asked if he could go on tour as a guitar tech, while handing out his business cards to anyone who'd take them. Basically, he was networking on our date, and I was livid.

As I stood alone in the back of the crowded club, the thick fog finally lifted: I had been seduced by snowflakes. If it hadn't been Christmas in Chicago, I probably wouldn't have dated Daniel at all. I'd met him in the most romantic of situations, but the warm, fuzzy feelings had nothing to do with him. And yet after countless frustrating moments while we were together, I still tried to make it work in hopes of maybe helping him reach his full potential. Sadly, I've had a bout or two of Florence Nightingale Syndrome in the past. Sometimes you think your influence can help a guy become the boyfriend he has the potential to be. Big mistake.

Daniel must have sensed the end was coming. He told me he was so happy with me that he'd written a pop song just for me. And he even suggested praying together regularly and doing a Bible study by phone each week to incorporate a more spiritual element into our relationship. While that was certainly a sweet gesture, not to mention an essential one if we *were* to continue, I couldn't believe he tried to play the spiritual card. It was too late. Clearly, I couldn't provide what he needed most. Like a lot of guys I've dated in the past, he really needed to grow up and get his priorities straight before he dated anyone again.

So I wished him the best of everything. Then I rented my old standbys, *Four Weddings and a Funeral* and *Sleepless in Seattle*, using my Valentine's Day gift card, and cried. Even though I was relieved that Daniel and I had broken up, I was left with that lingering question: Are there really any good Christian guys left out there?

✳   ✳   ✳

Meanwhile, in Arden Hills about twenty minutes away . . .

Sydney's sister, Samantha, was answering a few questions of her own as she wrapped up her midterm for her Personality Disorders class.

Sam is still a year away from graduating with two bachelor's degrees—one in psychology, the other in communications—but when Sydney needs a shrink (or just some girl-talk), she knows that Samantha, a crackerjack psychologist in training, is wise beyond her years. When it comes to dating, she's a bit more, well, clinical. And don't mistake that for boring! She's just cautious, where Sydney is more of a risk taker.

For instance, in one of her early psych classes she discovered a theory on the correlation between birth order and long-term compatibility. After reading countless case studies on failed relationships between an oldest child and another oldest child or a youngest child and a middle child, Sam is now convinced that in order for a relationship to work for her, she must date an oldest child, which is considered the best match for a youngest child like herself. While she's the first to admit that her devotion to the theory is a little odd, it all makes perfect sense to her. And though it pained her to do so, she once turned down a date with the hottest guy on campus because she found out he was the baby in a family of four kids. She takes this advice *very* seriously.

In fact, she told her sister several times that it wasn't going to work out with Daniel because he was an oldest child—and two oldest children together are doomed to failure. The primary problem is an issue of control. Two oldest children are far too competitive, butting heads at every turn. But a youngest child would provide a necessary dose of balance to Syd's slightly neurotic nature, something she needs from time to time.

As she filled in the last of the little circles on her test and turned it in, Samantha couldn't help but daydream about her favorite oldest child, Aidan. While it wasn't particularly serious yet, they were certainly spending a lot of time together.

Sam and Aidan had met cute like couples do in the best romantic comedies (think *How to Lose a Guy in 10 Days, You've Got Mail*, and *Must Love Dogs*). To earn extra cash, Samantha waits tables at an Applebee's near her school—not exactly the most glamorous gig in the neighborhood, but it helps pay the bills and as a bonus provides some pretty great stories about really bad customers. One particular Saturday night after serving a couple who sent three appetizers back and left a seventy-five-cent tip on a check that she practically comped in the first place—a new low in her waitressing career—she had waited on Aidan and a bunch of his friends. While she instantly noticed how cute he was, it was his kindness when he returned—and return he did, several times that week—that *really* impressed her. Unlike the majority of the customers, he never complained, always left a generous tip (at least 20 percent), and made jokes and casual conversation whenever she'd bring him a refill of Cherry Coke. Needless to say, she looked forward to seeing him sitting in her section.

And when Aidan asked her to church the next week, it was an offer she couldn't refuse. Yet, despite her giddyness, she wondered what Eli would think.

CHAPTER 3

THERE'S WISDOM IN SOUP LABELS?

When you don't have anything, you don't have anything to
lose. Right?

—SAMANTHA BAKER (MOLLY RINGWALD) IN *SIXTEEN CANDLES*, 1984

A FEW DAYS AFTER DANIEL and I called it quits, my next-door
neighbor Rain (yes, she's just as much of a hippie chick as her
name suggests) decided to intervene—without my permission,
of course. As Helen Reddy's "I Am Woman" blared in the
background, she whipped up her typical breakfast of egg whites,
polenta, and tofu sausage, and not so politely told me it was time
to move on with my dating life.

Easy for her to say: She's been seeing her boyfriend, Nate,
for two years now. Kristin (my best friend from college) and I
affectionally refer to Nate as Stinky Nate because, like Rain,
he prefers the au naturel approach to personal hygiene (i.e., no
deodorant, cologne, or probably even soap, for that matter). Truth
be told, Nate has strange thoughts on just about everything. He
says his thinking behind the whole hygiene issue was inspired by
his cat, Curious. One day as he watched Curious clean himself the
feline way—by licking as much of his body as possible—Nate
wondered if there is a more natural way for humans to clean

themselves. So until he figures out what that is, he's stopped showering. And that was five months ago. Five *long* months ago.

"Well, what are you suggesting?" I asked as I glanced over at a framed picture of Rain and Nate. "I don't exactly have any prospects at the moment."

Rain clicked through the address book on her MacBook, occasionally looking thoughtfully over the top of it at me. Finally she snapped her fingers. "I can't believe I didn't think of this sooner . . . Justin! Yes, Justin would be perfect."

"Justin who?" I asked skeptically. After all, this was Rain trying to set me up—Rain, who listens to Billy Joel nonstop, wears her waist-length, dirty blonde hair in pigtails, and decorates her kitchen with Campbell's soup labels as wallpaper. But even though we were polar opposites and I often question her judgment on many matters of importance, she was the first friend I made in Minneapolis. And even when I wasn't exactly new to town any longer, she always called to check up on how I was doing. That kind of friendship, aside from Kristin and Samantha, of course, is a rarity in my life. As outgoing as I am, it's never been easy for me to make friends. Acquaintances, yes; I've always had plenty of those. But true friends, especially true friends who happen to be girls, that's another story.

As Rain ate her atrocious excuse for a breakfast, I surveyed the wall o' soup labels. Since the last time I was over, she'd filled another wall full. Her affinity for soup labels is more than a cheap way of avoiding a trip to Home Depot. Her theory is that every man's personality corresponds with a certain kind of Campbell's. For instance, she's always said her dream man would be split pea because it takes a leap of faith to enjoy it, with its unconventional color and texture and all. But then once you get over the greenness of it, it has a smoky and unexpectedly wonderful taste. Kind of like Nate, I guess.

When I asked her about good old-fashioned chicken noodle soup (my personal favorite), she scrunched up her nose and said a chicken noodle man would be pleasant enough, nicely broken in like an old shoe. He'd lack the excitement of, say, a tomato basil or lemongrass chicken, but he'd be more stable in the long run. When I told her I liked the sound of that, she defiantly shook her head. Apparently, she thought my ideal man would be more along the lines of a meatball alphabet: strong, full of warmth, a favorite with kids, and a lover of words. I liked the sound of that even better.

As for Justin, Rain informed me that he was thirty, cute but not *too* cute, worked at the local PBS station, liked indie rock music, and wasn't a Christian but was "a really good person." He also just ended a two-year engagement and desperately needed to get out of the house after sulking in front of the TV for the past two weeks.

While I certainly felt bad for him, I couldn't help but remember my resolve to not date non-Christians. I knew it couldn't lead to anything lasting, so why even start? I also wasn't a fan of missionary dating, even with its good intentions. Back in high school, my youth pastor had given a sermon on the concept of being unequally yoked, something I'd never really understood until he explained it that evening. He said he knew plenty of girls who dated non-Christian guys, hoping to eventually convert them to Christianity, but that missionary dating seldom worked. And for whatever reason, I heard his voice in my head whenever I considered dating someone who didn't believe as I did.

But Rain was persistent, and after mentally weighing the pros and cons, I decided that dinner with Justin didn't have to be a big deal, right? It was just one meal, not a lifelong commitment.

"So how do we get in touch?" I asked as I snatched a few M&M'S from Rain's candy dish, quite possibly the only normal food she had in the place.

"Remember that pic we took together after the Beck concert last month?" Rain was staring intently at the screen. "Well, I was thinking I could send him an e-mail with that and your e-mail address, and he could probably take it from there."

Sounded simple enough, even though I seriously doubted I'd hear from him. Despite my reservations, I could tell Rain was happy with her matchmaking attempt. She was singing along—loudly—with the Piano Man classic "She's Got a Way" as I made my way out the door.

After leaving Rain's, I glanced down at my oversized pink watch and realized I'd procrastinated away nearly three hours on my deadlines for *Get Away*'s special "Spring Flings" edition. I really needed to get to work—thank goodness I've always thrived on short deadlines. There's just something about a ticking clock that gets my creative juices flowing, and I had three stories due by five. One was about the best coffee shops in Seattle (and trust me, there are plenty of caffeine purveyors to go around in the Emerald City). Another compared the top fusion restaurants in Belize, and the last was "Tips for Scoring Cheap Broadway Tickets in New York City." Even though it's hard to compete with an all-expenses-paid trip to Belize, this story was by far the most fun to research because I saw ten plays in three days without paying a dime. Gotta love job perks like that.

Once my computer started up, I checked my e-mail. I had five—one with discount travel deals at Travelocity, two that assured me that $10,654,341 from a wealthy Egyptian man would be deposited into my checking account as long as I provided my account number ASAP (wouldn't that be nice?), another from my oh-so-neurotic editor (more on her later, I promise), and one from a Justin Stanley.

Who is Justin Stanley?

Ah, yes. It finally hit me as I was about to push the delete button. He was Rain's friend. *Wow, that was quick.*

From: Justin Stanley <ihatebugsandlizards@hotmail.com>
To: Sydney Alexander <salexander@getawaymagazine.com>
Subject: So, Rain told me that . . .

you were cute, and you know what? She was right. I like your picture. I don't know how much Rain has told you about me, but I'm a little out of practice with dating. But I'm willing to give it another chance if you're available tomorrow night?

— Justin

Hmmm, what to do . . . what to do? I'm officially oh for twelve on blind dates, not a great track record. But then again, this would just be for fun — to show Rain, my sister, and all my other nosy friends that I'm ready to give it another go. So I waited a little more than ten minutes, drank a Diet Coke (my third of the day, it's definitely an addiction), and hit reply.

From: Sydney Alexander <salexander@getawaymagazine.com>
To: Justin Stanley <ihatebugsandlizards@hotmail.com>
Subject: Re: So, Rain told me that . . .

First things first, why do you hate bugs and lizards so much that you made your disdain part of your e-mail address? See, you're supposed to be able to protect me from such horrible creatures. Guess we'll have to rule out a picnic for tomorrow night.

By the way, I don't think it's very fair that you got to see my pic, and I haven't seen yours. So that it's truly not a blind date, you'll need to send me over a pic ASAP. Or else.

— Sydney

Then approximately fourteen minutes later, he e-mailed me back.

From: Justin Stanley <ihatebugsandlizards@hotmail.com>
To: Sydney Alexander <salexander@getawaymagazine.com>
Subject: I'm changing the subject line.

If you grew up in Phoenix, you'd understand why I hate bugs and lizards. Also, one of my ex-fiancee's pet peeves was people who had "silly" e-mail addresses. She's anal-retentive and thinks all e-mail addresses should follow a format like yours: first initial, last name @blahblahblah.com. So when we broke up, I decided I needed a silly one for myself, even though we haven't e-mailed each other once since then. Childish? Yes. But at the time it seemed like a really good idea, so sue me.

I don't have a pic to send you, so I'll have to face the wrath you threatened with "or else." But people say that I'm a cross between the Subway guy, Jared, and James Franco from Spider-Man, if that gives you an idea. I'm not the worst-looking guy, but I'm definitely not the best either.

— Justin

Well, that didn't sound too bad. James Franco was pretty cute, with those big puppy-dog brown eyes. But then I remembered that who Justin resembled was less important than whether he and I would find enough to talk about. When you're out with someone new, there is nothing worse than wanting to leave after twenty minutes. Recently, I've even hated revealing personal details like where I grew up, what my family is like, and so on just to make conversation when I *know* I won't see the guy a second time. Really, it is such a waste of time. Why can't there be some sort of panic button you can push when things are going nowhere?

Sometimes I wish I were as bold as Samantha. Whenever she's on a not-so-promising first date, I'm required to check in with her an hour after they meet. If things are going badly, she'll tell him that her boss needs her to come to work immediately or that a friend is sick and needs her to pick up a prescription immediately. Whatever the excuse is, she always adds "immediately" and manages to get out of her bad dates without much fanfare. But I, on the other hand, just can't bring myself to make something up — no matter how horrendous the date is.

Perhaps I need to reconsider my strategy to protect my own sanity.

From: Sydney Alexander <salexander@getawaymagazine.
    com>
To: Justin Stanley <ihatebugsandlizards@hotmail.com>
Subject: Re: I'm changing the subject line.

Thanks for changing the subject line. That other one was really beginning to bother me . . . ha ha. By the way, I don't think your retaliation against your ex was childish by any means. That actually sounds like something I'd do.

I think I can handle Jared the Subway guy meets James Franco. What time were you thinking?

— Syd

PS: My "or else" wasn't much of a threat, just a motivational tool to get you to send a picture. Obviously, I'll have to threaten bodily harm next time.

Since my deadline was getting closer and closer, I forced myself not to check my e-mail again until I was finished. Despite a little extra stress, it was fun flirting a little on the clock, even if my boss's notoriously evil stare kept flashing through my mind as the minutes cruised by.

CHAPTER 4

BREAKING UP BEFORE THE FIRST DATE

Why can't I have a normal boyfriend? Just a regular
boyfriend, one that doesn't go nuts on me!
— CAROL CONNELLY (HELEN HUNT) IN *AS GOOD AS IT GETS*, 1997

While Sydney wasted time cyberflirting . . .

SAMANTHA WAS ENJOYING NONFAT white mochas with Aidan for the third time in a week, something Eli did not exactly approve of—not the mochas, but the fact that she was enjoying them with Aidan.

Eli has been Samantha's best friend since her first year of college, that time of life when one tends to make friends that last for life. And while she and Eli have never dated officially, there's definitely something there that's not platonic. Observing from a cool distance, both her mother—who is generally a little slow to figure out most things of this nature—and Sydney wonder when the wedding will be, even as Samantha chatters on and on about some new guy like Aidan.

What's especially cute (and equally annoying) about the whole Samantha/Eli scenario, however, is that neither of them has ever been gutsy enough to admit his or her true feelings. According to

Eli, there's just too much at stake. In fact, during a particularly introspective moment, he'd written down a few of his concerns in the ratty old journal he keeps in his car's glove compartment.

Why I Can't Date Samantha

1. Getting into a serious relationship could ruin our friendship.
2. I've never had a girlfriend before.
3. My job only pays $7 an hour, which severely limits dating opportunities.
4. I'm not sure how she feels about me.
5. Sometimes she annoys me so much that I want to throw things.

Eli is certain that he cares about Samantha in a more-than-friends way, but his inexperience in relationships causes him to be unsure of how to proceed. Sure, he drops hints from time to time about his feelings and always makes sure to compliment her outfit, especially if she's wearing something he hasn't seen before. He'll drop whatever he's doing to help her — no matter what time it is. Case in point: While he was in the middle of a game of Halo (his highest score yet!), she called to see if he could help take her clogged kitchen sink apart. It was one in the morning. When Eli asked how it got messed up in the first place, she replied that she "didn't know that chicken fat would be bad for the sink." And while he couldn't fathom how she came to *that* conclusion, he got up and went to her place to fix the sink. At one in the morning.

But despite all he and Samantha have been through in college — clogged sinks, changing majors, and nursing her broken heart after a series of breakups — he still can't bring himself to tell her how much he loves her. Or that he's scared she'll move far away after she graduates and he'll never see her again.

Instead, when the conversation gets too heated, he picks a fight—and he's done that a lot since Aidan entered the picture. See, Eli's seen Aidan at the gym, where he seems to flirt more than actually work out. But Samantha assures him he doesn't need to be so protective, and then Eli gets offended and says something along the lines of, "Well, I'm not sure why I bother anyway," and abruptly hangs up. Mature, huh?

Even though Samatha knows Eli has her best interests in mind, she stubbornly refuses to talk to him for the next few days. Then she inevitably feels bad (or Eli does, take your pick), they apologize, and they quickly resume their friendship. And in case you wondered, this happens *all the time*. It's like *Dawson's Creek* meets *Groundhog Day* with an even more predictable plot.

Despite Eli's constant warnings, there is something about Aidan that makes Samantha seriously weak—not only in the knees, but pretty much everywhere. And God only knows why, considering Aidan's background isn't anything like hers. He'd grown up in a Christian home but succumbed in his early twenties to many of the temptations he'd been warned to stay away from. He'd been in jail twice, once for driving under the influence and the other for public drunkenness. When he was arrested the third time for driving without a license (and with more than the legal limit of alcohol in his bloodstream), he was sent to rehab for six months. Thanks to his mom's persistent prayers and long talks with his former youth pastor, Aidan finally turned his life around. It didn't happen overnight, though. It came after nights and nights of regrets about how he'd hurt his parents, his younger brother and sister, and his ex-girlfriend, Sasha. After regret came shame and plenty of tears. He had known the way but abandoned it—and for what?

Aidan isn't sure what it is about Samantha, but she's easy to talk to. She's a really good listener and doesn't judge him, despite the fact that she seems completely straightlaced and probably doesn't have one rebellious bone in her body. Maybe *this* is the girl he should be dating—as opposed to the vacant party girls he's preferred in the past. He loves her big blue eyes and her beautiful smile. He loves the way she talks. Samantha is one of those expressive types who talks with her hands and rattles on about anything—and everything—without missing a beat. And then there is her laugh. Even when it's much too loud, it is positively infectious.

It also amuses Aidan how Samantha puts so much sugar and cream in her coffee that it barely resembles coffee at all. He's thought about taking her out on a real date, to dinner and maybe a movie, but so far they've just met for coffee. And that has seemed fine with Sam.

While this is all endearing, Aidan still feels uneasy—deep in the pit of his stomach uneasy. Bottom line: He is scared. What if this fling with Samantha turns into something lasting? What if she is the right one, the one he'll spend his life with? No, no, no, he just isn't ready for that. So Aidan sticks with smiling, flirting, and sharing his stories. No dinners. No commitment. And without even knowing it, Aidan will break Samantha's heart before long.

Sydney has this theory that guys grow up six years later than girls do, which makes Aidan the perfect age for Samantha. But the cold, hard facts of Aidan have caused her to seriously reconsider the six-year differential. Syd thinks that Aidan is probably ten years behind, which is sad, given the fact that he's already twenty-eight—and while she'll admit it's probably a little unfair to assume he should be at a certain place in life as he approaches thirty, she just doesn't trust him.

Sure, he *is* pretty easy on the eyes with his tall, surfer-like build, wide smile, and piercing blue eyes, and it doesn't hurt his cause that he constantly talks about wanting to be a missionary in India. This is something significant he shares with Sam—she plans to do the same after she finishes college and is already taking mission-readiness classes. But despite a few shared interests and the fun times he and Sam have had together, Sydney suspects that Aidan isn't all that different from lots of guys. He wants his freedom and the girl too. And big sister Syd wonders if his desire to move to India doesn't have more to do with impressing Sam than actually wanting to help.

* * *

Whew, with two minutes to spare I e-mailed my stories to my editor. With those deadlines out of the way, I could finally kick back. But just as I was about to warm up some leftover Chinese takeout and watch an episode of *The Office* I TiVo'ed last week, my cell phone rang. It wasn't a number I recognized, but I picked up anyway.

It was Justin.

We talked for two hours—about his work (he can't wait for the current piranha of a boss to wrap up his two weeks' notice), his family (still together, but he doesn't understand why, since they fight about the silliest things, like who drank the rest of the milk and put the empty carton back in the fridge), his breakup with his fiancée (she was high maintenance and they'd been growing apart for a long time, but he was much too lazy to end it). It all went really well—until he asked me about my faith.

"Okay, I have to ask, Syd, are you more like Rain, who says she's a Christian but doesn't really go to church, or are you one of those die-hard Christians who only dates Christians, marries Christians, doesn't drink, smoke, or lie, and goes to church all the time? Because to be honest, I don't believe in God at all. So if that's a problem, I think we probably shouldn't even go out."

I couldn't help but laugh. He was breaking up with me before our first date. And he also seemed to be hyperventilating.

"Justin, I can't really speak for where Rain's at in her life, but, yeah, my faith is very important to me. It's the most important thing. I try to go to church whenever I can. I don't drink very often, and I don't smoke because I find it repulsive.

"And, yes, you're right, when I do get married, it will be to someone who shares my faith. But I don't think that just because you don't believe in God means we can't be friends and go out and have a good time together. That wouldn't be very cool of me to discriminate, now would it?"

He sounded surprised by my lack of judgment. "Oh, I just thought that might be a problem, and I wanted to be straight with you because I really don't plan on changing."

With that cleared up, we decided to meet at P. F. Chang's on Friday night.

Exhausted from trying to convince Justin that I was a Christian and still relatively normal, I thought about how weird the whole dating thing is. Seriously, dating is hard enough, but when you're a Christian, there are a slew of new factors that come into play.

But at least things are slightly more sane now than when I was in Bible college. While I wouldn't trade my college experience for the world, it certainly didn't help me develop a rational perspective on relationships. I mean, the whole Christian university scene is isolated enough already, but on top of that, people are hooking up like it's a warm spring day on the set of *Bambi*. In fact, I had a few friends on my dorm floor who confessed that finding a man (or, as it's known in Bible college circles, getting the MRS degree) was the primary reason they enrolled in the first place. Now, that's what some might call one expensive dating service!

And even if you actually *had* career goals and planned to use your degree (like me), marriage was usually on your mind — despite the fact that you didn't want it to be. I mean, three girls on my floor actually had a subscription to *Brides* — even though they weren't dating anyone at the moment — in anticipation of the "big day"! You just couldn't escape it because that's what the majority of girls were thinking and talking and obsessing about. And I couldn't help but wonder what was wrong with me when I didn't get twitterpated like the rest of them.

But more and more, I'm beginning to see the wisdom in not getting hitched by the age of twenty-two. Unfortunately, many of those Bible college marriages didn't last long. Olivia and Nick split after four months. Emily and Eric made it eight and a half months. Cassidy and Cameron stayed together a year, had a baby, then called it quits three months later. It was so sad. Thankfully, there were a few good stories too. I have two friends who met in Penteteuch right before Christmas their first semester, got engaged over break, and have been happily married for four years now. I guess when you know, *you know*, right?

Despite the moments of frustration I've confessed to Samantha countless times, I know there are plenty of great things about being single — even in my loneliest moments. For example, I can do whatever I want without having to ask anyone. I can have chocolate chip cookie dough for breakfast ten days in a row. (It's not particularly healthy, but sometimes a girl just craves cookie dough, okay?) Or watch a *Project Runway* marathon or a really bad Lifetime made-for-TV movie without worrying what some guy thinks. Most important, I am free to pursue exactly what God has for me in this season of my life.

And as I curled up on my comfortable IKEA couch with my plate of sweet and sour chicken and watched Steve Carell make a fool out of himself at Dunder Mifflin, I thanked God for all my blessings . . . even (gasp) my singleness.

CHAPTER 5

THE TIMES THEY ARE A CHANGIN'

Life has to be a little nuts sometimes. Otherwise it's just a bunch of Thursdays strung together.

— BEAU BURROUGHS (KEVIN COSTNER) IN *RUMOR HAS IT*, 2005

IT WAS ONLY SEVEN fifteen, and I already suspected that it was going to be one of those days. It all started with a nerve-wracking dream that kept me awake most of the night. Then in my sleep-deprived state, I accidentally jabbed myself with my favorite MAC eye pencil while getting ready for work. And if that sudden burst of pain in my left eye wasn't enough, the tears inevitably started rolling, causing the eyeliner to run right down my freshly applied foundation. Trust me, I was quite the sight to behold.

Despite my best efforts to calm down, I couldn't get that nightmare out of my mind. Like many of my waking thoughts these days, it involved work. Things had been especially tense at *Get Away* lately, and I wasn't exactly sure why. Everyone around the office had a theory, but there just weren't enough facts to string together for me to formulate one of my own. Still, the constant closed-door meetings and muffled whispers of my superiors didn't ease my escalating fears, and whenever I asked my boss what was going on, she'd quickly change the subject and give me more work to do. So needless to say, I'd stopped asking.

In my dream, my boss, the infamous Lucinda A. Buffington—purveyor of evil stares, a fake British accent (Who knows? Maybe she borrowed it from Madonna), and passive-aggressive behavior—caught me e-mailing one of those get-to-know-your-friends surveys back to Kristin, who teaches fourth grade at Maranatha Christian Academy. Since Kristin spends her time with rowdy kids all day, she unwinds during her prep period by forwarding me cutesy poems, links to online quizzes like "Is He Boyfriend Material? Find Out in Ten Minutes or Less," and the aforementioned surveys. While I immediately delete the poems and only take about half of the quizzes, I secretly love filling out the questionnaires, even if they're a complete waste of time.

As Lucinda plopped the third round of proofs on my desk for the upcoming "Italy Extravaganza" issue, she "accidentally" peeked at a couple of my answers—which meant she wasn't particularly understanding when I tried to explain how much fun these things are.

1. FIRST NAME? Sydney
2. WERE YOU NAMED AFTER ANYONE? Not officially, but it would've been cool to be named after Sydney Bristow on "Alias"
3. WHEN DID YOU CRY LAST? Yesterday, when my boss humiliated me yet again in a staff meeting
4. DO YOU LIKE YOUR HANDWRITING? Sure, why not? I type really well in Lucida Grande
5. WHAT IS YOUR FAVORITE LUNCH MEAT? Smoked turkey
6. KIDS? Not yet, but I hope someday
7. IF YOU WERE ANOTHER PERSON WOULD YOU BE

FRIENDS WITH YOU? Of course

8. DO YOU HAVE A JOURNAL? Yes, but I've also discovered the fun of blogging these days

9. DO YOU USE SARCASM? Yes, especially to irritate my boss

10. DO YOU STILL HAVE YOUR TONSILS? Yes

11. WOULD YOU BUNGEE JUMP? Probably not, unless large sums of money were involved

12. WHAT IS YOUR FAVORITE CEREAL? Can't decide on one so I'll go with Frosted Mini-Wheats, Honey Nut Cheerios, or Banana Nut Crunch

13. DO YOU UNTIE YOUR SHOES WHEN YOU TAKE THEM OFF? Yes, doesn't everyone?

14. DO YOU THINK YOU ARE STRONG? Physically? No. Emotionally? Most of the time. Spiritually? That's my goal.

15. WHAT IS YOUR FAVORITE ICE CREAM? Ben & Jerry's Half Baked if I'm being good, Maggie Moo's cinnamon if I'm being bad

16. WHAT IS THE FIRST THING YOU NOTICE ABOUT PEOPLE? Probably their eyes

17. RED OR PINK? Definitely pink

18. WHAT IS THE LEAST FAVORITE THING ABOUT YOURSELF? See #9

19. ANY BROTHERS OR SISTERS? A younger sister, Samantha

20. DO YOU WANT EVERYONE TO SEND THIS BACK TO YOU? Who's everyone?

21. WHAT ARE YOU WEARING RIGHT NOW? Faded blue jeans, a brown and white striped sweater, and my new brown suede boots

22. THE LAST THING YOU ATE? A raspberry Nutri-Grain

bar from my desk drawer

23. WHAT ARE YOU LISTENING TO RIGHT NOW? The graphic designer yelling at one of the editors

24. IF YOU WERE A CRAYON, WHAT COLOR WOULD YOU BE? Magenta

25. WHAT'S YOUR FAVORITE SMELL? Burberry London perfume, fresh-baked bread, or the air just before it rains

26. WHO WAS THE LAST PERSON YOU TALKED TO ON THE PHONE? Justin

27. DO YOU LIKE THE PERSON WHO SENT THIS TO YOU? Definitely

28. FAVORITE DRINK? A frou-frou drink from Starbucks, Diet Coke, Dasani water

29. FAVORITE DESSERT? Creme brulee

30. ROLLING STONES OR BEATLES? The Beatles!

31. WHERE WERE YOU BORN? Ladysmith, Wisconsin

"Well, well, well, it looks like you're far too busy complaining about me to actually work," she began as she tapped her perfectly French-manicured fingers on my computer screen. "So why don't you do us both a favor and pack up your stuff?" And just like that I was out of a job.

Ever have a dream that feels so real that you wake up sweating? Well, that's what happened to me—the whole scenario felt all too real. Maybe it was a sign of events about to unfold. Maybe Lucinda was planning to fire me. What would I do? How would I pay my bills? Why was this all happening?

Okay, Sydney, calm down, it was just a dream. I hopped into my car, cranked up the classical station to sooth my frazzled nerves, and started the familiar fifteen-minute drive to the office.

* * *

Across town . . .

Aidan was thinking about Samantha (something that was happening more and more frequently) as he wrapped up his financial report for Wells Fargo Mortgage, the company he'd been with for three and a half years. The work wasn't inspiring (or even challenging, for that matter), but he didn't mind the luxuries that came with a six-figure salary. However, even with a closet full of snazzy suits, a state-of-the-art seventy-inch plasma screen TV, and the Jag he'd recently acquired, he'd still been considering giving it all up to be a missionary in India.

Truthfully, it was a desire that caught him by surprise. It had all begun when he skipped the Sunday night football highlights on ESPN (since he knew his beloved Vikings had won anyway) and went to church. But instead of his pastor behind the pulpit, a representative from Searching for Justice had spoken about the organization's efforts to rescue children caught up in sex trafficking. Although Aidan had heard a few of these alarming statistics when watching a *Law & Order* rerun a few months before, the horrific stories presented at church that night permanently pierced his heart. He couldn't get the images of all the suffering children out of his head — no matter how hard he tried.

That was a year ago. And while he still felt God's persistent tug on his heart, he wasn't ready to take the plunge and convert intentions to actions. Not yet. Instead, he chose to support SFJ's efforts through generous financial contributions, which Samantha had reminded him "was something" as they'd enjoyed a leisurely afternoon at the park a couple of days before. Now Aidan reflected again how Samantha had this way of encouraging him to do more, to step out of his comfort zone and embrace the call God had clearly put on his life. And when he was with her, he genuinely felt like he could do that. But once he got back into the rhythm of his usual routines, going to India was, well, about as likely as his settling down with a wife and starting a family any time soon. (Although he'd admit—only to himself, of course, since his mother would probably pass out from shock—that Samantha did make a compelling case for at least considering marriage.)

✸ ✸ ✸

When I arrived at the *Get Away* office, I was thrilled to find that I hadn't been fired yet. Aside from another hush-hush meeting going on in the conference room, it was a pretty average day at the office. We met at Starbucks for our morning editorial meeting and brainstormed ideas for our upcoming "London's Calling" issue. I can't wait for that one because London has always been on the top of my list of Places I Absolutely, Positively Must Visit Before I Die. While my coworkers chattered around me, I opened my laptop and pulled up the list.

Places I Absolutely, Positively Must Visit Before I Die

1. London, England (A no-brainer; it's got everything a girl like me could want . . . culture, history, those fabulous British accents)
2. Rome, Italy (I'd have to include Tuscany, Venice, and Florence on this trip, of course)
3. Prague, Czech Republic (I've heard the shopping and Bohemian culture is to die for)

4. Paris, France (How fun would it be to write and drink cappuccinos at a French café like Hemingway did?)

5. The Greek Islands (Three words: cradle of civilization)

6. Madrid, Spain (To check out the culture, of course, or at least the Antonio Banderas look-alikes)

7. Cozumel, Mexico (Well, because I've never been to Mexico, and the brochures we get at the office always look incredible)

8. Anywhere in Hawaii (Seems like beachy-type fun, plus one of my favorite TV shows, *Lost*, is filmed there . . . maybe I'd run into Matthew Fox, Josh Holloway, or that guy who played a hobbit in *The Lord of the Rings*)

9. Tour of the East coast (Particularly Massachusetts, Vermont, and Maine since I haven't been there yet)

10. The Caribbean (Same rationale as #7 minus the Mexico part)

It's funny—even though I get to travel frequently for my job, I still haven't crossed any of these destinations off my list. I was still daydreaming about London when the meeting ended and we returned to the office.

Three hours and three cups of coffee later, I'd officially read all seventy-five pages of copy for the Italy issue three times and signed off on each one. Since I hadn't left the confines of my comfy desk chair all afternoon, save a trip to the kitchen to fill my French press, I was sluggish and desperately needed a break. Just as I was about to check my e-mail, our receptionist/administrative assistant, Nan, who has to be the sweetest, most patient lady on the planet (or at least in the publishing biz), bolted into my office. She shut the door.

"Have you heard the news?" she asked breathlessly.

"What news?" I asked as I smoothed out my black, ankle-length Banana Republic skirt admiringly. I found it on clearance last week for only twenty-four dollars—a steal considering it was sixty-eight dollars to begin with.

"Wow, you *have* been busy!" Nan said with a hearty laugh. "Lucinda walked out today. She got in a huge fight with upper management and stormed out. No notice—just good-bye!"

Words couldn't even begin to describe how happy I was at that moment. I had dreamed that I'd gotten fired, and Lucinda ended up leaving instead. But who was going to be my boss now? What if it was someone even worse? Someone more moody. A worse micromanager. Yikes, it hurt my head to even consider it.

But before I had any more time to worry, Thomas Waggs, the president and publisher, called me into his office for "a little chat."

CHAPTER 6

UNEXPECTED PROMOTIONS AND HEARTBREAK

People are always telling me that change is good. But all that means is that something you didn't want to happen has happened.

— KATHLEEN KELLY (MEG RYAN) IN *YOU'VE GOT MAIL*, 1998

ALTHOUGH *GET AWAY* HAS a fairly small staff for an international travel magazine (there're only thirty-five of us, including the head honchos, sales, marketing, design, and editorial), I've only spoken to Thomas three times (and one of those was during the interview process, so that doesn't even count, right?). It's not that he's unapproachable per se—although his strictly Armani wardrobe definitely gives him an air of being untouchable—but I've heard from very reliable sources (i.e., the other editorial peeps) that he's terribly impatient and despises small talk.

Since I don't know Thomas all that well, small talk would probably be the only way to go. So to avoid extending any unwelcome pleasantries his way, I've always made a point to avoid him at all costs, lest I get the verbal lashing the marketing team faced last Monday morning when they dared to discuss the previous night's Packers/Vikings game instead of new advertising opportunities for *Get Away.*

Feeling a little nervous, I quickly made my way to his well-lit corner office and firmly knocked on the door. "Come in and sit down, Sydney," he said with a hint of a smile. "We've got lots to talk about."

Wasting no time getting started, he began, "As you probably already know, Lucinda made an unexpected departure from the company today, so that leaves a few important matters up in the air."

"Yes, that came as a big surprise to me too," I replied, trying not to sound *too* cheerful. "I wonder what—"

Without providing any further insight, Thomas proceeded in all-business fashion. "After talking it over with the team this afternoon, we've decided to promote you to senior writer. We're confident you won't have any trouble assuming the majority of Lucinda's duties. Then if all goes well in the next few months, we'll officially move you into her position."

I was speechless. And as you know, that doesn't happen often.

"Oh, and we're going to need you to fly to London next week to write and research our cover story for the 'London's Calling' issue. The deadline is a quick turnaround, but you're up to the task."

"Wow!" was about all I could muster. "Thank you so much for the opportunity."

"I know you can do it." He smiled. "Accounting has booked your airfare and hotel. You can get the details from them."

"I will," I stammered. "I won't let you down, Thomas. Thank you. Thank you!"

"You're welcome," he said hurriedly as he rearranged the paperwork on his desk, picked up his leather briefcase (Armani, of course), and left the office for the day.

I couldn't believe it. I was being promoted *and* going to London! How much better could life get?

An hour later I was still reeling with excitement. As I left the office, I suddenly remembered that I had dinner plans with Justin. Under normal circumstances, I would've been far too ecstatic about *having* a date to forget it. But between the events at work and my belief that Justin and I weren't exactly in this for the long haul, I guess I shouldn't have been surprised that our date almost slipped my mind. Despite my misgivings, however, I was happy that I had a couple of hours to head home, and, yes, primp a little. After all, a girl should look her best—even if her date is probably doomed, right?

After checking my mail (two magazines, a Sephora catalog—yay!—and my electric bill) and putting away a giant load of whites that had been sitting in a laundry basket at the foot of my bed for days, I opened the door to my spacious walk-in closet and debated what to wear. I didn't want to look like I tried too hard, so my new knee-length black Marc Jacobs dress and silver-accented Manolo Blahnik knock-off pumps (gotta love outlet stores with great sales) were definitely out. Ditto for my red beaded wrap dress that I'd worn to the Christmas party three months ago. On the other hand, my favorite outfit—plaid pajama pants, an oversized gray hooded sweatshirt with my alma mater's logo on the front, and pink fuzzy slippers—wasn't going to cut it either.

So with what felt like a million options and not much time, I eventually decided on a look that I'd describe as "understated chic" if I worked in the fashion biz. I chose my always-forgiving black pants from The Limited with a silky peasant top that was more cranberry than red and dangly silver earrings with beads that perfectly matched my shirt. My long brown hair was covering my ears, making my choice of earrings irrelevant, so I speedily took a flatiron to it, pulled up the sides, and fastened it with a barely noticeable black barrette. Then with a quick brush of my teeth, a couple of sprays of perfume, and one last application of cherry-flavored lip gloss, I was on my way to P. F. Chang's.

Much to my amazement, I was running early, even after I found a parking spot at Southdale Mall, so I walked over to the nearby Barnes & Noble to scan the newsstand and pick up a new *AP Style Guide*. I was scouting out what a few of *Get Away*'s competitors were spotlighting this month when I felt a tap on my shoulder. And as I turned around, I dropped all the magazines I was holding.

It was my ex-boyfriend, Liam Engleton.

"Surprised to see me?" he said with a laugh as he bent down to pick up the magazines.

Here's a little perspective on just how horrifying it was to see Liam: You see, there's a reason I chose Minneapolis over any other city—and it wasn't for the weather. Yes, I'll admit right now that when I moved to Minneapolis after college, my motives weren't entirely pure, or even work-related. They were, well, Liam-related. I dated him for about six months right after I started working at *Get Away* (a little more than three years ago).

But the story goes back even further. Back when I was still in college, right before my senior year, I moved to Nashville for a summer internship at *7 Ball*, a Christian music mag. I spent the first two weeks organizing the massive file cabinet of artists' press materials (i.e., eight-by-ten glossy photos, CDs, and promotional bios) and getting coffee for the editors (their requests made me wonder if they were shooting for the longest Starbucks order in history: my editor's drink of choice was a grande, extra hot, no foam, two Splenda, sugar-free hazelnut latte) before they finally decided I'd paid my dues and gave me my first writing assignment.

"We need an eight-hundred-word profile on Stars Collide," editor-in-chief Cameron Stringer barked as we walked toward the conference room for an afternoon brainstorming session. "They're recording at the Sound Kitchen, so give their publicist, Jackie Sachs, a call to set things up. Oh — and we need the story by tomorrow morning."

"Sure, I've got it covered," I replied in my most self-assured voice. Of course, that was the exact opposite of what I was feeling. Even as a rookie, I knew Cameron's request was near impossible. Tomorrow morning? Seriously?

When I gave Jackie a call, however, she was more than understanding about the last-minute request. She asked if I could meet the guys at Mafiaoza's for pizza at six. "Sure thing," I said as I googled Mafiaoza's and wrote down the address. Turns out it was only a fifteen-minute drive from the apartment I was renting near Vanderbilt.

And that's when I met Liam, the lead singer of Stars Collide. I wouldn't call it love at first sight, but there was an immediate attraction. Now, I know a writer isn't ever supposed to fall for her interview subject, just like J.Lo wasn't supposed to commit the cardinal sin of falling for the groom, Matthew McConaughey, in *The Wedding Planner*, but my crush on Liam was the rare exception, right? I just couldn't help it. He was incredibly witty, had great taste in music (we shared many of the same favorite bands, mostly British, of course), and the pièce de résistance was the mysterious twinkle in his blue eyes whenever he spoke. Call me sappy, but I hung on every word the guy said. And even with my "professional" hat on, it felt like it was just Liam and me, even if there were four other band members, a manager, and a few other spectators in the room.

Of course, I never believed there was a chance in the world that he'd notice me. But he did. Or at least that's what I discovered the day after our interview when a huge bouquet of red roses arrived at the office as I put the finishing touches on my story. With all eyes on me, I blushed with nervous anticipation as I opened the card.

Roses are red,
Yesterday's interview was fun,
When you get off work on Friday,
Can we have dinner when you're done?
Liam (612) 300-0096

Okay, it wasn't exactly Lord Byron, but sweet all the same.

"So who was *that* from?" Cara Benner, *7 Ball*'s assistant editor, asked.

"Um, no one you know," I answered, stumbling over my words. Thank goodness she took the hint and left me alone, or my career might have ended before it got started.

As you can probably guess, I called Liam back later that day (I chose four forty-five because I wanted to strike that crucial balance between being overeager and aloof), thanked him for the flowers, and took him up on his offer to buy me dinner on Friday. "I hope going out with you isn't a breach of journalism etiquette," he said before asking if I liked Indian food.

"Well, since I am an intern who works for a slave's wages, I'm willing to take my chances," I answered, surprised by the ease of the conversation. "By the way, Indian food sounds great."

After a few minutes of chitchat, the countdown to Friday night officially began. Of course, the week passed at a snail's pace with deadlines and such, but the thought of spending time with Liam kept me going as I dutifully crossed off the tasks on my to-do list. Like any girl with a new crush, I daydreamed about our upcoming date countless times and ran through several scenarios in my mind, wondering how things would go. I hoped the conversation would be as exciting and effortless as it had been during the interview. But the more I thought about it, the more I was convinced that Liam the rock star wouldn't be impressed with little ol' me.

Even back then, Samantha was my confidante. "C'mon, Syd," she said when we spoke that night. "You're gorgeous! You're just used to going out with guys you're not all that wild about. Don't overthink this."

"Ah, there's my favorite little psychologist-wannabe," I replied.

She sighed. "I don't know. It's just obvious that you like him, so you're trying to . . . to sabotage it or something."

Even though my first date with Liam was ages ago, I still remember how nervous I was. I skipped breakfast and lunch, something I never do. I picked at my cuticles relentlessly. At work, I straightened my desk drawers, each and every one. But despite the lightness I felt from not eating, my frazzled nerves, and the rather large knot in my stomach, my fears slowly subsided a few hours later when I opened the door and saw Liam. Dressed in faded blue jeans, a fitted black T-shirt, and black Vans, he looked rock-star casual. "Ready to go, gorgeous?" he asked.

Blushing, I was too nervous to speak as I followed him to his beat-up Land Rover. I know he noticed too because when he opened the car door, he said, "I just call 'em like I see 'em; you look great."

"Thanks," I said shyly. "You don't look so bad yourself."

With pleasantries out of the way, our Friday night together—he took me to Sitar, a great Indian restaurant not far from my apartment—was just as incredible as I'd imagined countless times in my head. Well, it *was* incredible . . . until he told me that Stars Collide was almost finished recording and he'd be heading back to his hometown in a couple of days.

"Oh, so you don't live here then?" I asked, sure that my disappointment was far too transparent.

"Afraid not," he said. "As much fun as it is to hang here, I could never imagine living in Nashville. It would be way too easy for the music thing to consume you. My home's in Minneapolis."

I was seriously smitten. "So you're sure you don't have to do a photo shoot or something before you head home?"

He laughed. "No, that comes much later in the process," he said as he polished off a bowl of mango pudding. "But I'm sure I'll visit sometime before the promo tour kicks off."

"Well, that's no good, I'll be back in school by then—in Illinois."

"You're still in college?" he asked. I could tell he was surprised. Shocked. Disappointed?

"Yeah, I still have my senior year left," I said. He looked so somber all of a sudden.

In retrospect, I should have taken that clue and forgotten all about him. I know now that Liam's parents already disapproved of his "gypsy lifestyle" as a traveling musician and were putting a lot of pressure on him to pursue a "respectable" career. And even though he was twenty-five and liked to believe he didn't care what his parents thought, he really did. He desperately longed for their approval — probably too much. And they were helping him financially too. Contrary to popular belief, having a record deal doesn't necessarily mean you are wealthy — in fact, Liam was still struggling to make his rent payments. He certainly couldn't afford a long-distance relationship with a student, and he knew it.

Oh, if only I'd known all that then!

When he dropped me off at my apartment and kissed me on the cheek, I suppose Liam thought our paths would never cross again. He didn't bother calling or e-mailing. Instead, he just continued crisscrossing the country, enjoying his rising notoriety as a Christian rock star.

I didn't fare quite as well, though. No matter how hard I tried, I couldn't forget Liam. When I wasn't studying or working on my latest column for the *Wheaton Record*, I was wondering if things would've worked out if I'd been a little bit older. More established. Or if we actually lived in the same city. It was a thought that kept me awake all hours of the night, a thought I contemplated time and again in my journal. I even started listening to his music constantly, hoping for a new insight — *what* I'm not really sure, but I was convinced I could find something if I listened hard enough. And my friends — especially Kristin — couldn't help but notice.

Kristin was the first friend I met in college. It was an accident of proximity, really. Her dorm room was across the hall from mine. And on the hot August day I moved from small-town Wisconsin to the "big city," Kristin was moving in too. As usual, I was playing my music much too loud, which certainly got Kristin's attention as she passed by carrying boxes of her stuff. Curious about who would listen to music *that* loud, she poked her head in my open door and said hello. Two hours later, we were still gabbing away and have been great friends ever since.

And I mean really great friends: Almost two years ago she decided, on a whim, to relocate to Minneapolis from Chicago so we could hang out more. Lucky for me they need schoolteachers everywhere, huh? There are loads of amazing things about Kristin, but one of her best qualities is her straightforward, tell-it-like-it-is nature. While I'm not particularly good about being confrontational, Kristin doesn't have any problem telling me when I'm being ridiculous—and she didn't have any problem all those years ago when I was pining after Liam my senior year.

"Stars Collide *again?*" she asked (while rolling her eyes, something that happened more and more as we talked about Liam). "Can't we listen to something else? I'm going to be honest, Syd. It's time for you to move on. I have *never* seen you like this." She was right. I had never been like this about a guy. "If he's going to be a jerk and not bother to write or call, he's not worth your time anyway," she added in her best Dr. Phil voice.

Grrrr. I hated her Dr. Phil voice.

Hoping for *someone* who could empathize with my plight, I called a few old friends repeatedly. But all I got was voice mail. I mean, I knew what Kristin was saying was totally on target, and I appreciated her patience in listening to me drone on day after day. But I still couldn't convince my heart that Liam and I weren't meant to be.

Then one month before graduation, I had an epiphany, an epiphany that Kristin thought was ridiculous. Instead of trying to get a job at a magazine in nearby Chicago, I could try my luck in

Minneapolis. I had to work somewhere, so why not there? A move would certainly provide a nice change of scenery, and perhaps I could finally figure out if Liam and I had a shot. (I'll admit the idea wasn't completely my own. I borrowed it from Felicity Porter, the curly-haired college-student protagonist from another one of my favorite TV shows. There's an episode in which she decides to do the unthinkable and move to New York City to be close to her high school crush, Ben Covington, instead of staying close to home in California. When I saw it, everything seemed clear: All that's truly amazing in life doesn't come without risk, right?)

Of course, what happened on *Felicity* was fictional, and this was *my* life, so things didn't exactly go according to script. Like I said earlier, my first two years in Minneapolis were so consumed with staying above water financially that I didn't have much time for anything but work. But no matter what I was working on, I thought of Liam often. Even though I hadn't seen him in a long time.

Then, shortly after I got the job at *Get Away*, an event of cataclysmic proportions happened. Okay, maybe not cataclysmic, but, hey, it felt that way to me. I was sitting in the upper deck of the Metrodome at a Twins game with my friend Andrea, an editor whose office is across from mine. Of course, we were really only halfway rooting for the Twins (it was a slow, slow game, and we were up one to nothing) while we spent the majority of the evening venting about work-related stuff (like Lucinda's random outbursts). But despite all the complaining, we were having a great time. Sometimes it's just good to let it all out.

As for that cataclysmic part: Midway through the seventh inning, when I tried to flag down the concessions guy (my Diet Coke addiction needed to be satiated, and fast—my head was pounding something fierce!), I thought I saw Liam sitting two rows in front of me, and my heart started to race. So I walked a bit closer, and, yes, it was definitely him. And he was sitting next to a pretty blonde.

I tried my best not to overreact. The Cameron Diaz look-alike could be his sister. A cousin. Or better yet, a friend he'd known forever who understood, as he did, that romance was completely out of the question. Of course, there was no reason why someone as amazing as Liam wouldn't be dating, but I sure had hoped he wasn't.

After I gave Andrea a quick rundown of the situation, she agreed that I must walk over immediately and say hello. She believed that if Liam and I reconnected it would be "one of the defining moments of my life." (She's definitely a kindred spirit: Like me, she's always had a flair for the dramatic.) And while I wasn't convinced it would be a "defining moment of my life," I thought it was worth a shot.

I was nervous — sweaty palm nervous. Even worse, I was sure there were visible pit stains on my white T-shirt and that my lips were all gunky from the chemical reaction of humidity and MAC lip gloss. But that was a chance I was willing to take as I inched toward Liam's row.

With Liam and the mystery woman's heads both turned attentively toward the scoreboard, I had the perfect opportunity to nonchalantly tap him on the shoulder. "Liam?" I said, my voice sounding a little shaky. "So are you rooting for the Twins or the Brewers?"

"Hey, I know that voice, but it can't be . . . Sydney!" Liam nearly shouted as he jumped up and gave me a big hug and a friendly peck on the cheek. "Wow, it's been a long time."

"Yeah, it has. So . . . how are you? What are you doing these days?"

"Oh, the usual: touring, making records. I just got back from Amsterdam," he said excitedly as he played with the flippy ends of his hair. It was still dirty blond with light blond highlights, but it was a lot longer than I remembered. It suited his rock star demeanor.

"How have things been going for you, Syd?"

As I was about to answer, I heard the impatient sigh of someone who felt a little out of the loop. "I think he forgot to mention that he's been busy planning a wedding. Or have you already forgotten, Liam?"

"Of course I haven't forgotten, darling," he said patiently, ignoring the snappy tone of Miss Thang's voice. "Sydney, I'm sorry I didn't introduce you sooner. This is my fiancée, Anneka."

"Charmed," she said as she limply shook my hand and gave me the once-over, surely noticing my pit stains, my unsightly lip gloss, and the fact that I'd skipped my last two weeks of Pilates.

"Well, congratulations," I offered with enthusiasm about as genuine as the small diamond studs in my ears. "When's the big day?"

And before Liam got a chance to speak, Anneka jumped in. "We're getting married in Bora Bora in two weeks," she announced as she smoothed her long hair, making sure I got a glimpse of her three-carat princess-cut diamond ring. "It's going to be amazing. I'm wearing Vera."

Of course she was . . . nothing but a Vera Wang gown would do for someone like her. As I wondered what it was about her (aside from the obvious physical attributes) that captured Liam's attention, let alone his heart, I said, "Well, I'd better get back to the game. Congratulations again. I hope your wedding is beautiful."

Fighting back tears, I walked back to my seat and told Andrea everything. And we left the game shortly thereafter. I still don't know who won.

As you can imagine, I was a mess. The fantasy that brought me to Minneapolis in the first place was over. Liam was marrying Anneka. And there was nothing I could do to stop it.

CHAPTER 7

DO YOU LIKE ME? CHECK YES OR NO.

It's not a date. We're just agreeing to eat at the same table.

—ROSE MORGAN (BARBRA STREISAND) IN *THE MIRROR HAS TWO FACES*, 1996

TAKE TWO ASPIRIN AND you'll feel much better in the morning."

That's what Andrea told me as soon as I got home from the Twins game. Here I'd thought she understood everything so perfectly. But she had no idea how deeply, how profoundly, this whole Liam situation had rocked my world. After pining after him for so long, he was marrying another woman. A woman who couldn't possibly care about him the way I did. Yes, I know I was being melodramatic; after all, I'd only gone out with him once. But I'd spent the last three years fantasizing about him. That counts for something, right?

To be fair, Andrea tried her best to cheer me up. She gave me the whole he-isn't-worth-your-time speech like a pro, but all I could do was cry. I needed air, and I needed it fast. So I grabbed a jacket and my favorite black and white striped scarf and walked around downtown Minneapolis. It probably wasn't the safest thing to do that time of night, but I didn't care. I needed to clear my mind.

While Minneapolis and I were strangers when we met, it didn't take long for me to fall in love with the place. Like the best cities, it never sleeps. There's always something going on, whether it's the Goth kids wandering out of First Avenue after a rock show or the more distinguished types who've dressed up for a night of classical music at Orchestra Hall. There's theater — amateur and off-Broadway alike — and art museums, and for shoppers like myself, there are plenty of places to spend money. And while I've never been much for architecture, I love how the buildings are a mix of old and new design, each having a distinct personality all its own. The IDS Tower is sleek and European, the Foshay Tower vintage and utilitarian. And on Washington Avenue, high-rise apartment buildings and trendy lofts are a stone's throw from industrial mills and old red-brick railroad stations.

On nights when I feel particularly depressed about the state of my life, however, I power-walk (trust me, it's quite the calorie-burning experience) from my condo to Nicollet Mall on Seventh. It's not a mall in the traditional sense. Rather, it's an extended row of restaurants and shops that give those who work downtown something to enjoy between business meetings or during their lunch hour. And for me, it's always been a place to process my thoughts and escape my troubles. A creature of habit, I always start at Wild Pair (where they have the best selection of stilettos and boots in all of Minneapolis) and work my way down toward Macy's.

Since Wild Pair was closed at that hour, I immediately walked toward Rush's, a hip bridal shop that always has the coolest dresses. While I've never been obsessed with wedding dresses the way my Bible college peers were, I love checking out their window display. Sometimes the dresses are outrageous, more feasible on the runway than wearable in real life, but other times they are so beautiful you can't help but stare. Of course, the night I discovered that Liam was no longer an option, I saw the crème de la crème, a silk floor-length, off-the-shoulder gown with gorgeous beading (probably hand-sewn) around the waist and hem. A matching chapel-length veil and blusher and white silk Jimmy Choo heels completed the bridal ensemble, giving it the perfect balance of something old and something new.

I stared at the gorgeous gown and thought of Liam, and a fresh batch of tears streamed down my face. I really thought it was supposed to be me, not someone like Anneka. No matter how disastrous a date was with someone else—and there had been a few—thoughts of Liam had always comforted me. I'd been certain that when I couldn't possibly handle being single one more day, he'd rescue me, and I wouldn't have to worry about dating any longer.

After staring at *the* dress for probably fifteen minutes, I tore myself away and breezed by Crate & Barrel. On a typical day, seeing the assortment of KitchenAid mixers and colorful dishes in the window quickly turns my thoughts all domestic. I dream of making pies from scratch and throwing lavish dinner parties with homemade lobster bisque and cheddar bay biscuits. If I feel especially adventurous, I think about whipping up some chocolate fondue to dip strawberries in for dessert. But that evening, Crate & Barrel was nothing more than a reminder of what I didn't have: domestic bliss.

There were two more stops to go on my tour-de-Nicollet Mall. After ordering hot chocolate at Barnes & Noble, something I never do unless I'm in mourning (don't ask me why, it's just tradition), I walked over to the Mary Tyler Moore statue in front of Macy's. I've always liked MTM, even if I've only seen the show in reruns.

The character she made famous, Mary Richards, was chic (I mean, c'mon, she had a killer wardrobe, even if the majority of it was plaid), classy, and a career woman (in journalism—just like me!), but she often found herself in impossible situations, especially with men. Yet no matter how crazy things got in dating and in everyday life, she was the ultimate good girl, something I could certainly relate to. And as I looked at her in all her bronzed glory, throwing her hat in the air, I thought I might actually make it after all.

* * *

So if you've been following closely, which I'm sure you have, you're probably wondering how in the world I ended up dating Liam when he was about to marry Anneka. Well, as it turns out, saying hello to him at the game *did* have a profound effect on my life—and his. Three weeks after the Twins game, he called me on a Saturday morning to see if I had lunch plans. While normally I would've been elated about such a spontaneous gesture, I was still a little on edge from our last encounter.

"Don't you have a wedding to plan or something, Liam?"

"Actually no," he answered in a hushed tone. "Anneka and I broke up. After seeing her respond to you the way she did, I realized how much we'd grown apart. She was so fixated on the wedding that I'm pretty sure she forgot who she was actually marrying," he added in his best self-deprecating manner. "I guess all the flowers and bridal showers and wedding cake do that to girls, huh?"

"Well, I'm not sure," I countered. "It could've been the fact that she was wearing Vera."

"Vera who?" Liam asked.

I love how guys can be so clueless.

So we went to lunch and picked up right where we'd left off that summer so long ago. And for six months everything was exactly how I'd dreamed it would be. Fun. Romantic. Exhilarating. I didn't even have to make the walk to Nicollet Mall once. Instead, we got to know each other in the same city—go figure—when he wasn't traveling with the band.

And when he was on the road, I'd meet him in various cities (and a few small towns too) from time to time to see him play. Let's just say that in six months I'd logged more miles in Illinois, Iowa, Nebraska, and North Dakota than I ever expected to. But to see Liam, even for only a few hours, it was worth the effort.

But much to my chagrin, the fairy tale didn't last forever. Four days before what would've been our seven-month anniversary, Liam's manager, Stan Sommers, dropped a major bomb during the band's weekly meeting. With the success of Stars Collide's latest radio single, "Superstar," the record label execs thought it was time for Liam and the boys to make their big move to Nashville. Stan said that despite Liam's previous concerns, living in Nashville would be the key to taking his career to the "next level."

And everyone wanted to make it to the "next level," right?

While I wanted to believe that he'd say no on principle (or better yet, for us), somehow I knew it was an offer he wouldn't refuse. And he told me just as much later that night. "It's something I *have* to do, Syd. I can't avoid it any longer," Liam said as he strummed his guitar. "You could always move there too."

Well, I could. But there was the small matter of quitting my job, selling my condo, leaving my church, my friends, and my family, and starting a new life for the second time in three years.

This wasn't exactly a marriage proposal after all; it was a you-could-always-move-there-too. Frankly, I was hurt.

And then, without even giving it much thought, I actually grew a spine. "Wow, Liam. I'd love for us to stay together. . . . I know we could try the whole long-distance thing, but your music is more important than I'll ever be." I paused, and for a moment I allowed myself to hope he'd contradict me. He didn't. "But you gave in to Stan so easily. I just hoped I ranked a little higher on your list of priorities. But I don't, so why don't we just call this what it is — a permanent break."

There was a long silence. He'd even quit running his fingers across the strings of the guitar.

"Well, if that's really what you want," he answered without a hint of sadness. "I mean, I have to think about the long-term. Can't you see that?"

"Yeah, and so do I. Good-bye, Liam."

And I walked out of his apartment and tried to forget him (again) as quickly as I could. Sure, walking out was a little melodramatic, but it had to be done. I'm sure if our breakup had been a scene in a movie, they would've cued Aretha Franklin's "R-E-S-P-E-C-T" by now, and the girls in the audience would've cheered. But unfortunately, as good as it feels to stand up for yourself, getting over someone you love for the second time isn't easy.

* * *

So as you can imagine, seeing him now was, well . . . *hmmm* . . . complicated. "Hi, Liam," I said, my voice a bit wobbly. "You must be in town for a show, huh?"

"Actually, I moved back here a few months ago. Nashville wasn't exactly all I had hoped for."

Gosh, he looked good.

"I'm sorry to hear that," I offered sympathetically. Wow, it was weird seeing him again.

He stared at me intently, his blue eyes sparkling as brightly as they had when we dated. "You look beautiful tonight, by the way. Got a hot date or something?"

"It's actually a blind date, so I'm a little nervous. I'm meeting him in a few minutes."

"You have nothing to be nervous about. I'm sure it'll be great. Well, unless he's a serial killer or something."

"Oh, *thanks*. I'm hoping he doesn't stuff me in his trunk," I said with a laugh. Okay, the ice was thawing a little.

"Hey, I know you have to get going, but can I call you sometime? I hate how things ended between us, and I'd like to—"

"Sure," I interrupted. "Feel free to call anytime. I'll be leaving for London in less than a week though." I took a step backward. A step toward the door.

"I'll give you a call before you go."

I got into the checkout line and took a deep breath. Of all the people living on the same planet, why did I have to run into Liam? I mean, it was nice to see him and all, but I had *finally* moved on.

✻ ✻ ✻

Meanwhile, in a parking lot not that far away . . .

Justin checked himself out in his rearview mirror and wondered what Sydney would be like in person. She sounded nice enough on the phone, even if she seemed a little overspiritual. He wasn't sure what to make of all that—the whole belief in Jesus thing. Sure, like most kids, he'd been to Sunday school a time or two and knew a few Bible stories—Noah and the ark, Samson and Delilah, David and Goliath. But he wasn't sure how that knowledge translated to real life. If God was so great, why did tsunamis happen? Or school shootings, where innocent children died way before their time? Better yet, why were there so many church denominations? It seemed like all these Christians did was fight over silly theological details, even if they roughly believed the same things. He made a mental note to ask Sydney about these issues. That, and why so many smarmy televangelists seemed to be on television all hours of the night. In his opinion, it was people like that who made Christianity about as appealing as the road kill he passed on 35W.

❋　❋　❋

After paying for the style guide, a tin of Altoids, and the latest *Us Weekly*, I made my way to P. F. Chang's. We'd agreed to meet at the bar, but just as I was walking toward the restaurant, a guy got out of a beat-up Toyota Corolla. Noticing his big brown eyes, which were definitely more James Franco than the Subway guy, I knew it had to be Justin. He was tall, slightly muscular, and surprisingly cute, even if his perfectly pressed khakis and navy-striped Polo button-up didn't seem to fit the whole tough-guy persona he'd perfected on the phone.

As I headed toward him, he smiled and extended his hand. "Hi, I'm Justin."

Taking his cue, I shook his hand firmly. "Well, I guess that makes me Sydney."

He laughed, and we didn't say another word as we walked the twenty-five or so steps to the restaurant's front door. After opening the door for me, Justin made a beeline for the hostess's station. "We've got a reservation for two under Stanley," he said to the bubbly blonde greeter who couldn't have been more than seventeen.

"Right this way, you two," she replied as she led us to a small corner table. "Enjoy your meal."

"Oh, we will," Justin offered absently. "I'm starving."

"Me too," I agreed, hoping our conversation would eventually pick up. Because if it didn't, it was going to be a *very* long, very painful night. "So what's your favorite thing on the menu?" I asked. "I always get the same dish."

"Believe it or not, I've never eaten here before. When I go out, I grab a burger, fries, and a few beers at Brit's Pub. This is highbrow for me."

"Well, if you're looking for a recommendation, the kung pao shrimp is delicious."

"What exactly does kung pao mean? It sounds like a karate move."

"Ha! It does have a little kick," I said.

"Ah, kick . . . karate . . . I like how you put those words together. You must be a writer or something."

"Trust me, that wasn't intentional. I'm officially off the clock."

As we continued to make small talk, Justin looked over the menu. After inquiring about the difference between dan-dan noodles and regular spaghetti noodles, he confessed he wasn't good at making decisions—especially at new restaurants.

"No worries," I offered reassuringly. "How about we try a

little of everything since they serve it up family style?" Deciding that would probably be the best way for Justin to sample a variety of items, we settled on chicken lettuce wraps, kung pao shrimp, garlic snap peas, and lo mein chicken.

With ordering out of the way, I wondered what we'd talk about next. Before I could give it any further thought, however, Justin spoke up. "I have an idea. Let's play Twenty Questions."

Vaguely familiar with the game, I asked him to explain the rules, just in case.

"It's pretty simple. You ask a question and I answer. Then I ask a question and you answer. We keep asking and answering until we've each asked and answered twenty questions."

Okay, that sounded easy enough. "And you want me to start?"

"Yeah, I figured since you do interviews for a living, you'd be pretty good at thinking of questions," he said with a wink.

"I'll start off easy. If you were given a free plane ticket to any destination of your choice, where would you go?"

"I like it, you're starting off in neutral territory. Amsterdam," he answered quickly.

"Why Amsterdam?"

"I can't answer that, Sydney; that would be your *second* question." He smiled. "I need to ask you one before I can divulge that information."

"Ah, so you're a militant, stick-to-the-rules kind of guy then?"

"Not exactly," he said. "Okay, it's my turn now. Sydney, why did you decide to become a Christian rather than a Buddhist, Mormon, Hindu, or, heck, even a Scientologist?"

Wow, he certainly didn't waste any time, now did he? But rather than make some snappy retort about the seriousness of his first question, I decided this was a prime opportunity to share my faith—especially since *he* asked rather than me forcing the issue.

"Well, I guess I have my dad to thank for steering me in the right direction," I said. Then I proceeded to tell him how my dad was the first one in our family to become a Christian. "After growing up in a pretty crazy family with ten brothers and sisters and leading a wild life in his twenties and early thirties, he began to wonder if there was something more to life. He just couldn't reconcile the idea of living to die."

Since Justin was still giving me his undivided attention, I told him the rest of the story, that about the time he was thinking about all of this, James, one of his coworkers at the small paper company he worked at, began to tell him about having a personal relationship with Jesus. While my dad thought it sounded a little crazy at first, he saw the joy that James had despite the fact that he didn't have many friends or much in the way of material possessions. What he appreciated about James the most was the little kindnesses. One day James brought him a cup of his favorite dark roast coffee. Another day, it was James' wife's world-famous fudge brownies. And finally, a few weeks later, James brought my dad a Bible.

"My dad wasn't necessarily excited about reading it at first, but one morning he opened up to the gospel of John, just like James had recommended," I told Justin. "Reading about Jesus and learning about the forgiveness that's available through God's unexplainable grace really began to change him and how he thought about things. Before long, he was getting up at five o'clock every morning before work to read more. Eventually, he knew he wanted God's forgiveness for what he'd done wrong in the past, so he prayed with James and became a Christian."

"But how did his decision affect you?" Justin asked.

"I don't know if I can tell you *that*," I said with a smile. "That's technically another question."

"Yeah, you're right," he said. "Maybe you could make an exception."

So I told Justin how the changes in my dad's life were so significant that I couldn't help but notice. How we'd never made it a habit to go to church, then how we went every Sunday. How my dad led Bible studies in our living room at night when my mom was away. "I was only ten or eleven at the time, but even then, I knew there was something different going on," I said.

"Every night he'd ask me, 'Sydney, why wouldn't you want tonight to be the night that you ask Jesus to come into your heart?' I'm not sure why I didn't want that. Maybe I was scared or something. But one night, a night he didn't actually ask, I told him that I was ready. So he prayed with me, and I accepted Jesus into my heart."

And then I told Justin about the most difficult time of my life, the time my faith became more personal—when my dad was diagnosed with terminal cancer at age thirty-six. He wasn't given long to live; there wasn't much hope for healing, although we knew that God was certainly capable of it. But through all the pain he experienced—the chemotherapy, the surgeries, even during the last few months when he had to use a cane to walk—you never heard him grumble or complain. A friend of his who often visited him in the hospital said during his eulogy that he remembered how my dad would sing his favorite hymns and pray for God's will to be done. And if someone could have that kind of faith, even through an unfair ordeal like that, well, I knew that was the God I wanted to serve.

Surely all this was a little more than Justin bargained for, information-wise. But when I looked over at him, I caught him brushing a tear away from his face. "That's a beautiful story, Sydney, I just wish it was that easy for me."

"You wish *what* was that easy?" I asked sympathetically.

"Believing in something. I'm not really into science, but I like tangible proof that things exist—not a feeling or a hunch, something I can see with my own eyes."

And as I was about to give him my best thoughts on the whole faith versus sight issue, our food arrived.

* * *

In a restaurant near the college,
a heart was about to be broken . . .

Aidan shifted uncomfortably in his seat. He'd been thinking about this all day and was just looking for a way to begin.

It had started yesterday. He and Samantha had been on their way to lunch when his phone rang.

"Hi, honey, it's Mom. Did you forget that we had a lunch date today?"

Of course Aidan had forgotten, but he couldn't bear to tell his mother that, so instead he told a white lie. "Um, no, I'm just running a little late. Mind if I bring a friend with me?"

"Of course not, see you in a few," she said.

Once she'd met Samantha, Aidan noticed how her mood quickly changed from chipper to downright euphoric. Like most moms, Aidan's wanted to see her son settled already, something she constantly reminded him of whenever she could. Unlike a lot of her neighbors, she was currently grandchildless and very, very antsy. And it didn't help that Mrs. Winkler had just announced that her son Tyler and his wife, Francie, were expecting their fourth. Four babies? It didn't seem fair to her. Aidan's mom would be thankful for one or even the promise of one.

And in what seemed like a constant reminder of how many little sweaters and blankets she'd knitted for other people's grandchildren, she felt a slight pit in her stomach whenever she stopped by Target and longingly strolled past the baby clothes section. Or whenever she saw a cute baby at the grocery store. Like many moms of a certain age, Aidan's mom wished her son didn't work so much so he'd meet a nice girl and start a family of his own — sooner rather than later.

But meeting Samantha had given her hope. She could tell right away that she wasn't just another pretty girl with mush for brains. She liked her smile and her sunny disposition. Plus, it was obvious that her beliefs were very important to her, something that was also a considerable improvement over Aidan's past girlfriends.

What Aidan's mom didn't understand was that despite her good intentions, the more she nagged, the less likely Aidan was to pursue a serious relationship with Samantha. And while Aidan definitely enjoyed Samantha's company and thought she was an incredible girl, it was much less complicated on his own.

So here he was at Applebee's on a Friday night, waiting for Samantha to get off work. It had become habit to hang out at a back table where she'd join him for late-night snacks when her shift ended. Truth be told, Sam didn't mind staying at Applebee's — as long as she was with Aidan.

But despite how much fun Samantha was having, she couldn't help but wonder what Aidan was thinking. Call it a girl thing or whatever you want—the more time she spent with him, the more she wanted to know. Were they dating? Just good friends? Friends with future potential? From past experience Samantha knew that guys didn't typically waste their time (and money) on someone they didn't care much about. But because Aidan hadn't exactly communicated his intentions, she didn't want to take anything for granted either.

Her friend Gretchen had suggested a DTR. For those unfamiliar with the term, that means *define the relationship*. Some even refer to it as "the talk." But whatever you want to call it, Samantha wasn't about to be the one to initiate it, no matter how much she wanted to know the state of the relationship. She was bold, but that wasn't her style.

Halfway through a gigantic plate of nachos, though, Samantha got her answer. He'd seemed on edge all night, and as soon as he opened his mouth, she knew something was wrong. Whenever Aidan was about to share something unpleasant, he crinkled his brow and spoke in a much softer tone.

"Samantha, I've really enjoyed hanging out," he began. "I haven't had this much fun in a while."

Now Samantha waited for the "but" she knew was coming.

"But I'm not ready for anything serious. It's not you; it's me," he said. "You're amazing; it's just not the right time."

Samantha hated the whole "it's not you; it's me" line. Sure, it sounded great in theory, but Samantha had heard it so many times before that she couldn't help but think it *was* her. But instead of voicing her frustration with Aidan, considering all the time they'd spent together, Samantha wanted to keep things amicable. She wasn't about to lose her cool or another good guy friend just because things didn't work out romantically.

"I understand," she said quietly, hiding her reaction to the emotional sucker punch he'd just thrown her way. "It's better to know now."

Considering how gracious Samantha was being about the whole situation, Aidan could've just dropped the subject. But instead, he felt the need to go on. What *is* it about guys?

"As far as women go, Samantha, you're a Ferrari. You're the exact model that every guy wants. You're beautiful, intelligent, you have everything going for you. You've even got all these little extras that would almost guarantee a great relationship. But even a Ferrari isn't always perfect. The seats are uncomfortable. There's not enough legroom. And there's far too much upkeep involved to keep it in mint condition. Sometimes what a guy really wants is a Honda."

"A Honda?" Samantha asked, her voice growing louder with every word. "Seriously, that's *all*?"

"Yeah, a Honda may not be as flashy as a Ferrari, but it's comfortable," Aidan said. "It doesn't take as much work. You don't feel bad throwing a gum wrapper or your empty coffee cup on the floor of a Honda. But you could never do that in good conscience in a Ferrari."

"Well, as enlightening as all this has been, I've gotta jet," Samantha said as she took a ten-dollar bill out of her purse and threw it on the table. "Just for the record, a woman—any woman—should never be compared to a car. Good luck finding a Honda, by the way. I hear there are plenty to go around."

❋   ❋   ❋

Back at P. F. Chang's, Justin polished off the last of the kung pao shrimp. "This was a good call," he said. "Beats a burger at Brit's any time."

"Well, I'm happy to hear that," I said. "Wanna try some banana spring rolls? The coconut pineapple ice cream that comes with them is to die for."

"I'm pretty sure I can't fit one more thing in my stomach, but why not? You know, 'When at P. F. Chang's . . .'"

"Do as the Romans do?" I asked.

"Yeah, that expression probably doesn't work as well here," Justin said. "You're the wordsmith, after all."

Despite a few (okay, several) awkward moments during dinner, there was something about Justin that was sweet. While I still couldn't believe he asked if I was "the big V" during Twenty Questions, I guess that came with the whole mysterious being-a-Christian territory. Even though it's not something I'd shout from the rooftops, I didn't mind sharing my conviction about something that's so important to me. I've always believed that sex is something not to be considered lightly. I vowed to God long ago that no matter how tempting the circumstances, I'd reserve sex for my husband on my wedding night. And since I hadn't met my hubby yet, well, it was completely off limits. Of course, Justin could hardly believe that was the case, "especially in this day and age," as he put it, but I could tell in some small way he respected me, even if that sort of resolve didn't make any sense to him.

* * *

He was just across the table, but a long way away . . .

Although Justin couldn't relate to Sydney's Christian faith, there was something pure about her that he liked. She was funny and self-deprecating, but she also wasn't afraid to stand up for her beliefs, no matter how insane they were. And even though he probably should have ended the date now, he wanted to spend more time with her.

✳ ✳ ✳

After paying the check, Justin asked if I'd like to browse at Barnes & Noble. "Sure," I said, thinking about my rather memorable visit there earlier.

Justin told me there's just something he loves about bookstores, even though he doesn't consider himself a big reader. He said when he's stressed, "there's something peaceful, calm, and enchanting about them." I told him I couldn't agree more—because reading is one of my favorite pastimes. In fact, if money weren't an object, I wouldn't mind owning a bookstore myself. And if I couldn't do that? A wall-to-wall collection of books in my condo would do.

As we walked through the children's section, we pointed at the books we liked best when we were kids. While I was a Dr. Seuss, Beverly Cleary, and Beatrix Potter fan, Justin said he preferred "anything Curious George" and couldn't get enough of *Old Yeller*.

Then as we worked our way to the young adults section (home of my beloved Judy Blume titles, like *Tales of a Fourth Grade Nothing* and *Otherwise Known as Sheila the Great*), we spotted an endcap with Mad Libs—something I hadn't seen in ages. "I *loved* doing these," I said with a laugh. "I'd try to come up with the most ridiculous stories possible."

"Well, I think we should play," Justin said as he picked up a book called *100 Monstrously Amusing Mad Libs*. After paying for the book, we headed next door to Starbucks and borrowed a pen from the barista. And before long, we were instantly transported back to our youth as we filled in the blanks with adverbs, adjectives, and nouns of our choosing to craft the crazy stories.

Our first Mad Lib went off without a hitch. We laughed uncontrollably as I read the silly space alien–themed story back to Justin. While this was good clean fun, Justin was quick to test the waters with his word choices to see if he could rattle me. Instead of the usual options, he decided to go a more risqué route. At first I didn't say anything as I diligently filled in the blanks with the words he'd chosen. But when I was forced to read it aloud, it didn't take long for my face to turn crimson. Justin must have noticed my embarrassment too because before long, he said, "That's probably enough Mad Libs for one night."

Thank goodness, I thought as we chatted a little longer. But like the Mad Libs, the conversation quickly made its way into TMI territory as he told me about a particularly randy roommate of his. If that wasn't enlightening enough, he confessed his inability to quit smoking pot. Then as I was about to suggest that we call it a night, he looked over at me and said, "I have a great idea."

"What's that?" I asked a little suspiciously.

"Do you have any paper in your purse?" he asked.

As a writer, there's usually a good chance I have a small pad of paper in my purse. And, yes, my reasoning is a bit nerdy. When I see a word or turn of phrase that I like, whether it's in the morning newspaper or a magazine, I write it down. So far I have about twenty-five pages full.

"Yes, I have some," I said as I removed the small leather-bound notebook from my black Nine West bag. "Will this work okay?"

"That's the perfect size," he said before giving further instruction. "Here's what I think we should do. We should assess how things went tonight. First, we'll write a one-sentence impression of the other person. Then we'll draw a solid line underneath and write down whether or not we'd like to see each other again."

Was he kidding?

"So what do you think?" he asked, looking quite pleased with himself.

While my first instinct was to write "NO!" in huge letters, throw the paper at him, and run out of Starbucks immediately, I said, "Sure, we can do that."

So I thought for a moment, picked up my pen, and started writing.

CHAPTER 8

NOTHING SAYS LOVE LIKE A
HEMP ENGAGEMENT RING

Impossible relationships. My special gift is impossible relationships.

— EDWARD LEWIS (RICHARD GERE) IN *PRETTY WOMAN*, 1990

I DIDN'T WANT TO HURT his feelings, but I knew I needed to be honest. Our date hadn't been a total bust, yet we weren't exactly what you might call a match made in heaven either. Some could even say it was a pretty successful ministry opportunity when it was all said and done. But did I want to go out with Justin again? Well, at least it would probably provide for some pretty interesting stories. Who knows? Maybe I could even turn my dating woes into a fiction book loosely based on some of my most traumatic experiences and become a best-selling author. Now, there's an exciting prospect!

But I couldn't think about that now. I needed to decide. I looked over at him and couldn't help but feel sympathetic. First dates are always a little awkward anyway, let alone going out with a girl who doesn't exactly share your worldview. Of course, I knew we didn't have this in common all along, but that didn't mean we couldn't hang out from time to time, right? I might even be a good influence on him, although I didn't want to assume that would be the case.

So I decided that my impression of Justin was this: He was thoughtful, a little nervous, and mischievous. And then I drew the line, crooked, of course, since I've never been able to draw a straight one freehand. Underneath I wrote, "It's worth another chance" with a smiley face next to it. Then I folded it in half and handed it to Justin.

"I think we should read them after we get home," he said with a sheepish grin.

"That's fine with me," I replied as I glanced at my watch. Eleven thirty. Wow, it had been a long day. I slipped his note into my pocket and said good-bye.

❋   ❋   ❋

I slept in until ten thirty the next morning, which is unusual for me, even on a Saturday. For better or worse, I've always been a morning person—with or without coffee. I just can't see the point in sleeping your life away. But what with all the excitement on Friday, I must have really needed the extra zzzs. And next week I was going to London, so it couldn't hurt to rest up.

Today I'd planned to go shopping with Samantha. It had been way too long since we'd seen each other, and we really needed to catch up.

We agreed to meet at the Mall of America at twelve thirty, which is early for a night owl like Samantha. I actually hadn't been shopping for a while (had Visa missed me?), so I was looking forward to checking out the presummer sales (after getting the latest dating dish from Samantha, of course). I had an hour to kill before I needed to head out, so I decided to check my e-mail.

Wow, eighteen new messages. The first was from Justin. As I glanced at his name, I realized I'd forgotten something. That slip of paper from last night's date was still in my pants pocket—unread. I quickly ran to the laundry room and retrieved it, wondering what it would say. But instead of some grand revelation, the only thing staring back at me was a giant question mark in blue ink. After asking me to give my first impression of him and a yes or no on whether I wanted to see him again, all he wrote was a question mark? What a letdown.

I'll admit I was a little upset, but maybe his e-mail would provide a little more clarity. Heck, anything would at this point.

From: Justin Stanley <ihatebugsandlizards@hotmail.com>
To: Sydney Alexander <salexander@getawaymagazine.com>
Subject: Last night

Sydney,

Hope you're doing okay after last night. I wanted you to know that I had a great time. You were so beautiful and poised, and I'll be the first to admit I was intimidated by that and your strong beliefs. But I'm pretty sure we've talked about that enough. I apologize for the moments when I was rude and for my ambiguous note. After suggesting we write down our impressions of each other, I realized that was pretty whacked and had no idea what to say. But I do hope that we can see each other again. Would you be up for a movie before you head to London?

— Justin

Now, I'm not a girl who necessarily abides by traditional dating rules, but I knew it was best not to write him back right away. I'd make him wait a little while. At least until I got home from the mall.

Speaking of the mall, can I just take a moment and say how incredible the Mall of America is? It's another perk of living in Minneapolis, that's for sure. No matter how many times I've been there (and trust me, I've been there a lot), it never ceases to excite me because I'm a born shopper. Having Sephora, Urban Outfitters, H&M, Bloomingdale's, Basin, Nordstrom, Coach, MAC, and so much more all in one place is downright heavenly. Even if I'm trying to save cash and just peek in the store windows.

Okay, there's my moment. Let's move on.

As usual, Samantha and I met at the third floor Caribou Coffee. I could tell immediately that she had a lot on her mind—her hug was perfuntory and limp, not up to her usual hearty standards. We ordered our drinks and quickly sat down at the corner table, typically the prime spot for people watching. But watching the tourists wouldn't be on today's agenda because Samantha clearly needed to talk.

I put on my big-sister voice. "What's up, honey?" I asked.

"So you can tell?" she said with a laugh. "Yeah, last night wasn't exactly the best night of my life."

"Okay, what did Aidan do?" I asked, knowing he was probably the reason she was feeling so crummy.

She proceeded to tell me the story (horrible car analogy included), and I just listened for a change. For some reason, I just wasn't in an advice-giving mood. "So what are you planning to do?" I asked. "And what does Eli think?"

I like Eli. And I've never been a huge fan of Aidan. Sure, Sam liked him, and I'd given him the benefit of the doubt, but there was just something that didn't seem right about him.

"I haven't told him," Sam said. "Don't want to hear 'I told you so.'"

"Do you want to make up with Aidan?"

Secretly, I hoped she wouldn't. The guy just wasn't a keeper.

"I'm certainly not going to be the one to call," she said tartly. "That whole 'You're a Ferrari; I just want to commit to a Honda thing' . . . *errr*, that really burned me up."

Yeah, I can't say I would've been pleased to hear that either. I've been compared to a lot of things in the past, but a car certainly isn't one of them.

After commiserating about our respective Friday nights (for the record, Samantha thought Justin seemed like a relatively good guy, despite his occasional forays into tacky behavior), we walked over to Sephora and bought new eye shadows before heading to Tucci Benucch to satisfy our carb addictions.

After a leisurely lunch, feeling heavy but satisfied, we walked a few laps around the mall. Although we both needed jeans, we skipped a trip to the Gap for fear we'd run into Eli, who works there. One look at Samantha's mopey face would be a dead giveaway that something was wrong, and Samantha just wasn't in the mood for one of his friendly lectures. So instead, we made our way to Bloomingdale's, where Samantha found a striped cashmere scarf for only fifteen dollars. Afterward, I picked up three skirts and a pair of earrings at H&M for less than fifty. You gotta love those end-of-season sales. Satisfied with our purchases, we then decided to kick back and see the latest Hugh Grant flick before Samantha had to leave.

Two hours later we were dabbing tears from our eyes. The

movie was sad. Okay, maybe not as much of a tearjerker as, say, *Steel Magnolias*, but it was melancholy all the same.

"It was so great to catch up," Samantha said as she gave me a hug (and it was a much better one this time). "This was the perfect distraction."

"My thoughts exactly," I replied. "Give me a call before I head to London next week. Let me know what's going on."

"Oh, *London*!" Samantha sighed. "Who knows? Maybe you'll meet Hugh Grant. Or someone just like him."

"Now wouldn't *that* be nice!" I began walking toward the east exit and headed home.

* * *

Three hours later, after three Diet Cokes and three trial attempts at packing my suitcase for London—I figured I'd better start early, and it's a good thing I did, because I just couldn't seem to get all the shoes and boots I wanted to take into my suitcase (imagine that!)—I decided to write Justin back. I didn't want to seem unresponsive to all the sweet things he'd said, but I didn't feel like addressing them either. So I kept my e-mail short and sweet, telling him that I enjoyed (most) of our evening out too and that I'd definitely be up for seeing a movie before I left town.

Not giving it much more thought, I pressed send and went back to packing. Obviously I'd need to pare down. Truth be told, I probably didn't need my black off-the-shoulder dress and matching black and white stilettos, even though they'd be perfect for a dressy night out. Or my gorgeous-but-high-maintenance tan suede skirt that looked so good with my Burberry scarf (after all, wouldn't everyone in London be wearing Burberry? I'd probably look like I was trying too hard to fit in). And given the rainy climate, a flatiron and straightening serum were probably a waste of space too. See, that was much better . . . now just a few more things out, and I was in business.

As I was deciding whether I'd really need five pairs of jeans for less than a week's stay, my cell phone rang. It was Rain. Skipping right past hello, she said, "So are you sitting down?"

"Rain? Actually, no, I'm packing for London—"

She was pretty excited. "Forget it, you don't have to be sitting, I'll just tell you. Nate asked me to marry him last night!"

"Oh, wow—that's incredible! What did he say?"

"It was so sweet," she said. "We were sharing some wheat germ muffins and berries for dessert, and out of the blue, Nate told me that he'd never believed in marriage until he met me. And you know me, Syd, I never cry, but I started bawling like the biggest baby," she continued.

"That must have been some proposal to make *you* cry," I said, still a little in shock. Rain had never seemed like the marrying type. She was "I am woman, hear me roar"—not exactly warm and cuddly wife material.

"Yeah, it was amazing, but I haven't even gotten to the best part," she said excitedly. "Right as I was about to take a bite out of my muffin, there was the ring, right on top of it."

"Uh—" I was wondering how in the world she didn't spot the ring immediately but didn't have a chance to ask.

"It's the most beautiful ring, but I almost swallowed it because it blended in so perfectly with the muffin."

Blended in with the muffin? Most diamond rings I've seen don't exactly blend in with anything.

I had to ask. "How could the ring just blend in? Wasn't it a bit too, um, shiny?"

"No, silly," she answered. "It was made out of hemp, so it blended right in. Nate spent three whole weeks making it for me. He wanted to get it just right."

Hemp. I should've guessed. Not exactly my preference when it comes to engagement rings, but, hey, it fit Rain perfectly.

"So I was wondering, would you be a bridesmaid?" she asked. "We've set the date for next March—probably the second Saturday if everything works out. I'll let you know as soon as we nail down an exact date. We want to make sure we have plenty of time to plan. I want to book a great band for the ceremony and reception, find someone who can make a beautiful vegan cake . . . wow, there's just so much to think about."

Of all my friends, I never would've expected Rain to take so much interest in planning a wedding. She seemed more like the let's-jump-a-plane-to-Indonesia-on-a-Tuesday-afternoon-and-elope kind of girl. Or better yet, maybe she'd get married at a Woodstock revival with Bob Dylan as the minister and "Shelter from the Storm" as her wedding song. But she was actually planning a proper wedding, bridesmaids and all.

"I'd love to be in your wedding," I said.

"Good, good, good," she said enthusiastically. "And you know what's the coolest? You won't even have to worry about paying for the bridesmaid's dress because I'm going to crochet it myself."

"Crochet?" I asked, hoping my lack of enthusiasm wasn't too obvious.

"Yeah, I want this whole laidback hippie vibe," she said. "Trust me; you'll look beautiful with daisies woven into your hair."

Suddenly, being a bridesmaid couldn't have sounded more

unappealing. But I couldn't let her down. "Well, it sounds like you know exactly what you want. And congratulations, by the way. I'm really happy for you two."

"Thanks!" Rain said. "It's a dream come true, Syd. I can't wait for it to happen to you. By the way, how did your date with Justin go?"

"It was okay," I answered. "I'll fill you in on all the details later."

As I hung up and resumed packing my suitcase, I'll admit I felt a twinge of jealousy. Not because she was marrying Stinky Nate, of course. But because she'd found her soul mate — the man who fit her like a glove in all his split pea glory. And here I was dating, dating, and dating.

Sigh.

CHAPTER 9

MYSPACE OR YOURS?

I love this Internet. It's part fantasy, part community, and you
get to pay your bills naked.

— DOLLY (STOCKARD CHANNING) IN *MUST LOVE DOGS*, 2005

Aidan's apartment was a lonely place that day . . .

AIDAN PACED AROUND HIS apartment. He'd intended to
break it off with Samantha, sure—but he hadn't intended to
make her quite so mad. He kept going over and over the scene in
his mind . . . and was desperate to put it *out* of his mind. So he
grabbed the last beer in his fridge and logged on to MySpace.

When he'd first heard of MySpace, Aidan thought all the
buzz about it was just that—buzz. A temporary fad, like William
Hung from *American Idol*. (Remember him?) But one night,
while looking up one of his old college buddies, he noticed one of
the "cool new people" on the MySpace home page, a girl named
Paige. That was all it took; he decided to sign up.

Normally, a tiny picture of someone wouldn't have caused
such spontaneity in a guy who'd learned the hard way to control
his impulses. And besides, Aidan thought he was a bit too old to
have a MySpace page. But there was something about this little

photo, this Paige—an air of mystery that intrigued him. So he'd requested her as a friend. A couple of days later she added him, so he was finally able to send her a message. It was something cute and witty; he couldn't even remember it anymore. She wrote him back an hour later, not scared off at all by correspondence from a complete stranger. And within minutes they'd forged a friendship—albeit in cyberspace.

She lived in Lexington, Kentucky, hundreds of miles away from Minneapolis. They'd talked about meeting in person once or twice, but plans were never solidified for one reason or another. Well, actually Aidan knew why that was: He just wanted to keep things breezy and uncomplicated for a change. No commitments. A couple of months after the first e-mails were exchanged, Aidan had even confessed that he had a crush on someone. A girl he'd met at Applebee's. While that would've been the end of the friendship for some girls, Paige was happy to give him pointers. And since Aidan had no real experience dating girls with any sort of integrity, he'd happily accepted Paige's advice on the matter. (It's possible that Paige had an agenda of her own. Maybe she hoped their online intimacy would give her a shot. She loved reading his e-mails and kept him talking with advice about girls. Her life wasn't exactly exciting.)

In fact, Paige was to blame for the whole Ferrari/Honda fiasco. He'd logged on to MySpace before heading to Applebee's. Not surprisingly, Paige was online. So he'd typed her a message about how he needed to have "the talk" with Samantha. He wanted to let her down gently, so he thought of this car analogy. It conveyed that he really did care about her but wasn't ready to invest in someone of her caliber—or so he thought.

And Paige had told him it was brilliant. "That's the perfect way to let her down," she'd written. "Nice and gentle."

Since Paige had been right about everything else, Aidan had run with it. And boy, had it backfired. Big time. He could blame his lapse in judgment on Paige. But deep down in his heart he knew he'd really messed things up with Samantha. Probably permanently.

Meanwhile, Paige couldn't have been happier with the news. Aidan had been an unexpected surprise right after her six-year relationship with her high school sweetheart had gone kaput. She was amazed how quickly she could fall for someone again; even if their interaction only happened online, it felt very, very real. Paige was an entry-level reporter at a small-town newspaper near Lexington, and she covered all the beats reserved for the people on the bottom of the totem pole. She checked in daily with the fire department, weekly with the school board, and for "special" assignments, she'd check on speeding tickets and traffic fatalities at the local police department. She even wrote obituaries. She'd studied journalism at Northwestern University, and this wasn't exactly what she'd envisioned. But maybe Aidan would take her away from all that. Now, if she only knew what he was thinking.

❋   ❋   ❋

Back in Samantha's neighborhood . . .

When she got back from the mall, Samantha checked her own MySpace. Looking at her home page, Samantha noticed that Aidan was online and made a mental note to change her Top 8 friends. He was currently in the number one slot, which was hardly representative of how she felt about him right now. But even though she was still angry with him, she couldn't resist clicking on his pic and perusing his site. His pictures were adorable.

And then she noticed *his* Top 8 friends list. She'd already been removed from the top spot and been replaced by some girl named Paige. Who was Paige? Aidan had never talked about a girl named Paige before. He didn't have any sisters or relatives with that name. Getting more curious by the second, Samantha clicked on the picture of this mysterious blonde. *Hmmm.* She was from Kentucky, so they must have met online. But as Samantha read through Paige's blogs and the comments she left on Aidan's site, she couldn't really make the connection between them.

Then, like many girls, Samantha's tendency to overanalyze things kicked in with a vengeance. Maybe Paige was the reason Aidan had been so quick to end things. While he'd been hanging out with Samantha night after night, he must have had this little online thing on the side. *Uh-huh.* And when it came time to make a decision, of course it was easier to choose Paige because he wouldn't have to deal with the day-to-day realities. Okay, it was finally all making sense.

Or was it?

          ✳   ✳   ✳

The Mall of America is a busy, busy place . . .

It had been jeans-folding day at the Gap, and Eli couldn't have loathed it more. Working at the Gap wasn't exactly the part-time job of his dreams. Or even the one he wanted for now. But it was all that had been available when he was looking for a way to make extra cash when he'd started college. He'd tried waiting tables, but he could never remember people's orders. There was also that brief stint in telemarketing, but, well, he tried not to think about that. The real low point had come when he was on regular rotation for donating plasma at Hennepin County Medical Center. He'd made one hundred dollars a week, but finally the dizzy spells made him stop. Not long after, he'd found himself walking through the mall, résumé in hand, hoping for a steady gig to keep him in spending money.

None of the sports equipment stores he wanted to work at were hiring, so he went to the Gap—they actually had a Help Wanted sign in the window. Eli got the job that afternoon and started the following day. At first he didn't think the job was that bad: He was around people and got a great discount on clothes. But the store manager drove him nuts. Chelsea took her job a little too seriously—or, as Eli thought privately, she was just a teensy-weensy bit anal-retentive. C'mon, we're talking jeans and T-shirts here, not a cure for cancer, right? For instance, on Friday night Chelsea had called an emergency staff meeting for seven thirty on Saturday. And, yes, that's a.m.

"Look at this; *look at this*!" she'd begun. "Men's boot-cuts *have* to be folded a certain way. Look at how these are folded. This is not acceptable." A dozen sleepy-eyed staffers clutched their cups of Starbucks and cringed at the decibel of her voice.

But Chelsea was just getting started. "I don't know how many times I have to tell you guys, but we have a standard to uphold." She stomped back and forth in front of the jeans wall. "People can buy a pair of jeans anywhere. But at the Gap, it's supposed to be an unforgettable experience. When we have sloppily executed jeans-folding, it takes away from our standard. And take a look at these T-shirts!" Chelsea worked her way around the store, getting louder and louder. "This is pathetic. I know we can do better!"

By the time the mall opened at ten o'clock, Eli had been folding jeans for over an hour. And all day he thought long and hard about telling Chelsea exactly what she could do with all the boot-cut jeans.

So at the end of a very long, pride-swallowing day at the Gap, Eli just wanted to relax. At home at last, he surfed over to MySpace to admire the pictures of Samantha he'd taken on a road trip to a Snow Patrol show in Chicago with Samantha's Bible study group. He'd put together an online photo album and posted it, along with a bunch of other shots of his friends, on his page. Not surprisingly, most of the photos were of Samantha. And as he looked at her gorgeous smile, he missed her.

Out of habit, he clicked on her page. She still listed her relationship status as "single." And wait a minute . . . was Aidan really not her top friend anymore? What had happened? Could this be good news? Not that he wanted to see her get hurt, of course.

Perhaps it was time he gave her a call. Tomorrow. When he was fresh and would know exactly what to say. Yes, tomorrow.

❊ ❊ ❊

On Tuesday Justin picked me up at 6:50 for our seven o'clock movie. I wasn't thrilled. In addition to being one of those freakishly happy morning people, I also don't like being late. Or when anybody else is. Now, I *knew* by the time we got to the theater all we'd miss were the previews, but I actually *like* the previews. (Not commercials, mind you. I hate those, especially the ones with the singing and dancing paper-bag puppets that remind you to use Fandango.) But previews are part of the whole movie-going experience, as far as I'm concerned. Of course, I mentioned none of this to Justin, who couldn't seem to stop fiddling with the radio.

"I meant to ask you the other night, do you like any bands that aren't British?" he said as he finally settled on a classic rock station. Steppenwolf's "Magic Carpet Ride" filled the car.

"Yeah, of course I do," I answered.

"I just couldn't remember if you mentioned any favorites that weren't from the UK or Ireland," he said.

"Oh, I like plenty of artists from the good ol' US of A too. Sarah McLachlan, for one."

"She's from Canada. I'm not sure if that counts," he said, smiling.

"Okay, okay, you're right. Let me think . . . I like The Killers, Jars of Clay, and Death Cab for Cutie. There."

"Death Cab for *who*?" He looked puzzled.

"Cutie," I said. "You haven't heard of them?"

He sighed. "Is it mopey rock where they're all sensitive and stuff?"

I had to laugh.

When we arrived at the movie theater in Roseville, there was actually a parking spot toward the front. But then, it was Tuesday. Traffic had been light. Maybe we wouldn't miss as much as I'd thought. After picking up movie snacks, we made our way into the dark theater, and amazingly, we caught the last trailer. It was for the rerelease of Mel Gibson's *The Passion of the Christ*. Just as I was wondering what Justin would think of it, he leaned over and whispered, "Would you see that with me sometime?"

"I'd love to," I whispered back, remembering the first time I'd seen it and how emotional I'd gotten.

Wow. Was Justin thinking about some of the things we'd talked about on our last date? Certainly suggesting we see *The Passion of the Christ* had to be a step in the right direction.

* * *

"Tomorrow" had gotten away from him,
   but he was ready now . . .

Eli had gotten caught up in church and homework and, well, a little indecision before he finally got around to dialing Samantha's number a few days later. He was sure his call would go straight to voice mail, which was usually the case because Samantha was a popular girl. But this time she picked up on the second ring.

"Hi, Eli," she said, her voice more cheery than he expected.

"Hi! What are you up to right now? Wanna go bowling?"

"Oooh, that sounds like fun," Sam answered. "Can we grab something to eat first? I'm starving."

"Of course," he said. "I'll pick you up in ten minutes or so?"

"Sounds great," she said as she shut her laptop and walked to the bathroom to brush her teeth and touch up her makeup.

CHAPTER 10

A KISS TO BUILD A DREAM ON

It's all happening!

— POLEXIA APHRODISIA (ANNA PAQUIN) IN *ALMOST FAMOUS*, 2000

'D ONLY BEEN IN London for two hours, but I was already in love. It seriously has to be one of the coolest places on earth.

I'll admit that things didn't exactly get off to a promising start, though. First off, I brought way too much stuff with me. Yes, I'd packed and repacked my suitcase probably ten times before leaving Minnesota, but *still* I overpacked. It's ironic, really, because I write articles about travel for a living—heck, I even wrote a "Pack Smarter" guide a few months back. And yet I can't pack my own suitcase efficiently. Go figure. So instead of choosing clothes I could mix and match or leaving behind the maybe-I'll-have-time-for-these things, like the several issues of *In Style* magazine, well . . . I brought them along.

Luggage—it's heavy. And I had a really, really big suitcase.

After clearing customs, I bought a ticket for the Heathrow Express train. I'd hoped to take one of those cool black taxis that I'd seen in countless English movies, but as it turns out, they're very expensive. It would cost close to seventy-five pounds (about 149 dollars) to get to my hotel, and I was sure that accounting wouldn't exactly approve *that* expense. Before I left for the airport, Thomas Waggs had called to remind me yet again to have an "amazing time that would make for a zesty article" (on a side note, who describes articles as *zesty*, anyway?) but to use common sense when it came to expenses. He also said that it was "crucial that I keep every receipt." Got it. For the fifteenth time.

So I didn't think it would be prudent to spend 149 dollars for a thirty-minute cab ride — especially when I could take the Heathrow Express for fifteen pounds (about thirty dollars) and get there in half the time. Ah, but then I had to get all my stuff in the tiny storage space allotted for luggage. As I wrangled my suitcase onto the train, making sure to "mind the gap" as the electronic voice instructed, I probably got no less than five dirty looks from other passengers. I could only imagine what they were thinking: *Those crazy Americans . . . must they bring everything they own on vacation?*

But once I sat down and settled in, my anticipation grew. I couldn't wait to see my hotel. I was staying at the Royal Eagle, a place I'd found on GoThrifty.com. Not only was it a great price, but it was described as "cute, clean, and charming" on the website, which sounded absolutely idyllic. I wasn't exactly expecting the lap of luxury given the economical price tag, but it would be fun to see where I'd be hanging out.

The train ride went by fast — much too fast in my estimation. It was so much fun to eavesdrop on all the conversations going on in those fabulous British accents. But like it or not, my snooping was interrupted by our arrival at Paddington station, and there I was with my heavy suitcase and no idea where my hotel was. I asked a couple of official-looking types with badges as I made my way to the exit. They didn't have the foggiest idea. A couple passing by on the street wasn't much help either. But I found my salvation, or so I thought, when I spotted a black cab on the corner. "Where are you going, love?" the older gentleman asked as he put my suitcase in the backseat. "The Royal Eagle Hotel," I replied, thankful that I'd be there sooner rather than later.

"It's only two blocks away, miss, you could just walk," he said, looking a bit grumpy.

"Thanks, but I have so much stuff, and I'm not really sure where . . ." I gave him my very best lost little girl look.

"Fine, jump in," he said, looking more irritated by the minute.

But five minutes later I surprised him with a tip the same amount as the fare. "Thanks so much," I said. "May I have a receipt?"

"Here you go," he said. "Cheers."

Twenty minutes later I was officially checked into my room and resting on my twin-size bed. The hotel was very cute, just as advertised, but there were a few marked differences between hotels in England and hotels back home. First, unlike the "bigger is better" thinking in the States, everything there was so much smaller: the hotel elevator, my bed (my legs actually extended beyond the length of it), the dorm room–sized TV. But the biggest surprise of all, not to mention the most comical, was my first English shower.

I was so eager to freshen up. But the shower wasn't much help. No bigger than a phone booth, it must have been designed with an anorexic supermodel in mind. Basically, it was a nightmare for anyone with curvy hips or claustrophobia. And since I've never been a huge fan of tightly confined spaces, the experience wasn't exactly relaxing. Plus, there was no place for my shampoo, conditioner, or bath products, so I had to bend down and reach for whatever I needed. How convenient. And if that wasn't entertaining enough, there was the water. As I stood there, nearly hyperventilating from standing in the coffin—I mean shower—I discovered the water temperature left a little to be desired. On my left side there was a stream of freezing cold water, and on the right, a stream of scalding water. I didn't know what was worse, freezing or burning, but I did know one thing—if they were hoping to conserve water by ensuring short showers, they'd succeeded. That may have been the shortest shower in my life.

Deflated by the shower experience, I had to take a look at old London town just to get my groove back. After all, it may have been eleven p.m. for the locals, but I was still on Minneapolis time—and ravenous. I walked past a couple of pubs, just wanting to stay in the neighborhood, and stumbled upon a cozy trattoria called Bizzarro. Italian cuisine—my favorite!

"Table for one?" the host asked as I walked through the front door.

"Yes," I replied. I really hate the way "table for one" sounds.

Most of the time, dining by myself doesn't bother me, especially since I travel frequently for work. But this was one of those nights when I really wished there was someone sitting across from me—a girlfriend, a boyfriend, my mom. . . . As I looked around the restaurant, I realized I was the only one sitting alone. There was a cute couple to my left who appeared to be on their first date. It seemed to be going well. They were asking all kinds of getting-to-know-you questions and giggling a lot. She tossed her hair; he leaned in whenever she spoke. Sparks were definitely flying.

On my right, there was an older couple sharing appetizer portions of calamari and bruschetta. They were so sweet. He had a strong British accent, and she beamed whenever he spoke. They flirted and touched like newlyweds, and I couldn't wait for the day I'd join their esteemed ranks.

* * *

Across the pond at Flaherty's Arden Bowl near the college campus . . .

Eli had beaten Samantha for the third time—this time by two strikes.

"I ate too much at dinner—that hindered my game," Samantha half-joked as Eli put the last brightly colored bowling ball back on the rack.

"Excuses, excuses." He laughed. "Although you did eat *a lot* of french fries."

Sam just rolled her eyes and sighed.

It was like old times, and Samantha couldn't have been happier. Okay, maybe it was Eli who was happier. Whatever the case, they were having fun, something Samantha definitely needed. But Eli still wondered. . . .

"Um . . . can I ask you something?" he began as they returned their rented shoes and headed out to his car. "Are you and Aidan still, you know, hanging out? Or whatever?"

Samantha looked over at Eli and smiled. How cute! He looked nervous. "Nope, that's definitely over, whatever it was," she answered. And as much as it pained her to admit it, she added, "You were right about him, you know. He wasn't worth my time."

Eli stifled the impulse to say "I told you so" and instinctively grabbed her hand. "I'm so sorry about whatever he did."

"Ah, thanks," she offered, content to hold Eli's warm, comforting hand.

"Want to come over and watch a movie, Sam? Something funny?"

"Sure, that would be fun," she said, so happy the evening was continuing.

✳   ✳   ✳

A few miles from Arden Hills . . .

Kristin was correcting papers at Caribou Coffee in Roseville, the place she and Sydney usually met for evening coffee and conversation. Since Sydney was in England, Kristin had opted to go alone—something she rarely did—but after a long day of hanging out with fourth graders, she desperately needed to be among adults, even if they were just sharing a coffee shop.

She was grading science projects. Her class was studying the solar system, and she'd asked each student to write a report on one of the planets. She loved her job, but this was slow going.

Ten minutes later, as she stood up to stretch her legs, an unfamiliar male voice addressed her. "So are you reading some Pulitzer Prize award–winning journalism there?"

Hey, he was pretty cute. She always had been a sucker for big brown eyes. "Um, not exactly, just my kids' science reports," she replied, noticing his thoughtful attention to every word she said.

"Wow, how many kids do you have?" he asked. "That's a lot of science reports."

"Oh," she said shyly, her face flushed red with embarrassment. "They aren't *my* kids. I'm a teacher. But I get attached to them."

"I guess that means you're a good teacher then," he replied. "I'm Justin, by the way."

"I'm Kristin," she replied. "Care to join me?"

"I'd like that," he said. "Want a refill of what you're drinking?"

"I'd love one."

In Kristin's experience, nothing this spontaneous had *ever* happened to her. She wasn't used to meeting random guys or doing anything she hadn't already scheduled in her dayplanner. But Justin seemed nice, and, hey, she was getting another Caramel High Rise for free. At the moment, life was pretty good.

✻ ✻ ✻

I'd consumed enough garlic to scare away any potential suitors. But oooooh, it was so good.

"Cleaned your plate I see, love," the waiter said as he dropped off the check.

"Yeah, I didn't really care for it at all." Looking at me, then my plate, and back at me, he shot me a confused look and walked away. Apparently he didn't understand my American sense of humor, which is rare, since the Brits are generally known as the clever ones.

After I'd paid the check and walked the few blocks back to the Royal Eagle, I discovered I was exhausted. So I changed into my favorite plaid pajamas, turned down the covers, and fell asleep on my very small bed.

✻ ✻ ✻

Back at Eli's apartment . . .

Samantha and Eli were trying to decide what movie to watch. "How about *Anchorman*?" he suggested as he riffled through his extensive collection of DVDs.

"Nah," she replied. "Not in the mood for that. How about *Clueless*?"

"No way, you'll just quote every line," he said.

"Okay, how about *Pride and Prejudice*?"

"I don't even own that," he said defensively.

"*Hmmm*, what's *this*?" she asked, holding up the case. "Caught you!"

"All right, all right, I used to have a small crush on Keira Knightley," he confessed, smiling.

"You're kidding."

"Yeah, she's pretty hot," Eli said.

"Used to?" Samantha asked. "Sounds serious to me."

"What makes you think that?" Eli asked innocently.

"It's called present tense," Samantha said. "Saying 'yeah, she's pretty hot' means you still think so."

"Fine, you're right," Eli said. "But then again, you usually always are."

"Usually?" Samantha said. "*Usually* doesn't go with always."

"Blah, blah, blah," Eli retorted. "So are we going to decide on a movie or what?"

An hour passed this way. Since they couldn't agree on anything from Eli's DVD collection, they decided to flip channels. *The Notebook* was just starting on CBS, and Samantha suggested they watch it.

"I've never seen it before. What's it about?" Eli asked quizzically. "What's so special about a notebook that they decided to make an entire movie about it?"

"I guess you're just going to have to watch it to find out," Samantha said with a smile. "And you might want to grab a box of Kleenex."

"This had better not be some sappy chick flick!"

Oh, he had no idea how sappy a chick flick it was, but he was about to find out—and Samantha wanted to watch it.

"Want some popcorn?" Eli asked. "Or I have Pringles, Doritos, and Sun Chips. Want me to bake some chocolate chip cookies? Or brownies?"

"You're going to miss the beginning, Eli," Samantha said. "Grab those Doritos and come here."

"I'm just trying to be a good host," he said with a smile. Then he shut off the lights and sat on the couch.

As the movie started, Eli moved a little closer to Samantha. The faint smell of her perfume and her intensity as she watched the movie made him smile. To Eli, Samantha was perfect. And finally, after all this time, Eli was getting to spend the evening with her. Alone. Well, together.

He didn't know what it was exactly, but something about the story of Allie and Noah inspired him. Maybe it was how they had to fight through so many obstacles for their love. Maybe it was because Allie was so feisty—just like Samantha. But whatever it was, he knew it was time to declare his intentions.

It was almost the end of the movie—the part where Allie has to choose between Noah and Lon. Allie was about to leave, but she was not entirely convinced that things could work between her and her first love until Noah said, "We're going to have to work at this every day, but I want to do that because I want you." Eli looked over at Samantha, who was brushing tears away from her face. Then she tried to hide the fact that she was crying, but the tears kept rolling.

Without hesitation, Eli made eye contact with her. Sam looked up at him and smiled, a little embarrassed that her black-brown mascara was running down her cheeks. Eli didn't care; she was beautiful, mascara streaks and all. And he told her so as he softly tilted her chin up and met her lips with his own.

The kiss lasted a few glorious seconds, and Samantha couldn't believe how much she enjoyed it. She had never thought a kiss from Eli could be so passionate, so romantic. But it was.

❋ ❋ ❋

Meanwhile, the staff at Caribou Coffee was trying to close up . . .

Kristin and Justin were having a great conversation. In fact, it went so well that the baristas finally had to kick them out.

Although Justin had gone on a couple of dates with another girl recently, there was something about Kristin that made him feel really comfortable; he felt an undeniable connection. She was pretty, smart, and easy to talk to, with something much deeper going on too. And he hoped to get to the bottom of it.

As he walked Kristin to her car, Justin thanked her for an "unexpectedly wonderful evening" and asked her if she was free for dinner sometime soon.

"Well, I guess you'll have to call and ask," she replied, loving how a mundane night of correcting papers had evolved so nicely into a quasi-date.

"I will," he said. And when he stepped closer to give her a quick hug good-bye, it ended up being a long, lingering kiss instead.

CHAPTER 11

LONDON'S CALLING (AND CALLING)

> You know I used to wait two days to call anybody, but now
> it's like everyone in town waits two days. So I think three
> days is kind of money. What do you think?
>
> — TRENT WALKER (VINCE VAUGHN) IN *SWINGERS*, 1996

A S A TRAVEL WRITER, it's my job to absorb the local flavor of a location and provide a compelling report for the readers of *Get Away*. So instead of making my usual Starbucks run for breakfast, I needed to check out some of the local fare. But as much as I wanted to provide the readers a true picture of London life, my preliminary research had really put me off the notion of a traditional English breakfast. I mean, their idea of breakfast is fried eggs, fried bread, black pudding hash and sausage (or as the Brits say, bangers), baked beans, and mushrooms — not exactly my idea of a good way to start the day. It was almost enough to make me want to skip breakfast altogether. But I'd heard great things from several respected food critics about Electric Brasserie in Notting Hill, so I headed that way.

As I walked the couple of blocks to Paddington station, I noticed that everyone who walked by had an umbrella (they'd call it a brolly). When a light drizzle began to fall, I understood why. And even though it was a gray day, which is par for the course in London, there was still something enchanting about it. I could picture myself sitting with the locals in a coffee shop with my laptop, drinking cappuccinos and working on the novel I've always dreamed about writing. I'd work for hours and hours, blithely unaware of the passing time, and it would be glorious.

My daydreams were so vivid that it seemed like only seconds had passed when I arrived at the Notting Hill Gate tube stop. There were rows and rows of pastel-colored houses in this quaint neighborhood (just like in the movie *Notting Hill*—imagine that!). I decided I was partial to the pink flat in the middle as I looked around for the famed "house with the blue door" that Hugh Grant's character, William Thacker, had lived in. (I found out later that the blue door had been auctioned off at Christie's a year after the movie was made.)

After looking around Portobello Road Market and picking up a handmade wallet, a paisley scarf for Kristin, and a cool antique clock the merchant said was "at least one hundred years old, miss," I tracked down Electric Brasserie. There was a twenty-minute wait, but I'd expected it since I'd read that there's always a line. So I walked over to the Travel Bookshop and browsed while I waited. I couldn't believe how many books there were about travel—and how varied and interesting they all were. There were memoirs, maps, and guides to just about any place imaginable, no matter how remote. And unlike Barnes & Noble, finding the books—which weren't in any particular order—was an integral part of the experience.

In addition to the *Mr. & Mrs. Smith Hotel Collection*, which highlighted the best places to stay in Ireland and the UK, I also picked up a beautiful coffee table book about Tuscany and a collection of black-and-white photographs of Kenya, Tanzania, and the Congo taken by African children. I don't know what it is about books, but I can never have enough of them. And since these were about travel, well, they were an investment in my career too, right?

Don't you just love how I justify my purchases?

Anyway, exactly twenty-five minutes later, I was sitting at a corner table at Electric Brasserie, sipping some of the most delicious coffee I've ever tasted. It was so rich and aromatic, it didn't even need cream or sugar. And trust me, that usually isn't my preferred java experience. And as I looked over the exhaustive menu, I was pleasantly surprised by the variety of options. Sure, there were plenty of bangers and black pudding hash (if you really must have that sort of thing), but there was also cinnamon-crusted French toast with warm blackberry compote, scrambled eggs with rosemary-sautéed Portobello mushrooms, and chunky hash browns with crumbly bacon and homemade sourdough toast. Everything sounded so delicious, but I finally settled on Belgian waffles and strawberries.

"I hope you're hungry, love," the waiter said as he wrote down my order on his small green and white tablet.

"Oh, I am," I answered with a smile.

He refilled my coffee. "I'm sure everything will be to your liking."

Yeah, I was sure it would be too; I was starting to feel a bit lightheaded.

Then as I paged through the *Daily Express*, which reads more like a tabloid that only seems to cover Prince William and Posh Spice than an actual newspaper, I scribbled down a few notes for my article.

* * *

Back in Minneapolis . . .

Midway through her language arts lesson (in other words, grammar), Kristin yawned for the third time, and it was only ten o'clock. And after a while, a few of her students caught on.

"Did you stay up too late, Miss Brown?" asked Lily, one of her favorite students. "You seem really tired."

"Yeah, I did stay up way past my bedtime," Kristin answered, allowing herself to think about Justin, just for a minute. She hadn't had that much fun in a long time, and oh, how incredible was that kiss? But she'd had trouble falling asleep. See, Kristin just isn't the kind of girl who is free with her kisses. This . . . whatever-it-was with Justin was definitely uncharted territory.

Kristin's life as a teacher is pretty planned out; she doesn't have room for random interruptions. When she isn't preparing for parent/teacher conferences, grading papers, or figuring out grades for report cards, she attends teaching seminars and volunteers to set up food drives at her church. After her breakup with Landon a year ago (they'd dated for five years before he announced he "never wanted to get married"), she vowed she wouldn't see someone again if she was certain she could live without him. But here she was going to Justin's for dinner next week. And it scared her how excited she was.

* * *

Sometimes girls just want to have fun . . .

The always-responsible Samantha decided to break character today: She (gasp) skipped her Psychology Today practicum. In the course of her college career, she'd probably only ditched a handful of classes — she just loved to learn. But she felt like she needed to kick back and relax because, well, she had a lot to think about. Should she accept the internship in Europe she'd been offered? And what about that whole crazy kissing scene from last night? Were she and Eli just good friends who decided to add "benefits" for one night? Or should they pursue a relationship? Samantha wasn't sure, but she liked how everything had turned out the night before. It had been unexpected — yet it felt so natural. So she'd done what any gal with a lot on her mind would do: She'd booked a haircut and a mani-pedi at the Aveda Institute in Minneapolis.

✻ ✻ ✻

For my restaurant round-up, I was definitely writing up Electric Brassiere. The food was absolutely fabulous. (I'd definitely try to come back before the end of my stay.) Now I'd try to walk some of those calories off — next on my agenda was a walking tour. London is famous for them, so I thought I'd better sample one or two. The Jack the Ripper walk came highly recommended, but investigating all the murder sites where this notorious killer made his mark was hardly my idea of a good time. I decided I'd namedrop the Ripper tour in the article but devote my attention to much less controversial subjects — Charles Dickens and The Beatles.

The Charles Dickens tour was fascinating, and not only because I'm a writer too. It was a breathtaking change in scenery. Alongside our guide, Jean, who dressed in an antique shawl, apron, and even a bonnet, we visited what she called Dickens' London. We were transported to a world without cars, high-speed Internet, or noise pollution — just by getting a little off the beaten track. Much of the London that Dickens knew still survives in old narrow streets and alleyways if you know where to look (or have a good tour guide!). This was the London where Dickens wrote his classic works, the place where Pip from *Great Expectations* came to life.

I loved every moment of it.

Later that afternoon I brushed up on my Beatles history with the Magical Mystery Tour. Although I wasn't alive in their heyday, I still love the music and would say, hands down, that Paul is my favorite Beatle. Our group on this tour was much larger, led by an enthusiastic guide named Richard. Clearly, he was born to do this job. He rattled off Beatles facts like a preacher rattles off Scripture. And the crowd hung on every word he said, whether he talked about the first time he met Paul face-to-face or his memory of the day John Lennon was shot.

We moved from place to place quickly: the Apple offices where the Beatles played their famous rooftop session, Paul McCartney's offices (he's known to show up from time to time), the studio where "Hey Jude" was recorded. But the best part of the tour, in my humble opinion, of course, was when we checked out Abbey Road Studios and the famed crossing where the album cover was photographed. Despite the chilly weather, I took off my shoes and walked out of step just like Paul did, which amused Richard to no end.

After buying a few mementos at the gift shop, I hopped on the tube and went back to my hotel. My feet ached from all the walking, but it had been a fun day. As I walked through the front door, the doorman asked, "Are you Miss Alexander?"

"I am," I replied groggily. I needed a nap—and soon.

"There's a delivery for you, miss; would you like it in your room?"

Who would send me something in London? And how did he or she know where I was staying? "Um, sure," I said.

"Certainly," he said. "We'll take care of it right away."

It was cute how formal everyone was here. Maybe I'd integrate a few London-isms into my daily vocabulary once I got back to Minneapolis: "Why certainly, Thomas, I will complete even the most perfunctory tasks with speed and nobility, sir."

Yeah, he'd get a kick out of that.

I caught a few minutes of the BBC News before nodding off to dreamland. I was so tired I didn't even bother taking off my shoes or getting under the blankets. Twenty minutes later a loud banging on the door made me nearly jump out of my skin.

"Who is it?" I asked, trying to pull myself together.

"Concierge, miss," I heard a deep, John Cleese–like voice say. "I have a delivery for Miss Sydney Alexander."

I opened the door. "Here you are," he said. "It looks like someone cares about *you* a lot!" He thrust a huge vase of red roses into my hands.

I don't think I'd ever seen this many roses clustered together in my life, let alone had them delivered to me. But who could they be from? As soon as I saw the first line on the card, I knew:

> *Roses are red,*
> *Violets are blue,*
> *Minneapolis just ain't the same*
> *Without you.*

Sydney, I miss you, can we give it another chance?
Please call me when you're back from London.
   Liam

Wow. I've always been a sucker for a well-written note, you know? But as gorgeous as the flowers were (and trust me, they were truly something special) and as sweet as his note was, I wasn't sure I wanted him back. I definitely believed in forgiveness and in second chances . . . even third chances, if necessary. But I'd have to give it some serious thought.

In my experience, I've found that thinking goes well with pizza. So I rang Pizza Express.

After the pizza arrived, I tried making a list of the pros and cons of reviving a relationship with Liam. But it just wasn't working. The smell of roses and pizza fought in the tiny room and made me a little crazy. Growing more anxious by the moment, I did something I hadn't done in a while—I reached into my oversized Coach purse and pulled out my Bible.

I always keep a Bible in my purse because you never know when you're going to need it. I used to have my quiet time in my office—during my lunch break. But more often than not, a coworker would stop to say hello or ask a question, and I'd get distracted. For a while after that, I went to Starbucks before work to get some reading in. But one day, for whatever reason, I just went to work instead. And now it's probably been at least two weeks since I've taken my Bible out of my purse, which is sad, considering how much I truly enjoy reading it. But, hey, no time like the present. So I opened up my slightly worn Bible, the one my mom gave me when I was sixteen, and started reading the Psalms. The words were familiar, of course, but also fresh, like a cool drink of water. Isn't it amazing how only a few minutes in God's Word can have such a transformational effect? Tears rolled down my face, and I felt certain that God would give me the wisdom to make the right choice.

*   *   *

A particularly memorable Friday night in the life of Aidan Hudson . . .

Aidan still felt pretty bad about upsetting Samantha, although he was sure it had been the right decision. But rather than give Samantha a call, he signed on to MySpace and asked Paige if they could talk on the phone. In all the months they'd known each other, their conversations had been limited to e-mail or instant messaging. Paige was thrilled, of course—until she heard what he had to say. After they'd exchanged a few pleasantries and marveled at the sound of "real voices," Aidan got right to the point.

"I've needed to get my life back on track for a while," he confessed. "I really liked Samantha, and I messed it all up. And that's because *I'm* messed up. I've been only thinking of myself. And that concerns you too because now I know that I'm not ready for anything right now, with anyone. And for some reason, I really felt I needed to tell you that now, tonight, rather than two or three months down the road."

"I understand," she began. "I appreciate that you're telling me this now. Aidan, I can't lie, I've had feelings for you for a while. But I knew you really cared for Samantha, so I just wanted to be a friend. If you ever want to call me after you're done getting your head together, I'll be here."

"Thanks, Paige, that means a lot."

And that was that. A few minutes later, Aidan checked his e-mail, and while he was waiting for the page to load, he noticed a banner ad for Searching for Justice. Most nights he would've ignored it and gone on with his business, but on this particular Friday night he clicked on it and began researching the possibility of traveling to India.

At that moment, he knew Samantha would've been proud of him.

*   *   *

As I opened up the curtains the next morning, I saw something quite unusual for London: the bright glow of sunshine. It looked like it was going to be a beautiful day, and I wanted to make the most of it.

On the way to the tube station, I stopped at Accessorize. I'd peeked in the windows several times in the last couple of days, but never actually walked in. Even though the store was cluttered and the Euro pop music was playing far too loud, they had everything a girl loves: plenty of brightly colored scarves . . . earrings that sparkled and dangled . . . bangles, necklaces, rings, and watches. Even their ballet flats were adorable, with cool little embellishments that would dress up jeans or look great with a casual Bohemian skirt. And the best part of all was that everything was reasonably priced.

When it was all said and done, I was probably there for two hours. I picked up three pairs of earrings for Samantha, a silver, shabby-chic bracelet for Andrea, and a pair of emerald green ballet flats for myself. I have far too many shoes already, but they were so cute I just couldn't leave them at the store.

After my adventure at Accessorize, I made a quick jaunt to Lush for some fizzy bath bombs and a mud mask for my face, and then I was off to buy a train ticket—I was headed to Arundel for an up-close look at the English countryside. My train left in an hour, so I killed time by reading the British rag *Hello!*

Before I knew it we were boarding. My section was nearly vacant until a young English guy sat across from me. "Is this seat taken?" he politely asked as he adjusted his backpack.

"No, feel free to sit," I answered good-naturedly, secretly hoping he wasn't in the mood for conversation since I planned to start working on my article.

I breathed a sigh of relief when he sat down and immediately reached for a book in his backpack. Turns out he was reading *Jane Eyre*.

"Can you believe I've never finished this book?" he asked. "Most people read this in high school."

"Well, I didn't," I replied. "We were always stuck reading books like *Animal Farm*. And I thought it was horrible."

"I'll just have to take your word for it on that," he said. "I try to avoid reading anything with the word *farm* in the title."

"That's a shame," I said. "You might be missing out."

I had no idea why I was saying this. I just kept babbling on and on and on.

"So are you a fan of Hemingway?" I asked. "I just finished *A Moveable Feast*, and it made me want to move to Paris immediately."

"Um, I think Hemingway's a little overrated," he said. "I just finished *A Farewell to Arms* and was quite disappointed."

"Well, I'm sorry to hear that," I said. "That must have been . . . horrific."

"Do I detect a little sarcasm there, Miss America?" he asked with a laugh.

"*Nooooo*," I replied.

"I'm Gareth, by the way," he offered. "Do you have a name?"

"Why, yes, I do."

"Would you like to share?" he asked, obviously enjoying our flirty banter.

"Sure, why not, since it's not likely we'll see each other again," I said. "I'm Sydney."

"Sydney? I like that name—reminds me of one of my favorite cities," he said.

"Hmmm, let me guess, could that be in Australia?"

"Ever been there?" he asked.

"No," I replied. "But I write for a travel magazine, so there's always that possibility."

As you can probably guess, I didn't read a word on my way to Arundel. Instead, Gareth and I talked and talked, which eventually culminated in a dinner invitation. "Have you had a chance to try fish and chips since you've been here?" he asked enthusiastically. "If not, I'm not sure you're qualified to write that fancy article of yours. England just isn't England unless you've had fish and chips."

"Honestly, I haven't tried them yet. I try my best to avoid grease in large amounts."

"Well, we need to take care of that," he said. "How 'bout it?"

It probably wasn't the smartest move to say yes. But—why not? He seemed nice, no bad vibes . . . and it could make a great addition to my London experience.

"I'm going to take you to Butlers," he said. "It's a pretty standard pub, but the fish and chips are outstanding."

"I'll take your word for it," I said. "I'm not what you'd call a pub expert."

*　*　*

Butlers was crowded and noisy, but I felt like I'd leave with a pretty good idea of what an average night was like there. Manchester United was playing Arsenal on the telly, as they call it, and the pub was clearly in favor of Arsenal.

"So what part of America are you from, anyway?" Gareth asked. "Anywhere I've heard of?"

"Well, what have you heard of?" I asked.

"I've never been to the States, but everyone's heard of New York City, Florida, and Las Vegas."

"You know Florida's a state, not a city, right?" I remarked with a laugh.

"There's a difference?" he said sarcastically.

So I told him all about Minnesota. He quickly informed me that he wasn't much of a shopper, so the Mall of America didn't appeal to him in the least. But the idea of all those lakes in one place? That truly excited him because he loved to fish.

"I love being on the water," he said. "It's when I feel the most at peace with the world."

Our conversation carried on for the better part of the afternoon and evening (so much for exploring the countryside), and we covered a lot of territory. On a side note, the fish and chips were just as delicious as he promised. And then things started to get a little weird.

At first I was positive that Gareth was joking when he asked me to marry him. But I began to take it a little more seriously when he started talking logistics. "Wouldn't it be fun to live in England part of the year and Minnesota the other half?" he asked.

"Incredible," I replied, playing along. "But I'd have to quit my job, and I have a mortgage to pay."

"I just got promoted, so you wouldn't even have to worry about working," he said. "Wouldn't that be a nice break for you? You sound like you're always busy."

"I don't mind being busy," I said. "Keeps me out of trouble."

But as we continued to talk, I realized that he was actually mulling all this over—it wasn't necessarily just for laughs. "It would be a great change for me to live in America," he said. "Would you wear my ring until I can afford to get you a prettier one?" He pointed to a thick silver band he wore on his right hand. "The engraving says 'Luck of the Irish'—isn't that cool?" he asked as he removed it from his finger. "I think it's pretty lucky that I met you today."

"Are you hoping to get a green card or what?" I asked as I took a sip of Diet Coke.

"No, that's not it at all," he said. "I just happen to think, well, maybe we met on the train for a reason."

"Don't you think it's a bit soon for marriage?" I laughed. "I just met you."

"Perhaps," he said. "But just consider it."

I'm not sure why, but I laughed when he said that. "I'll keep it in mind," I said. Aside from all the talk of matrimony, Gareth seemed like a nice guy. And it was certainly one of the more interesting dates I've had lately—how often does a girl get proposed to on the first date?

On the train back to London—and I was traveling alone—I got out my journal. Ever since I was ten years old, I've kept a running log of my life. And while lately I've discovered blogging, I still like getting my thoughts down in my own handwriting whenever I can. So I wrote about the interesting encounter with Gareth, the flowers from Liam, and how this whole trip had been the realization of a lifelong dream. It was fun and therapeutic, and the time passed quickly. Before I knew it, I was back at the hotel, watching some crazy British variety show until I nodded off.

* * *

It was date night in Minnesota too . . .

Eli and Samantha were having a great time at ComedySportz in Minneapolis. They'd both been to the popular comedy club before but never remembered it being *this* funny. Neither of them mentioned the kiss.

When the show ended around eleven, they drove to Perkins, the only place nearby that was open twenty-four hours. All that laughing had worked up their appetites. They settled into a booth and ordered the bottomless coffee, and then Eli asked Samantha if he could join her on her side of the booth.

"Sure," she said, startled.

"I just wanted to sit closer," he said, sliding in next to her. "I had a lot of fun hanging out tonight."

"Yeah, me too," she replied. Then, cautiously, "I think I like going on dates with you, Eli."

"Oh, so this was a date?" he asked, smiling.

"Yeah, I think it was," she said. "And it was nice."

Eli couldn't have agreed with her more.

＊　＊　＊

On Sunday, groggy as I was, I paid an early visit to St. James's Church, which wasn't far from the hotel. On my walk back I stopped at Starbucks—I was just ready for something familiar. I sank into a comfy couch with my coffee and the *London Times* and decided to spend a leisurely hour flipping pages of one of the world's most famous newspapers.

Before I'd left Minneapolis, Thomas had given me instructions about the article. "Nothing predictable," he'd said. "I don't want to see anything about Buckingham Palace, the Tower of London, the queen, or Harrods."

So only out-of-the-ordinary activities would do—things that my generation might find interesting. And I'd planned my attack for this afternoon.

My first stop was Bond Street, which I'll admit wasn't entirely for work purposes. A friend of mine had told me that Bond Street was the place du jour for shoes, and since shoes are one of my weaknesses, I had to have a look. I couldn't afford anything from Christian Louboutin, Prada, Burberry, or Jimmy Choo, but it was fun to window shop.

Far more practical in terms of my limited cash flow was Oxford Street, my second stop of the day. TopShop was everything I'd heard and so much more. I found three dresses, a spring coat, and the cutest pajamas ever. I couldn't wait to wear my new purchases to work. Aside from the pajamas, of course.

After TopShop, I hit up French Connection, Zara, and Selfridges, London's answer to Bloomingdale's. Just like Bloomie's, it was the sort of store you languidly look through department by department. And so I did. It turned out to be the start of an adventure I'm still laughing about. As I walked out, I was positive I spotted Hugh Grant. *Surely this is destined to be one of my life's greatest meetings*, I thought as I trailed him for six blocks and brainstormed about what I would say if I had the opportunity. (Incidentally, nothing brilliant or even remotely clever came to mind, but I persevered.) What I lacked in inspiration, though, I made up for in sheer determination as I sped up and walked ahead of him so I could get a better look. You can imagine my chagrin when I discovered that not only was it *not* Hugh Grant, it was an older British *woman*. Perhaps a trip to the optometrist is in order—and *soon*.

After my near run-in with Hugh, I was in desperate need of a midafternoon snack. So I grabbed a sandwich at Boots, an apothecary that's much cooler than Walgreens could ever be. Then I hopped on the tube for a trip to the Tate Modern, the museum I'd been told was one of London's must-sees.

Twenty minutes later I was checking out some of the most exquisite art by the likes of Picasso, Pollock, Matisse, and Warhol. Even the architecture of the building is interesting—especially since it's in a converted electrical power station. I stayed for a couple of hours, taking in everything. I could've easily spent an entire day, but I had to keep moving. My time in London was getting significantly shorter, so I had to pack as much into these remaining hours as I could.

When I got back to my hotel, there was a note for mc at the front desk. Folded up with it was a ticket for *The Rose Tattoo* at the Olivier Theatre. The note read:

> *Dear Sydney,*
> *I'd love for you to see this play with me. It's my*
> *absolute favourite. We could have a late dinner*

after the show. I'll be there tonight—I hope you'll
come sit in the seat next to me.
   Cheers,
   Gareth

The truth is, I love the theater, and it was a difficult decision to make. But I didn't want to give Gareth the wrong idea either, and, frankly, he was coming on just a little too strong. I'd enjoyed my time with him, but that's all it was—time spent with a stranger. My thoughts, I realized, were thousands of miles away. All I could think of was Liam. And I wasn't about to share all of that with Gareth.

So instead of seeing the play, I took a ride on the London Eye, a gigantic Ferris wheel that gave me the best view of the city I'd seen yet. I enjoyed it so much that I actually rode twice, noticing new sights the second time around. Afterward, I went to Covent Garden, a shopping and entertainment district where people stay out until all hours. This particular evening there were street musicians covering everything from Sting to songs from *The Sound of Music*, which was very entertaining. After snapping a few pictures, I walked to the Covent Garden entrance to the Royal Opera House. Next time I came to town—how about that for confidence: *next time!*—I decided I had to see a show there.

It's funny—here I was in the city I'd always dreamed about, and all I could think of was home. I kept wondering if things could really be different this time with Liam if I gave it another chance . . . or if I was just wasting my time. Countless times during the evening I tried to talk myself out of my feelings for him, but I couldn't. Old love dies hard.

It was late when I got back to my hotel, and there was a phone message from Gareth. I deleted it. He didn't try again.

❋ ❋ ❋

Like the best adventures often do, the end of my London sojourn came far too quickly. On Monday morning I wandered around the neighborhood near my hotel one last time, and then I bought a small, cheap suitcase to pack all my new purchases in so that I wouldn't be over the weight limit. Then in the late afternoon, I lugged it all down to Paddington station for the ride out to Heathrow and my overnight flight to Minneapolis.

There's something about a train; the rhythmic clacking of the tracks put me in a pensive mood. My mind wandered in a million different directions. I thought about life, work, the future, and, yes, I thought about Liam too. Probably too much. But instead of ignoring my impulses this time, I decided at the airport to send him a postcard. I thanked him for the flowers and shared a few details about how incredible England was. And then quickly, before I could think better of it, I told him I missed him and signed my name.

CHAPTER 12

I'M NOT WITH THE BAND

What is it about love that makes us so stupid?

— FRANCES (DIANE LANE) IN *UNDER THE TUSCAN SUN*, 2003

THERE'S A REASON DOROTHY clicked her heels together and said, "There's no place like home." Although I love traveling and enjoying luxurious accommodations somewhere else, there's nothing quite like your own bed with your favorite down blanket and your own sheets softly scented just the way you like them (Downy Simple Pleasures does the trick for me). And the more I thought about it on the transatlantic flight, the more I wanted to be home. By now my plants could be dead, the mail would be piling up, and I knew my dishwasher was full of dirty dishes I forgot to take care of before I left. But I didn't care. I just wanted to kick back on my favorite couch and watch the E! channel to my heart's content. Or a bad Lifetime made-for-TV movie. Or . . . well, you see what I mean. I don't have the poshest place on the block, but it's mine, and I love everything about it.

As I riffled through all the magazines I'd already read on the way over, checking to see if there were any movies I hadn't already watched on the in-flight entertainment service, I noticed an incredibly good-looking man sitting back one row and across the aisle from me. He sat in the seat next to the aisle, and his row was empty except for his Martin guitar in the seat next to him. (I only knew it was a Martin because it said so on the case.) He had jet black hair and the most striking brown eyes I'd ever seen. And oh, he had a dazzling smile, which I caught sight of over the top of my magazine when he handed a rattle back to the frazzled mother of a baby across the aisle from him.

He was reading a magazine and writing things down in a small leather-bound book, just like the one I always carry with me. Normally, I might've devised some clever way to talk to him, but right then I didn't exactly feel like flirting. I was dressed in gray sweatpants and an oversized hooded sweatshirt that read *London, England* in huge black letters on the front. For the record, even a travel writer has a touristy moment or two when she is making the shopping rounds. That was one of the only cheesy souvenirs I bought, though . . . well, aside from a refrigerator magnet for my mom. While I get some pretty extravagant requests from friends whenever I travel, all my mom ever wants is a magnet. So I've bought her one from every place I've been to, meaning it won't be long before she may want to invest in a second refrigerator.

But Mr. Hottie, now, he was pretty fascinating to watch. Better than any movie. He finally finished with his magazine and got out a book. But before he started reading, he actually smelled it. Then, with a satisfied look on his face, he began to read, until the baby dropped her rattle again. This time when he picked it up, we made eye contact. Turns out his eyes were even more gorgeous when they were staring back at mine.

❋　❋　❋

Decisions, decisions . . .

Even though words like *determined*, *self-assured*, and *driven* are often used to describe Samantha, she sometimes has trouble making decisions just like everyone else. And boy, was she ever struggling with whether or not she should take the internship in Europe. It was still a few weeks away, but the chairman of the psychology department needed to know by the end of the week so he could give it to someone else if she chose not to accept it. Really, it was something she shouldn't pass up, a rare opportunity to partner with an overseas organization that helps missionaries acclimate to their new surroundings by teaching them the language and customs of the region and providing leadership training and crucial prayer support for the long months ahead.

While it matched up so well with what she hoped to do in the future, she worried about how it would affect her relationship with Eli. Because it *was* a relationship, she knew that now. It was a friendship blossoming into love, something that was very rare indeed. Was she willing to risk that by being away for three months?

Later that night when she and Eli met for dinner at his place, they talked about it extensively.

"Samantha, I can't think of anything that would be a better fit," Eli said. "Sure, I'm going to miss you like crazy, and I hate that we'll be spending the summer apart, but this is your future. There's no reason why you shouldn't go."

"But what about . . . us?" she asked as she twisted the fettuccine around her fork. "I was really looking forward to kickin' back with you, getting a tan, having fun."

"Well, I'll always be here, Sam; this opportunity may not,"

he said. "I'll just have to get a tan without you." He smiled. "And think of all the places you'll see."

"Yeah, it's a tough job, but someone's got to do it," she said with a laugh. "But I promise to bring you something back."

"I'll hold you to that," he said as he reached for her hand and kissed it. "It just better not be some tacky snow globe."

*   *   *

When I woke up an hour later, there was drool on my chin and funny marks on my cheek from the airplane pillow. Without even looking in a mirror, I sensed my own hideousness and hoped that Mr. Hottie hadn't walked by while I napped. I snuck a glance in his direction. He was fast asleep, looking positively angelic.

With two hours left, I took out my laptop and attempted to work on my story. But as hard as I tried, the words just wouldn't come. I was still processing my personal revelations, so I wrote about that instead. Getting my thoughts down on the screen was therapeutic. And for the first time in a few days, I thought about Justin. I wondered how he was doing, what he'd been up to while I was away, and if he'd missed me. I can't say that I missed him terribly. . . . Liam still had the power, after all this time, to completely capture my attention. It was exhilarating, but it was also frustrating—why couldn't I just be done with him?

As soon as we were on the ground, hundreds of cell phones were switched on in unison, including my own. I checked my messages; there were seven. Three were from Samantha, who said she was going to be late picking me up, not late picking me up, and, um, late picking me up. Gee, thanks for the clarification there, Sam. The other four were all about work.

After clearing customs and picking up my luggage, I waited for Samantha at baggage claim. And my phone started to ring. First I got a call from Justin to see if I'd made it back safely. How thoughtful of him! We talked for a few minutes and agreed to meet later in the week. Then Liam called . . . and try as I might to control it, my heart leaped—thank goodness he couldn't see me blushing—although I tried to play it cool. I thanked him for the flowers right away, knowing he wouldn't get my postcard anytime soon. And then he asked whether he'd be able to see me soon. I paused. "Sure," I replied. "That would be nice." *Be still my heart.*

I still wasn't sure how I felt about renewing . . . well, whatever we might be renewing, and I planned to tell him as much. But suddenly Samantha pulled up and jumped out of her car, popping the trunk as she walked to the curb. She picked up the largest suitcase. "Hey, sis, glad to be back home?" She grinned.

She had no idea. I was so ready to crash at home and do nothing for the rest of the day.

As she drove me to downtown Minneapolis, she filled me in on the dramatic turn her relationship with Eli had taken. As she talked about him, she was positively radiant. I can honestly say it was the happiest I'd ever seen her. Well, until she told me about Europe.

"Oh, boohoo, you get a once-in-a-lifetime opportunity, and Eli is supportive of it," I said. Do you think she picked up on my sarcasm? "What more could you want, girl?"

"I know, I'm just going to miss him, you know? I think this could be the start of something really important—and now I have to leave."

"If you don't go to Europe, you'll regret it," I replied.

"Everything's going to work out just as it should. You know that."

"Yeah, you're right. It's just hard," Samantha said. "After everything went wrong with Aidan, it was so nice to have a relationship with Eli develop completely out of the blue."

"I'm sure it was. And you'll still get to enjoy it for a few weeks before you go to Europe."

When I heard her sigh, I knew I'd gotten through to her.

A few minutes later I was back at home with my feet propped up on my ottoman. Ah, yes, this was the best. Well, okay, it would be better if Mr. Hottie were here, rubbing my feet. I was exhausted. I barely had the energy to flip the channels. One thing was sure: I wasn't going to the office tomorrow. I'd e-mail Thomas in the morning and ask to work from home.

✱ ✱ ✱

Decisions, decisions — part two . . .

After Samantha dropped her sister off, she went back to campus to catch her afternoon classes. When she was done, she called Eli to let him know she'd finally made her decision about Europe.

Eli was honestly thrilled that Samantha had decided to go. He knew she'd made the right decision.

"I want to celebrate this, Sam," he said. "Soon. But I have this paper. . . ." He wanted her to come over immediately, but he had to finish a paper for his Systematic Theology class. He'd already put it off for two weeks, and now he had to write fifteen pages before nine o'clock tomorrow morning.

"I'd come and help you," Samantha began, "but I don't want to be a distraction."

"Yeah, that's probably best," he said, "although I'd much rather have you distract me than write about the differences between justification and sanctification."

"Golly," she replied, "that sounds like all kinds of fun."

Eli hated writing papers. It just didn't come naturally like it did to Samantha. So she let him work on it a couple of hours while she baked him some of his favorite double chocolate brownies. When they were ready, she grabbed her French press and some coffee beans.

She knocked on his door with great anticipation. "Just a minute," she heard him say. As he opened the door, he was rubbing his eyes—how adorable was that?

"Sam! Wow!" he said. He opened the door to let her in, eyeing the plate of brownies. "For me?" he asked. "That was so sweet of you, Samantha—literally and figuratively."

She laughed at his joke and made the coffee. And before long, she was helping him wrap up his paper in record time.

* * *

I'd decided that if I didn't move to my bed, I'd end up asleep on the couch. Curled up under the covers, I was in that in-between phase—you know, where you're not quite asleep, but you're definitely not fully awake either. Moments before I was officially out for the evening, my cell phone rang.

"Hello?" I said groggily.

"It's Liam. I'm sorry—did I wake you?"

"Not really," I said. "Not quite."

"I'm so, so sorry," he said. "You do know it's only eight thirty, right?"

"Two words for you: jet lag," I answered with a laugh. "I'm exhausted."

"Well, maybe I should call tomorrow."

"No, no, we can talk now."

"Okay," he replied. "Stars Collide has just been invited out to LA to play a showcase for Atlantic Records at the Viper Room."

"Oh, Liam, that's wonderful."

"And, well, I was wondering if you'd like to fly out with me."

Now I was wide awake. "Wow." This felt really special. "When do you leave?"

"That's the thing," he began. "We're leaving tomorrow afternoon. We'll be there two days. I know you just got back from London, but you could sleep on the flight."

"Okay," I said, hesitating. "Can I get back to you tomorrow morning?"

"Of course you can, but you know I'll sleep better if you tell me now," he said, turning up the charm.

"I do love LA," I said.

"I know you do, now just say yes," he pleaded. "Pleeeeeeeease?"

I couldn't bear to hear him resort to whining. "What time are you picking me up?"

"Two o'clock sharp," he said.

"Okay, now let me get back to sleep," I said.

"Good night," he said. "Pleasant dreams."

If Liam had told me they were playing a showcase in South Dakota, I probably would've said no. But Los Angeles—who couldn't use a couple of days in LA? Sunshine, ocean, Rodeo Drive . . . what's not to love? Plus, I could take my laptop and work on my London article poolside (in the shade, of course, so I could actually see the screen).

And as I thought about the soothing waves of the Pacific, I drifted off into a deep sleep.

* * *

The next morning my alarm clock scared me half to death. I hadn't used one for the entire London trip because for once, I didn't have a set schedule. Instead, I decided to try to enjoy life more leisurely, like the Europeans do. And even though I love the morning, I probably could get used to life without an alarm clock.

I'd been spoiled with those hearty breakfasts in London, so I decided to whip up a batch of chocolate chip biscotti to go with my morning coffee. Then I flipped on the TV to check out what the girls were yapping about on *The View* and e-mailed Thomas to let him know I'd be working from home (or LA—I mean, what's the dif, anyway?).

As the biscotti baked and Barbara and Elisabeth argued about the virtues of plastic surgery, I started unpacking—and repacking—my suitcase. My London clothes weren't going to work for this trip—no bulky sweaters required in LA, *woo-hoo*! So basically I had to start from scratch. I packed a few lightweight skirts, some cute flowing tops, a couple of pairs of capri pants, and sandals. Lots of sandals. I also threw in some sunblock, a sundress, and a pretty sweater, just in case the weather was freakishly cold for some reason. I sure hoped it wouldn't be, but better safe than sorry, right?

Twenty minutes later I was ready to go, and that's when the butterflies started. Even though Liam wanted to give our relationship another chance, I couldn't help but remember all the reasons it hadn't worked the first time. Of course I knew he cared about me. He liked having me around. It was just the small matter of commitment that threw him for a loop. Any time a better offer came around (like the chance to make it big in Nashville), I was always the last one considered.

I wondered if he'd changed—if he'd finally gotten his priorities in order. Perhaps this trip was an indication that he'd grown, that he was thinking outside himself. Wouldn't it be great if he was? I needed to figure out this Liam thing once and for all.

Liam showed up at my door just when he said he would. "Why, hello, gorgeous," he said as he picked up my bulky suitcase. "You *know* we're only going to be gone for two days, right?"

"Yeah, but a girl's gotta have options," I replied.

"Of course. I should've known that, Syd," he said. "My apologies."

It hadn't been that long since I'd seen Liam, but he looked different. Strikingly different. And not necessarily in a good way. His hair was buzzed short, maybe a little longer than a standard-issue army crew cut, and was dyed jet black. Black! He was wearing a leather jacket with the sleeves pushed up on his arms, and I could see he'd gotten a tattoo, a Chinese symbol of some sort, on his forearm, just above his wrist. Now, it's not that I have anything against tattoos, but along with the black hair, it just didn't seem to suit him. "So when did you get a tattoo, Liam?" I asked as we merged onto 62 east toward the airport.

"I got it a week ago in Uptown. You like?" he asked proudly. "I didn't even cry, can you believe it? You know how much I hate needles."

"Well, you've got your rock-and-roll image to uphold, after all," I replied. "What does it stand for?"

"It's the Chinese symbol for strength," he said. "I figured I was going to need it since we're auditioning for a mainstream deal. This could really take us over the top, Syd. We could be on MTV and get to go on tour with groups like The Killers or The Fray."

"Is this what Stan told you to do, or did you initiate the move to mainstream?"

"Of course it was Stan. He's our manager. That's what we pay him to do, make the connections that are best for the band's career," Liam said.

"I hope this works out better than the move to Nashville did," I said. Inside, I was starting to wonder if this trip had been a mistake for me. Outside, tears started to form. I hoped Liam didn't notice.

"It will," Liam said. "And that's why I wanted you along with me. If we're ever going to make this relationship work, I need you to see everything as it unfolds."

Well. How considerate of him.

We made small talk the rest of the way to the airport. I told him about London. He played me some MP3s of the new songs he'd been working on. Liam's always had a knack for writing catchy lyrics. They stick in your head for days because he has a way of stringing words together that tell a story so cleverly. But these new songs he was playing? They sounded forced, like he was selling out his soul in pursuit of something bigger, commercially speaking.

Now, don't get me wrong. I know people can't go peddling their wares around for free and expect to make a decent living. I certainly don't do my job for free, and I wouldn't expect anyone else to either. And there's nothing innately wrong with wanting to have your music, paintings, writing—what have you—enjoyed by the masses. But what Liam was writing about and how he was doing it, well, it sorely lacked the conviction and strong Christian worldview of his previous efforts. And I told him so after he played his demos for me.

"They definitely sound like pop hits, but there's just something missing," I said.

"Well, they're not mastered yet, Syd. We plan to bump up the vocals, add some strings and additional production. These are only rough cuts."

"I know that," I said. "That's not what I meant. I meant there's something missing on the lyrical side. These songs are so superficial. Anyone could've written them. They just aren't . . . *you*, Liam."

"Writing for the mainstream is different. I can't talk about God and my Christian beliefs; they just won't go for that," he said. "But love and relationships, that's universal. People always want to hear about that."

"You're right, people like hearing about that," I agreed. "But why not stretch people a little, give them something they're not expecting? I'm sure when Switchfoot recorded 'Meant to Live' or 'Dare You to Move,' they weren't exactly what their mainstream label expected to connect with people. But they did, and now the band has the respect of the Christian *and* general market audience. All without sugarcoating what the guys believe."

"I know, but what worked for Switchfoot might not work for me. I need a hit, Sydney. Something huge," Liam said emphatically. "Or I'm going to have to hang it up, which is the last thing I want to do."

Now his true motivation was finally out in the open.

He went on to tell me that after he and Anneka had broken off their engagement, his parents flew home early from a vacation to stage what Liam called an intervention. Ostensibly, the rush trip home was just to make sure he was okay after the breakup. But after the pleasantries had been exchanged, they gave him a lecture he'd never forget. "It was something along the lines of 'If you're ever going to make something of yourself and have anything of value in life, such as a family, then it's time to evaluate what you're doing with your life,'" Liam said with a sigh.

"I've worked really hard since then. Harder than ever before. And that's why I'm going to LA now. I need to make it in the mainstream, and this is my chance," he added. "Plus, I couldn't wait another two days to spend some time with you."

Awww.

The warm and fuzzy sentiment didn't stick with me long. *I'm not going to let his charm get the best of me*, I thought as we boarded the plane. *Not this time.*

After we situated our carry-on items in the overhead compartments, I decided to catch a quick nap. Liam handed me a pillow and blanket, and before long, I was out.

Three hours later, as I slowly opened my eyes, Liam smiled. "Well, good morning, sunshine, you went out like a light. I thought you'd sleep all the way to LA."

"You mean we're not there yet?" I asked.

"No, but we're definitely getting closer," he said.

As I smoothed out my hair and wondered if I'd snored or done anything weird while I was asleep, Liam flagged down the flight attendant. "Could I get a Diet Coke for my friend, please?"

"Well, look at you," I said. "You remembered."

He smiled. "Of course I did."

For the duration of the flight, Liam and I caught up on everything. Two years' worth of everything. I told him about all the guys I'd dated, including Justin, and about that crazy first-date proposal from Gareth. He told me about a couple of bad dates he'd had and how his mom had suggested he sign up for eHarmony immediately. "I think she's scared that she's never going to have grandchildren," he said.

"You've realized, of course, that as an only child, providing your mother with grandchildren does fall squarely on your shoulders," I said playfully.

"How could I forget?" he said. "She reminds me on a weekly basis."

"I bet she does."

I've met Liam's mother only once, back when we dated the first time. She was sweet enough on the surface but pretty high maintenance once you got to know her. When I met her, she rather conspicuously gave me the once-over and seemed to be assessing whether I was good enough for Liam. She asked me a steady stream of questions as we ate lunch. In fact, they got so detailed and overbearing that Liam finally asked her to stop. When I'd first noticed Liam and Anneka together at the Twins game about three years ago, my first thought was to wonder if Anneka was more what his mom had in mind.

Of course, that didn't matter now, but there wasn't any doubt in my mind why Liam felt constant pressure to please his mother. And she wasn't pleased easily.

We were standing in the lobby of the hotel when Stan walked up. "Hello, Sydney," he said flatly, looking a little annoyed that I was there. "Liam, I had a few thoughts about the showcase on the plane. Want to hear them?"

"I'd love to," he said. "C'mon, Syd."

"This doesn't involve Sydney," Stan told Liam. Then he looked at me and said, "No offense, sweetheart, but this is business."

Liam looked over and shrugged his shoulders as if to say he couldn't help what was going on. Instead of standing up to Stan, and in doing so standing up for us, Liam followed him like a little lost puppy to a circle of overstuffed chairs in the lobby, where the rest of the band had already gathered. And with each step Liam took away from me, I had the answer that I'd flown five hours to discover. Liam's music would always come first, and his continued attempts to win me back weren't going to convince me otherwise.

So while Liam was engrossed in his meeting, I rolled my suitcase back out to the curb and got into the first cab that pulled up.

I could've purchased the next flight out to Minneapolis, but it was late, and I decided to treat myself to a night at the Beverly Hills Four Seasons instead. Since I'd come to Los Angeles for work on occasion in the past and had raved about the hotel in one of my articles, they'd given me a 50 percent discount on any future stays. It's a pretty sweet perk, considering how expensive the rooms are normally. I called the hotel from the cab, and by the time I arrived, everything was all set. When the door closed behind the bellman and I was alone in one of the most beautiful rooms in LA, I started to cry.

I couldn't get over the fact that it was over between Liam and me . . . again. This situation fell in the "three strikes, you're out" category. Deep down I knew that even as much as I cared about him, Liam and I just weren't meant to be. And I'd been ignoring that for the last couple of weeks while I fantasized about getting back together with him. Now it was clear to me that that had been nothing but a fantasy, and it hurt.

I turned off my cell phone, called room service, and ordered ice cream and coffee. After it arrived, I curled up in bed with the remote. When I found *Cold Mountain* just starting on HBO, I stopped changing channels. After all, isn't the first rule of recovery for a broken heart to watch as much Jude Law as humanly possible? Yeah, I was pretty sure it was.

* * *

Earlier in the evening, fifteen hundred miles away . . .

Napkins? *Check.* Homemade bread baking in the oven? *Check.* Knives, forks, and spoons in all the right places on the dining room table? *Check.* Okay, so he'd gotten a little help from Pillsbury on the bread, but in all seriousness, Justin hadn't gone to this much trouble to make dinner for a girl since he had for his fiancée. And for Kristin, he wanted everything to be right. He'd really enjoyed hanging out with her the other night and wanted desperately to impress her. Initially, he'd made reservations at Pazzaluna in downtown St. Paul. But after watching Emeril whip up some homemade rosemary-scented ravioli on the Food Network, he'd decided to break out his barely used set of All-Clad pans and work some culinary magic of his own.

Not that he was brave enough to make homemade ravioli. (Discretion, after all, is the better part of valor.) No, Justin thought he'd go with his grandmother's legendary chicken cacciatore recipe instead. Along with some perfectly cooked al dente rotini, the aforementioned bread, and freshly grated Parmesan, the cacciatore would be the centerpiece of the meal. With that out of the way, the only menu course he'd yet to consider was dessert. While he could make a pretty tasty pie (a hidden talent that nobody knew about—even his mother), he didn't have time.

So after considering all the options, he'd whipped up a batch of chocolate chip cookies—simple, yet loved by almost everyone.

By six thirty everything was ready, so he had exactly a half hour to shower and change before Kristin arrived. For some reason, he knew she wasn't the type to be late, so he had to hurry. Fortunately he wasn't into primping. A metrosexual he was not.

Sure enough, Kristin knocked at the door at seven sharp.

"Hi." Justin opened the door wide, wondering if he should kiss her hello. Perhaps not. Take it slow.

"I brought this for you," Kristin said, handing him an antique-looking wine bottle. But it was sparkling apple cider, not the great vintage wine he'd assumed it was. "I don't drink, so that's the next best thing," she added as he took her coat.

She didn't drink? Aside from Sydney, Justin didn't know anyone who didn't drink. *Kristin just gets more interesting all the time*, he thought to himself.

"Wow, it smells wonderful in here!" Kristin looked around Justin's place. "What are we having?"

"You're just going to have to wait and taste," Justin said with a grin. "But I'm pretty sure you'll like it. If not, you'll have to tell my eighty-eight-year-old grandmother. It's her recipe."

"If it's your grandmother's recipe, I'm sure I'll love it," Kristin added, noting how cute Justin looked wearing a marinara-stained apron as he diligently stirred the sauce.

"All right, everything's ready," Justin said as he poured her some of the cider. "Have a seat, and I'll serve."

Even though it was technically their first date, Kristin was surprised at how relaxed she felt with Justin. She liked the way he served her so attentively (and put enough food on her plate to feed a small country, but, hey, she wouldn't complain)—and it was really sweet that he'd gone to the trouble of making a home-cooked meal.

"So do you cook a lot?" she asked as she tried the pasta and cacciatore. "I mean, this could really spoil a girl . . . and it's scrumptious!"

Her comment made him blush, although he wasn't sure why. "Why, thank you, thank you," he said in a fake Italian accent. "If you keep saying things like that, my head will get big and you'll never want to hang out with me again."

She laughed—a big hearty laugh. "I doubt that'll happen."

Over the course of dinner, they picked right back up from where they'd left off last week at Caribou Coffee with nonstop conversation about seemingly every topic under the sun. Everything was going extremely well—they ate; they laughed; they ate some more. But as soon as Kristin asked, "So do you go to church anywhere?" Justin clammed up.

He should've known. She didn't drink. She dressed modestly. She mentioned not liking movies with a lot of violence or bad language. She was probably a Christian. What was it with him and Christians these days? First Sydney—and now Kristin.

"Actually I don't go to church anywhere," he explained. "I guess I'd describe myself as an atheist. I'd like to believe in God, but I don't think I do."

She hadn't seen that one coming, so his answer really threw her for a loop, but she didn't let it show. "Wow, that takes a lot of faith," she said with a smile.

"What do you mean?" he replied as he reached for a third helping of pasta.

"I've always thought that it would take more faith to not believe in God than to believe," she continued. "Look at nature.

There has to be a creator, some grand designer. Everything's so perfectly in sync and complex in structure that it couldn't have just appeared out of nowhere. Don't you agree?"

He'd never really thought about it, to be honest. "Um, I guess so," he said. "But the thing is, I really don't want to change anything about myself. I have my own set of rules, I'm happy, and I don't want to answer to anyone. Oh, and I don't, for any reason, want to miss a Vikings game—ever. If I went to church, that might be a problem."

Kristin laughed. "Well, I guess that's that. A simple yes or no would've probably been fine."

"I'm sorry," Justin said. "I'm just a little sensitive about all of this right now. A couple of weeks ago I went on a date with a girl who is a Christian, and she got me thinking about this crazy stuff. And I'm just annoyed with myself because I was happy just the way I was before I met her. Now I'm getting concerned about things like where I'm going to end up when I die. I mean, I'm not so sure how I feel about any of it," he said. "Basically, I'm one giant mess."

"We all are in our own way," Kristin began. "That's why we need Jesus."

"That sounds great in theory," he said. "But I don't know how that would help."

As he was talking, something finally clicked in Kristin's head, and she had to know. "Justin, can I ask you something?"

"Shoot," he said. "Anything you want."

"Was the girl you went out with named Sydney?"

"How did you know?" he asked, hoping the Lord wasn't revealing stuff to her about him or something weird like that.

"Well, she's my best friend, and she told me about your dates.

I don't know why I didn't make the connection sooner."

She had to be kidding, right? Justin couldn't believe what he was hearing. "So now I've essentially gone out with two best friends—without their knowledge?"

"Afraid so," she said.

＊ ＊ ＊

I had a good cry over *Cold Mountain*, which was exactly what I needed. But still I lay in the king-sized bed and mourned a little longer. *Move on, Sydney.* Who knows? Maybe Liam will get famous one day, and I can say, "I knew him when . . ."

＊ ＊ ＊

Setting the record straight . . .

"So . . . were you planning to go out with Sydney again?" Kristin asked, still just a little in shock that she'd kissed the guy Sydney had gone out with twice.

"Yeah, we were going to see the rerelease of *The Passion of the Christ* when she got back from England," he said.

"Really? You were going to see that with her? That must mean you like her. And if that's the case, why did you ask me over for dinner?"

"I hadn't exactly planned on meeting you, Kristin. I've been out with Sydney twice, I barely know her, and we're certainly not exclusive. So why not?" he answered. "I had no idea you were her best friend. But that's just my luck now, isn't it?"

Kristin laughed. "Yeah, that is pretty unlikely."

"But here's the thing." Justin leaned forward intently. "I really like *you*. I really *want* to see you again."

"I like you too," Kristin said shyly, surprised at how transparent she was being. "But you and Sydney need to work things out first. After that's all sorted out, give me a call. But do see *The Passion of the Christ* with her. It's a great film, and I can't wait to hear what you think about it."

"I will," he said. He could tell that this date that had started with so much promise was coming to an end. He didn't want it to, but he was at peace with the way things needed to progress. "Thanks for coming over for dinner. I had a great time."

"Thanks for cooking for me; it was wonderful," Kristin said.

"I'll plan on cooking for you again then. Soon." Justin held her eyes and tried to telegraph his good intentions.

With that, Kristin grabbed her coat and said good-bye.

And because of that unlikely twist of events, Justin ended up eating chocolate chip cookies all by himself as he sprawled on his couch watching *Friends* reruns.

CHAPTER 13

MOVING IN THE RIGHT DIRECTION?

This may sound like gibberish to you, but I think I'm in a tragedy.

—HAROLD CRICK (WILL FERRELL) IN *STRANGER THAN FICTION*, 2006

I TRIED TO SLEEP LATE, but my body was still on Minneapolis time. And as soon as I opened my eyes, reality started to kick in. As I thought about why I moved to Minneapolis in the first place—for Liam—it felt like someone had kicked me directly in the heart. Sure, life was great in so many ways, but I guess I always thought Liam would be part of it. And now that dream was lost forever.

So I did what every strong woman does: I got up and got to work. There were two messages from Liam on my cell phone, but I deleted them without listening. For the next few hours, I sat poolside with my laptop, working on my London story. It was coming together surprisingly fast, despite my heartsickness, and I loved every minute of writing it. I almost forgot where I was because I was so lost in thought. When I finally looked up, I noticed Enrique Iglesias (sans Anna Kournikova) sitting in a partially secluded section and eating a cheeseburger. Not far from him was Harry Connick Jr. and his family, which particularly thrilled me since I'm a huge fan of his music. I'd never walk up and ask for an autograph or anything, but it was fun to watch him as he hung out with his kids.

Three hours later I wrapped up my story and e-mailed it to Thomas.

Since I'd finished a day earlier than I expected, I decided to treat myself to a spectacular meal on my way to the airport for the red-eye back to Minneapolis (I was darned if I was going to ride back on the same flight with Liam, so I'd changed my ticket). After I'd packed up and checked out, the doorman hailed a cab, and I was off to Mr. Chow in Beverly Hills. It was the perfect time to eat there—the late, late lunch hour (okay, call it the very early dinner hour if you must) when it isn't packed like it usually is. The restaurant not only has a very classy ambience, with its black-and-white checkered tile floors, muted lighting, and simply adorned tables, but the food is just to die for. Calling it delicious is an understatement. Yes, I ate too much. I'll diet tomorrow.

At the airport I checked my e-mail. Thomas had read my London story and already sent it off to the art department. Even though he hadn't given any specific feedback, I knew he must have liked it. Otherwise he would've asked for a rewrite.

Liam had somehow managed to send an e-mail too, but I deleted it with a sigh. What a disappointment he had been! But I figured someday I'd look back at this and think, *Well, at least I got a couple of days in LA out of it.*

＊ ＊ ＊

I'm not sure how it happened, but as soon as I was back in Minneapolis the next day, my heart started to ache something fierce. Turns out I was going to need a little more Jude Law to fully recover from the disappointment with Liam (perhaps *Alfie* would set the right tone and put me on the road to recovery). After voice mail and e-mail, Liam tried text messages. I read them but chose not to reply. There was no point, really. I never wanted to talk to him again, and I certainly wasn't going to send *that* message if I answered him. I mean, what would I say? "Hey, don't worry about it, Liam — have a nice life"? No, I didn't think so.

Truthfully, in some small way I was glad it had happened. It wasn't fun to find out that I'd been right all along about Liam and the high premium he placed on his music career, but it was better to find out now rather than date again for several months only to break up and have to recover yet again. In short, I felt like I was finally moving on with this very long chapter of my dating life.

But even that realization couldn't curb my craving for Ghirardelli chocolate. Just as I was about to reach for my third square, an intervention came in the form of a phone call from Justin.

"What are you doing right now?" he asked.

"Gorging, actually," I said. "You may have actually saved me from death by chocolate."

"Sounds like you're in pretty rough shape," he said. "Why don't I pick you up in a half hour and get you out of the house?"

"Okay," I said, still feeling a little blue. And what if he asked what I'd been up to the last two days? We weren't exclusive or anything — how could we be after just two dates? — but I didn't want Justin to think I wasn't being open with him.

Since most of my clothes were dirty after traveling to London and Los Angeles in just a week, I didn't have many date-night options. But you know, I didn't care. So I decided on my stretchy

Gap jeans that were faded to perfection after two years of constant wear, a black-and-white pin-striped button-up, and my chunky black boots. My hair was still dry and frizzy from the flight, so I ran some Aveda leave-in conditioner through it, sprayed on a little perfume, and was ready in a record ten minutes' time. Of course, Justin wasn't coming over for another twenty minutes, so I killed time by updating my profile on MySpace. I hadn't logged on for months, and my relationship status still said "in a relationship." *Oops.* So I changed that, approved fifteen new friends, checked for messages in my in-box, and signed off.

A few minutes later Justin arrived. "This is for you," he said as he handed me a Sketchers shoebox.

"You bought me shoes?" I asked with a grin. "That's so sweet of you, Justin. But how did you know my size?"

"I didn't buy you shoes, silly," he said. "It's a breakup box. It's got everything you need to survive a breakup."

"Really?" I asked. Suddenly my interest was piqued—I was dying to know what was inside. "Does that mean we're breaking up?"

Justin flushed red, and I wondered if I'd struck a nerve. *Hmmm.*

"Well, I figured we weren't all that serious, really," Justin said. "So I thought I'd be a good friend instead."

"Did you want us to be serious?" I asked.

"I don't know," Justin said. "But the die is cast, so you need to open the box. The faster you open it, the faster you'll get cured. Of me."

"Well, in that case . . ." I said as I lifted the lid. "Okay, we've got Tylenol PM here. Are you trying to medicate me?"

"Nope, those are for the nights when it hurts so much that

you can't sleep," he said. "Because, you know, once I'm gone, it's gonna hurt." He smiled gently. "But seriously—I know how that is after breaking up with my ex-fiancée."

"And the Mad Libs?" I asked.

"Those are to remind you that our breakup will never be as bad as our first date," he said with a laugh.

"Ah, good thinking," I said as I reached for the paper plate with tin foil wrapped around it.

"That's a dozen of my famous chocolate chip cookies," he said. "I baked them for you."

"How sweet!" I said as I gave him a hug.

"And last but not least, the final remedy is in this envelope," he said. "It's not exactly escapist entertainment, but I bet you'll like it." It was two tickets for *The Passion of the Christ* for tonight. "I really hope tonight works for you," he said.

"I think tonight sounds great," I replied.

We grabbed some Thai food a few blocks from my place, then drove to the Mall of America for the movie. Since we were over an hour early, we started walking around the mall. "I really need some new shirts for work," Justin said. "Would you help me pick them out?"

"Sure," I said. "Do you know what kind of shirts you're looking for?"

"Nah, it's more of an 'I'll know them when I see them' deal," he said.

"Ah, okay," I replied. I could tell already he was going to be one of those difficult shoppers.

We started at J.Crew. Their clothes are more utilitarian than trendy but very well made, so I thought that might suit Justin. "Is it me, or does this store's stuff look a little too preppy for me?" he asked. "I feel like I'm getting ready to hang out with the Kennedys or something."

Point taken. "Do you like the Gap?" I asked as we left J.Crew.

"I think I've bought jeans there before," he commented.

"Well, that's a start," I said. "Maybe we'll find a shirt that works there too."

As we walked in, I noticed that Eli was the greeter. "Hi, welcome to the Gap," Eli said, barely making eye contact. "Everything in the store is 20 percent off today, so let me know if I can find a size for you."

"Hey! I didn't know you worked at this store," I said with a smile.

"Sydney? Wow, it's been a long time! How are you?"

"I'm great. Eli, this is my friend Justin. We're looking for shirts."

"What kind of shirts?" Eli asked.

"Why does everyone keep asking me that?" Justin whispered as we walked toward the men's section.

"Oh, I don't know, maybe because it's a fairly pertinent detail in the whole shirt search," I said.

"Always sarcastic, aren't you, Miss Alexander?" Justin said with a laugh.

"Yeah, it's one of my spiritual gifts," I said.

Of course, my comment went way over his head. It was an inside joke I have with my sister.

Being a psychology major, Samantha loves giving psychological tests. Personality tests. Career aptitude tests. Spiritual gifts tests. One day as we waited for her hair color to process at home (because that's what sisters do, right?—keep each other company while we color our hair!), she said, "C'mon, Syd, don't you want to know your spiritual gifts? You should really take this test. I learned so much from it." And after the third "oh c'mon," my resistance wore down.

"Okay, okay, what's the first question?" Patience, you might have already noted, is not one of my spiritual gifts.

After an hour of answering hundreds of questions that seemed like only slight variations of the one before, Samantha determined I was compassionate, hospitable, and good at teaching. While these are certainly admirable qualities and I'm proud to have them, I couldn't believe it took that long to figure out.

"Now if someone asks you what your spiritual gifts are, you know what to say," Sam said proudly.

"Yes, that has always been a concern of mine—what *would* I say if someone asked me that?" I replied.

"Sydney?" My sister smiled wisely at me. "Let's scratch what I said before. I've decided that your spiritual gifts are sarcasm and shopping. Does that make you feel better?"

Well, yes. So now anytime I have the opportunity, I joke about sarcasm being one of my spiritual gifts.

Anyway, on our shirt-finding mission, Eli successfully helped Justin find six different shirts that he actually liked. "Oh, let's just take all of them," Justin said as he slapped down his Visa.

"Wow, man, thanks! You're really going to help my sales draw for the day," Eli said. "My horrible boss said my numbers needed—"

"I heard that, Eli," a female voice shouted from the dressing rooms.

"Yeah, that's her," Eli whispered as he rang everything up. "That'll be $309.39."

"Sydney, remind me never to go shopping with you again," Justin said with a laugh. "I don't think I've ever spent that much on shirts in one day before."

After thanking Eli for his help, we wandered over to Barnes & Noble. "I've never figured out why girls like shopping so much," Justin commented. "For me, it's one giant hassle."

"That's because guys' stuff isn't as much fun to shop for," I began. "See, girls've got purses, makeup, accessories, and, well, let's not overlook *shoes*. Maybe if you had some variety like that, it would be more fun for you."

"Uh . . . I seriously doubt it, but nice try."

We browsed through the magazines, idly flipping the pages of things we'd never ordinarily buy.

"Heeeere's a fine publication," Justin said with a smirk. Holding up the latest issue of *Get Away*, he added in his best broadcasting voice, "'Enjoy the Big Apple on Only $50 a Day' by Sydney Alexander." I rolled my eyes.

"It's got to be fun to see your name in print each month, huh?" he asked as he skimmed my article. "I write our station's newsletter as part of my job, and I'm thrilled to see my byline."

"Yeah, I must admit, I still get pretty excited to see it," I said. "I thought it might get old after a while, but it never does."

After flipping through the latest issues of *People*, *Cooking Light*, and *Budget Travel* (which, in my humble opinion, pales in comparison to *Get Away* in quality, design, and writing), Justin and I hopped an escalator to the fourth floor and headed to the movie theater. Since this wasn't exactly a popcorn flick, we skipped the concessions and found a seat in the center of the theater. Yes, I always have to sit in the middle of a row at the movies. It doesn't matter if it's in the front, middle, or back of the theater, as long as I'm in the center of that particular row. In the same way I like all the furniture in my condo to be symmetrical, I also like to sit that way at the movies.

"A bit anal-retentive, aren't we?" Justin said with a grin as I counted the seats.

"Maybe so, but I just happen to think it's the best movie-watching experience this way," I replied.

"Whatever you say, Sydney," he said lightheartedly. But then his tone grew more sober. "So are you ready for this?" he asked.

"I am," I replied.

I'll admit that as much as I enjoyed *The Passion of the Christ* the first time I saw it, it was hard for me to watch, which I'm sure was exactly Mel Gibson's intent. Knowing that something as violent as a crucifixion wouldn't make for light entertainment by any means, I still wasn't prepared for the sheer brutality of it. One thing was sure, however: It gave me a visual of the experience that stuck with me for a very long time. And it probably made me even more aware of what Jesus went through to redeem mankind.

Just like the first time, I started to cry when I saw Mary's response to the situation. Of course, I've never been a mother, but I've taken care of enough kids to know how attached and protective you become — in a hurry. And if you were the one who carried him for nine months, gave birth, and raised him, I couldn't imagine how horrifying it would be to know your child was going to die in such a dramatic, painful fashion. When I glanced over at Justin, I noticed he was wiping tears from his eyes too, as discreetly as he could.

Then, as the scourging began, my tears flowed more freely, along with those of the majority of the people sitting in the theater. Again I heard Justin sniffling and wondered what he was thinking about all of this. Was he crying because the story of Jesus moved him? Would it cause him to think about the gospel in a new way? I wasn't sure, but I hoped he'd want to talk about it later.

By the end of the movie, we both were a mess. I excused myself and went to the bathroom to make sure the crying hadn't caused my makeup to run every which way. Of course it had, but it didn't take too long to fix. We had originally planned to go out for dinner afterward, but Justin said he didn't really feel up to it. "Syd, I think I might go to the office and wrap up a project I've been working on," he said. But I knew he needed to process what he'd seen without necessarily having to do it in public.

We didn't talk much on the way back to my place, but for some reason, the silence didn't bother either one of us. When we got there I asked if he wanted to come inside for a little.

"That would be nice," he said. "I guess work can wait a little longer."

Finally, as Justin settled in on the couch, he asked, "Did that pretty much follow the story in the Bible?"

"Well, I'm no Bible scholar," I admitted. "But that's how I've always understood it."

"Okay, so you believe that Jesus had to make that sacrifice for people's sins; otherwise, we'd all go to hell?" he asked. "There really was no other way?"

It's times like these I wish I knew Scripture a little better—that I had paid better attention in my Bible classes in college. But I did the best I could. I explained to him how Jesus' birth and death were foretold in the Old Testament, how Jesus was basically born to die so that we might have the opportunity for eternal life. I talked about the significance of the Resurrection and about the free gift we know as grace. And how that grace, something we did nothing to deserve, is what essentially separates Christianity from other more performance-oriented religions. It is our only way to God.

Even though I felt my explanations lacked specificity in certain areas, I could tell that Justin was receptive to what I said. As he asked more questions and I answered them from my own faith experience, he slowly began to open up about his own life. He recalled how from a young age his father didn't believe in God because he didn't have any empirical proof of his existence. While his mom didn't exactly agree with his dad that God didn't exist, she didn't have much interest in learning more about it either. So that disinterest in anything spiritual was inevitably passed down to Justin and his younger brother, Grant.

In high school, Justin said, he knew a girl who was a devout Christian, but the constant persecution she faced for her beliefs just made the whole thing unappealing. "Yeah, I know how that goes," I said with a laugh. "A little too well. She and I could've been good friends."

Even though it seemed odd to him that she brought her Bible to school and often read it during study hall, he said he respected her for "being different," even if that was something he never desired for himself.

"And what do you think about that now?" I asked, wondering how he'd respond.

"I guess I wish I'd been so committed to something that I'd have been willing to stand up for it, no matter what," he answered. "But I just wanted to fit in and do the same things everyone else did."

"Of course you did, Justin; it was high school," I said. "Don't you think I wished the same thing? Let me tell you this, just because you're a Christian doesn't mean that you don't sometimes struggle with it. But that's what is so amazing about Jesus. He actually spent time on earth so he could better identify with the human struggle. He didn't sin, but trust me, he was tempted beyond belief. And in many of the same ways that we are, actually."

Rather than saying anything more, Justin just soaked it all in. "Sydney, I've had a really good time tonight," he began. "But I think I'm going to get going."

"Okay," I said as I walked with him to the door. "Did I say something wrong?"

"Not at all," Justin said. "I'm just getting tired, and I have to go in to work tomorrow. Good night," he said. "And thanks again for everything."

Although he left abruptly, I knew our chat probably provided him plenty of food for thought. When we'd left for the movie earlier that evening, I'd really had no idea that it would affect both of us so dramatically. I'd hoped we would have a thought-provoking conversation later, but I wasn't sure that would happen. Now for the first time since we'd been out, I knew there could be some potential for a future together—if faith was something he wanted to explore further. But whether we ever went on another date or not, I felt like I'd done what I was supposed to do. And I thanked God for the opportunity to share my faith with Justin.

✸ ✸ ✸

It was a long ride home . . .

As Justin headed home, he thought about the movie and some of the things Sydney had said. Both she and Kristin were so different from other girls he knew. They seemed to have a very sure sense about what they believed, and it had a profound effect on the way they lived, the things they pursued. And he liked that. But as far as a relationship went, he finally knew which of them he wanted to pursue.

* * *

Meanwhile, the Metrodome was doing a lively business . . .

To keep from thinking too much about Justin and Sydney being out together, Kristin had invited her brother, Todd, and sister-in-law, Teresa, to a Minnesota Twins game. Other than professional tennis, where she enthusiastically rooted for Roger Federer, baseball was her favorite sport to watch—especially live. She loved a good pitching matchup like tonight, where the teams had only allowed two hits each, neither of which had resulted in a score. While some might consider a game without a score boring, it was exciting to her.

Kristin had cultivated her love of baseball in high school when she'd kept stats for the guys' squad as a senior. Normally, she'd run track in the spring, but after blowing out her ACL her junior year, she'd needed something to occupy her time, so she'd signed up for the open manager position. At first the guys had seemed skeptical about a girl keeping stats and accurate pitching charts. But after seeing her knowledge and love of the game in action during her first night on the job, they were not only impressed but had welcomed her into "the boys' club" with open arms. Heck, she'd even sat in the dugout and spit sunflower seeds with them.

And now that she was living in Minneapolis, Kristin faithfully went to a few Twins games each year. She actually hoped she could talk Justin into coming sometime. That is, if he hadn't fallen for Sydney.

At the moment, she couldn't help but feel a little jealous of her best friend. There was something about Sydney—her vivaciousness, not to mention her natural beauty and wit—that guys always seemed to fall for. And that's exactly what worried Kristin this particular evening. That's not to say she resented Sydney in any way, because that wasn't the case. She was her closest friend, after all, and she only wanted the best for her. But since this whole Justin thing came so blissfully out of the blue and, frankly, made her feel so amazing and alive, she didn't want it to end. At the same time, though, it was weird keeping something like this from Sydney, and she couldn't wait for the day she'd tell her everything.

CHAPTER 14

LOVE IS IN THE AIR

Don't cry at the beginning of a date. Cry at the end, like I
do.

— LAUREL (BONNIE HUNT) IN *JERRY MAGUIRE*, 1996

So much to consider . . .

JUSTIN, YOU KNOW WHAT your problem is? You never know
what you want!"

Those were the last words Justin's fiancée, Claire, had said
before he'd officially called off their wedding. While the end of
their engagement had been coming for a while (as much as Justin
tried to ignore the warning signs), those words had hit a little too
close for comfort. It was true: When it came to making crucial
decisions, Justin always wavered. And this night had been another
prime example. Just a few days after he'd decided that Kristin
was the one he wanted to pursue romantically, he'd called Sydney
again, on Sunday evening. When he'd called, he'd had every
intention of telling her about Kristin.

They talked for almost an hour before he realized he couldn't
tell her on the phone, so he asked if he could come over. As
accommodating as always, Sydney said yes without hesitation. Of

course, if she'd known he'd kissed her best friend while she was in London and was at this very minute trying to figure out a way to gently break it off with her, well, that would've been another story. But she didn't.

Sydney greeted him with a hug when she answered the door. "Hello, stranger," she said. "Guess you missed me already, huh?"

She had no idea.

* * *

"Would you like something to drink?" I asked as I hung up Justin's coat. "I don't have anything alcoholic, but I have Diet Coke, soy milk, orange juice, and some Starbucks mint mocha frappuccinos."

"Wow, that's quite the selection. Are those frappuccinos decaf by any chance?" he asked.

"Afraid not," I said. "It's the hard stuff."

"In that case, I'll have orange juice," he answered. "I'll be up all night if I have that amount of caffeine."

"Oh, the perils of getting old," I said playfully.

Justin just laughed. Ignoring my comment, he asked if I had any good movies we could watch.

"Depends on what your definition of good is," I said. "I have a few thrillers, a few dramas, and, like most girls, I'm well stocked in romantic comedies."

"Oh?" he said. "What's your favorite?

"*Roman Holiday*, but that's a boyfriend movie," I said. "I'll only watch it with someone I'm really serious about." Which means, I didn't add, that I usually watch it alone.

"Is that so?" he said. "That must be some movie."

"Oh, it is," I said. "It's Audrey Hepburn, and I just love her.

But more than that, I connect with it on such an emotional level." I told him how the main character, Ann, is a princess visiting Rome who decides to abandon her duties for one day so she can experience life's ordinary pleasures. "She gets her hair cut, eats ice cream, and, ultimately, she falls in love with the reporter who had been sent to write a story about her," I said.

"So what's the big deal about that? It sounds predictable to me," he said with a laugh.

"No, it's not predictable," I said defensively. "In the end Ann has to choose between having a life with her true love or going back to the castle to fulfill her duties. And much to the chagrin of *every* girl who has ever watched the movie, she chooses to complete her obligations instead. That resonates so much with me. She was willing to forsake true love for duty, and I want to be just as intentional about my relationships. I only want to share certain experiences, like Ann's day in Rome, with the love of my life." I guess that's why I haven't shown the movie to anyone I've dated — even Liam, whom I loved so much, because I was never sure he felt the same way. I just want more, like women did in old movies like *Roman Holiday*.

"What if I told you that I really cared about you but just haven't been very good at showing it?" he asked as he inched closer. "Then would you show me the movie?"

For once, I was fresh out of snappy replies, and that's when he kissed me.

I'll spare you the extraneous details because I'm sure you don't really want to know anyway. But I will say this: Justin's not half-bad at kissing. We didn't say much afterward, but he kept on smiling the rest of the night, so I assumed that was a good sign, right? A few minutes after our lip-lock, we sat on the couch and started watching a movie—a romantic comedy of my choosing. It wasn't *Roman Holiday*, but it was in my top ten favorites: *Two Weeks Notice* with Hugh Grant and Sandra Bullock.

If he hated the movie, he did a good job of convincing me otherwise because he laughed quite a few times. He did mention the movie's predictable ending, however, which made me laugh. "I'm afraid to say that's typical of the genre," I said. "We girls like our happy endings."

I wasn't sure why at the time, but when I said that, the expression on his face suddenly went cold and blank. I ignored it, though, and we hung out for another hour or so before calling it a night.

"I'd best get some shut-eye," I said. "I've got to go back to the office tomorrow."

"Good night, Sydney," he said as he kissed my forehead. "I really enjoyed our quiet night in."

       ❋   ❋   ❋

Same ol' story . . .

As Justin drove home, he felt unsettling pangs of guilt all over. What was he thinking? Once again, he'd intended to tell Sydney he wanted to pursue a relationship with Kristin, and once again he'd failed to do it. What's worse, he'd kissed her! He wasn't entirely sure how she felt about him . . . whether she thought he was someone she could truly love or perhaps just a "ministry project," but he knew he could never love her—he didn't feel the same spark of attraction with her that he'd felt so immediately with Kristin. He'd needed to tell her tonight, but he just couldn't do it. He berated himself all the way home.

* * *

Monday, Monday . . .

The next morning, exhausted and emotionally drained, Justin considered calling in sick for work. He planned to say he had a hangover because he knew his boss, a recovering alcoholic, would completely understand. But if he stayed at home, all he would do was wallow, worry, and watch lame TV shows like *The Jerry Springer Show* or, worse yet, soap operas. So he decided that a day at the office might actually be a better alternative.

Armed with two Mountain Dews (coffee just wasn't going to cut it today) and strawberry Pop-Tarts (his favorite since college), he quickly retreated to his office and checked his e-mail to see if he'd heard from either Sydney or Kristin.

He had zero new messages in his in-box. How depressing.

While stopping off at the break room to put his sack lunch in the fridge, Simon the tech guy (no one knew his last name, so everyone called him that) asked Justin why he hadn't been at the PBS crew's happy hour the previous night. Going to Brit's Pub had been a Sunday night tradition for more than two years now, and Justin had rarely missed an opportunity for all-you-can-drink Guinness on tap.

"I hung out with a friend last night," Justin said.

"Yeah, right." Simon snorted. "It must have been a chick if you skipped brew with the crew."

Did he really just say "brew with the crew"? Justin wondered. "Um . . ."

"I knew it!" Simon said. "How long has this been going on?"

"It's casual. A couple of dates. Dinner once. A movie—"

"Oooh. A mooovie. What did you see?"

Justin sighed as he considered whether or not to lie about what he'd seen.

"Actually, we saw the rerelease of *The Passion of the Christ*," Justin said defensively. "I didn't expect to enjoy it, but I really did. I thought it was well done."

"Boy, you must be serious about this chick," Simon said. "Otherwise, you'd never see *that*."

"If you knew this girl, you probably would've seen it too. She's hot." Justin squirmed a little inside, but what could he say?

"Sweeet," Simon said.

And with that said, Justin left the break room and retreated to his office, slamming the door behind him. All of this had to stop—and soon.

*　*　*

Later that day . . .

Around four o'clock, about fifteen minutes after she got home from work, Justin gave Kristin a call. Although she tried to act calm and composed on the phone, she was thrilled to hear his voice. And he enjoyed hearing hers as well. They caught up on the details of each other's day—she told him about the student who threw up on his desk right before the bell rang for lunch; he told her about today's episodes of *Sesame Street* and *Teletubbies*. Although it definitely fell into the category of small talk, it didn't matter to either of them. It just felt good and comfortable and right.

"Oh, I've been meaning to ask—what did you think of *The Passion of the Christ* the other night?" Kristin asked.

Justin had suspected she was going to ask that—even if he'd hoped she wouldn't. "I really enjoyed it," he said. "Believe it or not, I actually cried through most of it."

The thought of Justin crying almost made Kristin tear up herself. "I wish I could've been there," she said.

"Yeah, I wish you would've been there too," he answered, knowing if she had been there, things probably would've turned out much differently.

The conversation took a downward turn from there.

※　※　※

At the Mall of America . . .

"Should I go with silver or gold?" Eli was perusing the rings at Kay Jewelers. He'd dragged Rachel, one of his Gap coworkers who also happened to know Samantha, along for some female advice—because goodness knows he needed it.

"With Samantha's skin tone, I'd definitely go with silver," Rachel said. "Plus, silver's really trendy right now."

"Thanks, that's very helpful," he said. "Very, *very* helpful."

Eli didn't know much about jewelry, let alone love, but he was about to go out on a limb for Samantha. In a week she was going to leave for Europe for three months, and he didn't want her to go without knowing how he felt about her—once and for all. Obviously it was much too soon to propose (plus, the thought alone made him feel like he was about to break out in hives), but he wanted to give her a gift that said, *I'll be thinking about you constantly while you're away (and you'd better not forget about me either).* So he thought a pretty ring, something with sapphires to match her deep blue eyes, would be perfect.

After a half hour of deliberation and about a third of the funds he had been saving for a new laptop, he was now the proud owner of a gorgeous ring for Samantha. It was a not-too-thin, not-too-thick silver band with a half-carat sapphire in the middle and two very small diamonds on each side. Although Eli thought it was lovely, and for six hundred dollars plus tax he thought it *better* be, he asked a couple of other girls at work for affirmation.

"Oh my goodness, Eli, you must seriously love this girl," Ashley said.

One point for Eli.

"Eli, wow, if she doesn't take it, can I, like, have it?" Leanne asked.

"Um, no," he replied.

Two points for Eli.

"You'd better not be expecting a raise now that you've bought something so outrageous," Chelsea said.

Three points for Eli.

With enough kudos from his coworkers to feel good about his purchase, Eli's next stop was Hallmark. He always hated buying cards because they never seemed to say the right thing. So instead of wasting time reading the sappy sentiments some romantically challenged copywriter came up with, Eli selected a blank card with a simple black-and-white photo of a couple kissing in the rain in Paris. It was perfect, considering she was going to Europe. But wait—what if she fell for some French guy while she was in Paris and this card was a foreshadowing of that?

Seriously, he was overreacting a little. Okay, a lot. But he didn't want the card to inspire thoughts of some random French guy named Pierre who wowed her with his art collection and knowledge of fine wines and cheeses. No, this card simply wouldn't do. So he opted for another blank card with a picture of a golden retriever puppy wearing a red heart on its collar. All girls love dogs, right? There's nothing controversial about dogs—especially a golden retriever.

The last step was figuring out how to give her the ring. Presenting it to her during dinner would be far too cliché. Slipping it in her purse with no explanation would definitely be the chicken way out. Eli needed something in-between cliché and chickening out. Oh, he'd figure something out. He was confident of that. Maybe he'd just be spontaneous. Yeah, Eli the spontaneous, that had a nice ring to it.

❋   ❋   ❋

Just like old times—roast beef at Mom's house . . .

"Mind helping me mash these potatoes?" Aidan's mom asked as she checked on the roast.

"Sure," Aidan answered as he picked up the masher and went to work. "Mom, you know how I've been wanting to go to India, right? I'm actually going to do it. I—"

"What?" Aidan's mom asked, stricken by his news. "What about that nice Samantha? I thought things were going so well."

"Actually, we broke up, Mom," Aidan said softly. "Sorry to burst your bubble there. I know you were hoping for marriage, but this trip will be a really good thing for me."

"Well, I'm glad," she said. "You know I just want you to be happy."

❋   ❋   ❋

Sleepless in Minneapolis . . .

It was ten thirty a.m., and Kristin was still in her pajamas, an anomaly during the workweek of a schoolteacher. Despite her best efforts to pull herself together, she simply couldn't after Justin's long phone call last night. Tired of feeling like he was lying to everyone, including himself, Justin had confessed to Kristin that he'd kissed Sydney "by mistake."

"I know you probably won't believe me, but it meant nothing," he'd said. "I didn't exactly plan it."

"Kind of like our kiss, right?" Kristin had retorted.

"No, not like that at all. Our kiss meant a lot to me."

She hadn't been sure whether to believe him or not. So she'd just told him her own truth. "I was really hoping everything would work out with us. I haven't enjoyed someone's company this much in a long time. But . . . I can't be in a relationship when you're not being honest with me. Or with Sydney. And when I'm keeping secrets from my best friend. It's just not right."

"I know. It's not," Justin said. "Trust me, you're better off without me and all my issues."

"But I like you and your issues," Kristin added.

Justin laughed. He'd never heard someone say *that* before. "I think I just need some time, Kristin . . . time to think it out and work it out so that I don't hurt anyone. Will you allow me that?"

"Sure," she replied, wondering what other options she had.

Even though Justin hadn't officially ended a relationship that had barely begun, somehow she'd still felt it was over between them when they'd said good-bye. And as much as she tried to convince herself that she didn't need him anyway or that someone better would come along in the right time, she couldn't stop crying.

CHAPTER 15

A CHANGE OF SCENERY

It is a truth universally acknowledged that when one part of your life starts going okay, another falls spectacularly to pieces.

— BRIDGET JONES (RENÉE ZELLWEGER) IN *BRIDGET JONES'S DIARY*, 2001

WITH ANOTHER DEADLINE IN progress at *Get Away*, it was shaping up to be one insane week. That—combined with the fact that I wanted to find some time to help Samantha plan what to pack for her three-month internship—left me a little frazzled. But even in my most stressed-out moments, thoughts of Justin's kiss the other night kept me going. I loved how his walls were slowly coming down, how he was finally opening up. I was in such a good mood that I actually sang along with my *ABBA's Greatest Hits* CD (for reasons I can't fully explain, their music always makes me smile, especially "Dancing Queen"—which, as you might imagine, has the added effect of making me want to bust a move around the office) as I copyedited the upcoming cover story about India. I'm sure that Andrea—her office is across the hall—was scratching her head over that.

But in spite of my happiness, I noticed that something odd was happening around the office again. The mysterious closed-door meetings of a couple of weeks ago had resumed (or maybe they'd never stopped, since I'd been gone for over a week). The typical workday chatter around the office was missing too. Instead of being paranoid, though, I chalked it up to deadline week. Everyone is always a little on edge during deadline week. Surely that was all it was.

* * *

It was about an hour before lunch when my past suspicions were confirmed. Thomas knocked on my door just as I was coming up with the teaser copy for the table of contents page. "Sydney, we need to talk," he said brusquely as he slid into the chair across from my desk.

"What's going on?" I asked, suddenly very nervous, given the look on his face.

"There's really no way to sugarcoat it," he said. "Corporate has decided to pull the plug on *Get Away*. We weren't meeting financial expectations, especially in comparison to our competitors. So this issue will be our last."

Oh no, oh no, oh no! I couldn't believe my ears, so I did what most people do in this situation: I tried to argue over a decision that had already been made. "But wait a minute—I thought the circ numbers that just came in had actually doubled in comparison to last year," I said in disbelief.

"That's true, our circ numbers doubled," Thomas said. "But our advertising revenue—that's what's suffering."

"What if we did more advertorials? More supplements, more how-to guides?" I was still trying to bargain.

"We considered all of those options carefully," Thomas said.

"Unfortunately, corporate just doesn't have any patience left."

"So . . . I'm out of a job?" I asked, still in a state of shock. I was hoping that maybe the corporation that owned *Get Away* might have a place for me at one of its other publications.

"Yes," Thomas said. "I'm sorry." Easy for him to say—I'll bet he had a golden parachute lined up.

"There'll be the usual week of severance for every year of service." Ah, that would make my parachute, um, lead.

He kept talking because I'd been struck dumb with shock and fear. "You know I'll be happy to put in a good word for you somewhere else, write you a reference letter, whatever."

"Thanks, Thomas," I said meekly. "I appreciate that."

With that, he rose. "By the way, you wondered why Lucinda walked out that day," he said. "She knew the end of *Get Away* was inevitable and wanted to get a jump on finding a new position before the bottom fell out. She's at *Vogue* now."

I blinked. "How did she get a job at *Vogue*?"

"Oh, you know Lucinda—she's got a way about her."

Yeah, she certainly does.

Once Thomas left the room, I e-mailed Justin immediately and told him everything, hoping he'd want to go to lunch and maybe talk me down from the ledge I sensed I was on. As I waited for a reply, I tried to continue my work, but I kept getting distracted, thinking how this would be the last deadline week at *Get Away*, how it wouldn't be long before I would no longer be coming to this office every morning. Then it hit me and I started to stress out. Sure, there would be a severance package, but I hadn't been here all that long, so it wouldn't be a lot. And what would I do next? I stopped myself right there because I knew that somehow God would provide for me.

Fifteen minutes later Justin e-mailed me back. But rather than the consoling words I expected, he was giving me the brush off. For good.

From: Justin Stanley <ihatebugsandlizards@hotmail.com>
To: Sydney Alexander <salexander@getawaymagazine.com>
Subject: Re: The End of Get Away As We Know It

Sydney,

First off, I am sorry to hear about your job. But knowing you, you'll bounce back and probably do something even more exciting. I wish I had more to say about that, but there you go. I'm selfish as always, which I guess is why I'm writing you this rather than saying it over the phone or in person.

I wasn't lying when I said that I've enjoyed every second we've spent together. You're an amazing woman, truly a rare find. But I haven't been honest about something, and I want to tell you now so I can stop feeling bad about it. While you were in England, I met your friend Kristin at Caribou Coffee. She was correcting papers or something when I started talking to her. I really liked her company, for probably the same reasons you do (except for the fact I thought she was hot), so we ended up hanging out. No big deal, right? But then when I said good-bye to her that night, I kissed her. I hadn't planned to. It just happened. We both enjoyed it, at least I think she enjoyed it. She looked pretty happy. So I asked her out and cooked dinner for her. During the course of conversation, she eventually figured out that I was the same guy you'd been out with (what are the chances?). So she encouraged me to go to the movie with you and set the record straight about us. But I didn't, of course, and things got more confusing.

My hope is that you won't be mad at Kristin. I'm the one who dropped the ball. The truth is, if you'll actually believe me, I really like both of you. I'd planned to pursue her, but then I couldn't resist you either. Now there's a good chance I won't be with either of you. But I do want to thank you for our time together. I've learned and thought about things I never had before. Thanks for being such a strong believer in what you believe in and for being willing to share it.

— Justin

There's so much I could have said after reading his e-mail, but all I could do was tear up. He'd been going out with Kristin behind my back? And Kristin had never bothered to tell me? He thanked me for sharing my beliefs? This was too much. And without letting Thomas know, I snuck out of the office early. A few hours early. After all, what was he going to do — fire me?

Between sobs and repeatedly asking myself how this could happen, I decided on the drive home that a pity party was in order. I changed into my favorite pajamas, watched TV, and ordered takeout. But after a couple of hours of wallowing my sorrows in Chinese food, ice cream, and whatever else I could find, I realized how ridiculous I was being. So instead of continuing my "Everybody Hates Sydney" campaign, I decided to pray about everything—my job, my relationships, my future. And I don't want to go all hokey spiritual on you, but let me just say this was the best therapy of all. I poured out my heart, all my frustrations, all my fears, all my shortcomings. When I was done more than an hour later, I felt better. Not exactly bouncing-off-the-walls happy by any means, but I felt at peace, which, in some instances, is even better.

Later that evening I got dressed and hung out with Samantha at her place. I spared her all the gory details of what happened with Justin but told her about my impending unemployed status.

"So," she asked sympathetically, "what are you going to do now?"

"I'm not sure yet, but I'm positive it'll have something to do with writing," I said.

"Well, that goes without saying," Samantha said. "But what?"

"I wish I knew," I said and then sighed. My sister sighed too.

❋ ❋ ❋

The next day no one asked me about stepping out of the office for the afternoon—which was a relief since I really did want to hold on to my job as long as possible. Even though we were at the busiest stage of the deadline week process, all the work we had to do kept me pleasantly distracted. I didn't hear from Justin, which didn't surprise me, considering I hadn't said much in my reply to his e-mail. But far more unfortunate was that I hadn't heard from Kristin for days. So I decided to reach out by e-mail.

From: Sydney Alexander <salexander@getawaymagazine.com>
To: Kristin Brown <kbrown@maranatha.edu>
Subject: You must be dead.

Since I haven't heard from you in ages, I can only assume one of the following situations has occurred. (1) You are dead. (2) You are not dead, but you've run off with one of the Minnesota Twins players and are now on your honeymoon in Fiji. Of course, this scenario would make me very envious of you (well, except for the part about being married to a baseball player), so you've decided not to rub it in. (3) You're not dead, but you found out that Justin told me about your time together while I was away, and you're not sure how I feel about that. And rather than find out, you're opting for the old-fashioned avoidance method.

If any of these are the case, please feel free to contact me at your earliest convenience (unless it's option one, of course, since that would be impossible) because I'd really love to catch up. I miss you and hope all is going well.

— Sydney

A few minutes later Kristin called me. "Your e-mail cracked me up," she said. "Another fine performance by Ms. Sydney Alexander."

"Well, I'd like to thank the Aca—"

Kristin started to giggle.

"Okay, in all seriousness, I wanted to let you know that the whole thing with Justin is no big deal. Aside from the fact that you could've told me what was going on," I said. "If you and Justin had a great time together, you *know* I'd want the best for you."

"Oh, Syd, I really should've known that was how you'd respond," she replied. "But everything happened so fast and unexpectedly, and I just didn't know what to think."

"No worries," I said. "Do you want to grab an early dinner and catch up?"

* * *

Over near campus . . .

After picking up her mail (she was obsessively checking for her passport), Samantha had two hours to kill before Eli would arrive to take her to dinner. For some reason, Eli wouldn't tell her where they were going, so Samantha wasn't sure what to wear. But rather than worry about it, since she already had so much on her mind with finals and her trip coming up, she decided on something in between casual and dressed up.

As her European internship grew closer by the day, she felt a mix of nervousness and excitement. Except for a mission trip to Mexico when she was in eighth grade, she'd never left the country or the comfort of good friends and family before. And although she was sure it was going to be one of those defining life experiences, it wasn't going to be easy to leave everyone behind. Especially Eli.

* * *

Kristin and I met for dinner at Chili's. I was craving their chips and queso and chicken fajita quesadillas, and Kristin is a devoted fan of their Chicken Crispers and fries, so it was the perfect option. As always, we gabbed nonstop. We compared notes on Justin, talked about the new house Kristin might be buying, and brainstormed ridiculous ideas for jobs I could pursue after *Get Away*. My personal favorite was dog-walker to the stars, but we decided I probably couldn't make a living at it, considering how little I knew about dogs and the fact that Minneapolis isn't exactly swarming with celebrities—with the exception of musicians like Prince and Paul Westerberg, of course. Oh, and Bob Dylan, who is known to make a cameo in the area on special occasions. So that was out, leaving me with Mall of America tour guide, makeup artist for MAC cosmetics, or copywriter for Starbucks.

Gotta love having options.

※　※　※

Hello, young lovers, wherever you are . . .

While there'd never been any doubt in Samantha's mind that Eli was good-looking, he had never looked as good as he did tonight. In fact, when she opened the door, she nearly did a double take. Eli wasn't the sort of guy who'd ever get a facial, but he had this fresh-scrubbed glow Samantha hadn't seen before. Plus, the shirt he'd chosen, a striking shade of blue that matched his eyes, certainly didn't hurt his cause either. Oh, and he smelled heavenly too. But in order not to boost his ego to the stratosphere, she kept her compliment decidedly more low-key. "You look great tonight, Eli," she said as he opened the car door.

"You don't look so bad yourself, Sam," he said with a grin, noting how gorgeous her hair looked. Normally Samantha wore her hair up in a clip, but tonight she actually wore it down, which made her look sophisticated, regal even. Aside from the change in hairstyle, she'd apparently bought something new to wear too. He'd never seen her soft pink sweater before or the black dress pants that flared out at the bottom. They definitely weren't from the Gap. Probably Express, one of her favorite places to shop.

They talked nonstop on the way to the restaurant. Because

he'd been keeping their destination a surprise, Samantha didn't ask where they were going, which was extremely difficult for someone as curious as she. Finally he pulled up to Arezzo Ristorante in Edina, a suburb not far from Minneapolis. "Here we are," he said.

As they got seated, Samantha looked around admiringly and said, "This place is really nice. How did you find it?"

"Actually, I researched it online," he began. "Then I drove out here, sampled a meal, and asked around a little. You'd be amazed at how much information is available online these days."

"Wow — that was really thoughtful, Eli," Sam said, reaching across the table and taking his hand. "Seriously, this is great."

"And just wait till you taste the food," he said.

"*Mmm.*"

As they waited for their food, Eli held Samantha's hand. She loved that; there was something comforting about his touch — he made her feel safe. She knew that even though she would be gone for three months, he'd always be there for her. And that meant so much to her to have a friend — a friend with future potential, or whatever they were — like that.

After bread, appetizers, and the main course, Eli and Samantha couldn't eat another bite. But in spite of how full they were, the biggest surprise of the night was coming with dessert, so Eli talked Samantha into ordering the chocolate mousse, even if it was only for one bite. Not one to turn down chocolate, Samantha happily obliged.

"So . . . what are you most excited about seeing in Europe?" Eli asked as they waited for their dessert to arrive.

Samantha hadn't really thought about it much because she'd been frantically busy with school and preparations for a three-month trip, so it took a minute for her to answer. "Well, you know how much I love *The Sound of Music*," she began. "I know it's cheesy, but I think living in the Alps and exploring that area is going to be pretty marvelous."

"You won't exactly be roughing it there," Eli said. "So the Alps, anything else?"

"From what I've heard, Rome is pretty fantastic too. I can't wait to see all the famous places like the Coliseum, the Spanish Steps, all of that," Samantha continued.

As she finished her sentence, dessert arrived.

She spotted the black velvet box immediately and went into semi-shock, although Eli would've never guessed from how calm she looked. Was he going to propose? What should she say in response? Glancing at her hands, she also realized her nail polish was chipped, which was sad since she'd gotten a manicure only a few days ago. Why didn't she think to touch them up? *Well, because you never thought he'd propose tonight, silly*, she thought to herself as she glanced up at Eli.

Eli was beginning to get a little impatient. "Would you like to open the box, Samantha, or did you want to stare at it all night?" he said in a half-joking manner. "Or wait—read the card first."

"Yes, of course, I'm sorry, Eli. I was just, well . . ." she stammered as she opened the envelope. He'd never seen her so visibly flustered before. It was kind of cute.

> *Dearest Samantha,*
> *As always, I'm a little late in saying this. But*
> *before you leave for Europe, I have to say*
> *something. I haven't been very good at showing*
> *it sometimes, but I love and care about you more*
> *than any other person on the planet (except for*

*God, but that goes without saying). I've always
shied away from expressing my true feelings, hoping
maybe they'd go away and I'd still always have
the security of having you as a dear friend. But the
more time we've spent together, I've discovered that
I no longer want you as just a friend. I want you
to be my girlfriend. We've been acting like we've
been dating for so long, and trust me, countless
people have asked what the deal is, so I'm asking
you if you'd like to take the step with me.*

*And if you would, I'd like for you to have
what's in the box. Don't worry, it's not THAT.
But I hope you'll like it.*

  Love always,

  Eli

She had never read a more beautiful letter in her life. Who knew
that Eli could express himself so well in writing? Samantha certainly
didn't. But if the truth were told, she'd probably underestimated
him in many ways over the last three years. She was always looking
for the next unexpected surprise when it came to guys—the guy
who came out of the blue, charmed her, and then, without her
permission, broke her heart. It seemed to be a pattern with her.
Yet there was Eli, patiently waiting in the background all along,
waiting for her to come around and be his.

With tears in her eyes, she finally looked over at him. "That
was an incredible letter," she said. "And, yes, I'd be proud to be
your girlfriend." When she opened the box, she was stunned. The
ring was absolutely lovely, definitely not a cheapie that was bound
to turn her finger green. "Eli, this must have cost you a fortune,"

she said.

"That doesn't matter," he said. "I just hoped you'd love it and have something pretty to remember me by while you're away."

"Ring or not, I wouldn't have forgotten you, Eli," she added. "But I can't wait to wear it."

Eli removed the ring from the box and slipped it on her finger. It looked perfect. Then he leaned over and gave her a kiss.

As soon as Eli dropped Samantha off at home later that night, Samantha called her sister. It was late, but she knew Sydney wouldn't mind, given the circumstances. As they debated the pros and cons of starting a relationship, they eventually determined there were far more pros than cons.

"But he is a youngest child. Did you think of that, Sam?" Sydney said, loving that Sam was about to abandon the birth-order theory she'd defended so ardently.

"Yeah, I know—and I bet you're loving that!"

Sydney just laughed. She was genuinely happy as she listened to Samantha rattle on about Eli and finals and her upcoming trip.

※　※　※

After we hung up, I thought about how good it was to talk to Samantha. I love that she lives so close and that we can (and do!) hang out together. She was offered scholarships to several schools, some prestigious ones like Duke University even, but she wanted to live in Minnesota to be closer to me. Lots of sisters with so many years between them don't really click, but Sam and I always have. Maybe it's because we shared a room growing up. Or maybe it's our sarcastic sense of humor. But we make a point to stay in touch, no matter how busy we are.

Then I thought about Liam, but only briefly. I realized that he'd never really been my *friend*, the way Eli is Samantha's friend. And this made the sadness I felt about the situation begin to lighten.

A friend of mine once said to me that "the art of love is largely the art of persistence." I never thought it sounded all that romantic, but with Samantha and Eli as an example, I understood what she was talking about a little better.

CHAPTER 16

A NEW YORK STATE OF MIND

Maybe the absence of signs is a sign.

— JONATHAN TRAGER (JOHN CUSACK) IN *SERENDIPITY*, 2001

THREE DAYS AFTER WE put the final issue of *Get Away* to bed, a press release went out to announce our now-defunct status to the publishing world. It was sad, really. I loved my job, and now I was forced to regroup and look for something new. At least my severance package was more generous than Thomas had indicated. If I were frugal, it would tide me over for a couple of months, which was good, considering I hadn't even updated my résumé yet.

But the whole idea of not working was a little foreign to me, honestly. After working so hard day after day and week after week for the last five years, I wasn't exactly sure what to do with my spare time. I know, I know: I finally had time to, well, smell the roses . . . or whatever it is that people do when they aren't burning the midnight oil. But given all that had being going on in my personal life, I missed work as a place to escape to, as sad as that sounds.

What I really needed was a good spiritual retreat, some time away to pray about this next phase of my life, whatever it might be. When a girl in my Bible study faced a similar crossroads in her life, she went to a nearby monastery to pray and fast for an entire weekend. I knew it would be difficult for me to go without food for that long—and being silent would be even harder—but I thought I'd call her and find out more about it anyway.

Just as I was reaching for my phone, an unknown name appeared on my caller ID.

"Hello?"

"Hi, is this Sydney?"

"Sure is," I replied.

"This is Lawrence Landers. I'm the managing editor at *Out and About*," he said. "How's it going?"

Out and About? One of the big New York magazines. Oh my gosh! "I'm doing all right, considering all that's happened at *Get Away*," I said.

"That was a real shame," Lawrence said. "Especially for you. And that's why I'm calling. We have an assistant editor position available. We know your work, and we think you'd be a good fit. I'd like to fly you out to discuss your coming to work for *Out and About*—that is, if you'd be willing to relocate to New York."

I realized I'd been standing there with my mouth hanging open ("they" know my work?), so I shut it. Then I opened it again. "Wow! Yes, I'm game. When did you want me there?"

"How about tomorrow?" he asked. "We're on deadline next week, so that would be insane. You know how it is."

"Tomorrow works for me," I said.

"Okay, I'm going to go ahead and book you a flight right now and will e-mail you the info," he said. "What's your e-mail address?"

I paused. Oh yeah, my *Get Away* account wasn't working

anymore. "It's sydneyalexander@gmail.com," I said.

"Perfect, Sydney, see you in New York tomorrow," he said. "Safe travels."

"Thanks for considering me," I began. But by this point, I realized he'd already hung up.

*   *   *

That afternoon, at the Har Mar Mall . . .

As Kristin looked for something new to read at Northwestern Book Store, she had an epiphany when she passed the overstocked section of Bibles. For days now she'd been praying about ways she could make a breakthrough with Justin. In one sense, it was for selfish reasons—she really enjoyed his company. But she also wanted to continue to water all the seeds that she and Sydney had planted on their dates with him. And now that Kristin knew that she was the one he wanted to date—not Sydney—she thought a gesture such as getting him a Bible and writing something special in it might be exactly what was needed to make those seeds grow. And even if Justin never called again, he might still read it someday out of sheer curiosity.

With so many translations to choose from, it wasn't easy deciding which would be the best for Justin. She wanted him to be able to get the gist of what he was reading, so she decided against the King James Version, even if that's what her first Bible had been. She liked the contemporary feel of *The Message*, especially for someone who wasn't yet a believer, so that was an option. The NIV always worked well for her, so that might work too.

Ultimately, after glancing through ten different translations, she opted for a leather-bound copy of *The Message*. To personalize it, she had the salesgirl put Justin's name on the cover with silver foil lettering.

After paying for her purchase and heading back home, Kristin took out one of her favorite pens and wrote a quick note inside. She kept it short but sweet:

> *Justin,*
> *I care about you so much that I want to share one*
> *of my favorite things with you — God's Word. I*
> *hope that someday you'll join me on this amazing*
> *journey of faith.*
> *Love,*
> *Kristin*

In hindsight, *Love, Kristin* may have been a bit much. But there was no turning back now. Well, unless she scrapped the idea altogether. But rather than chicken out, she decided to go through with it, no matter how Justin ended up responding. So she found a mailing envelope, used the Internet to track down his work address, and made a note in her dayplanner to mail it in the morning.

* * *

After catching up with my mom on the phone for a little more than an hour (she just remodeled the house I grew up in and loves it, which makes me happy; she's worried about my job — or lack of it — which does not), I checked my e-mail for my New York itinerary for tomorrow. Frankly, I was still in a state of disbelief about the whole thing. After suddenly having no employment options, *poof,* this had come out of the blue. Maybe living in New York would be a good change for me. It certainly would be a huge difference from Minneapolis and much more expensive. I'd researched the cost of living online in preparation for my interview. Then again, I'm sure the salaries at *Out and About* take that into account. But, hey, I didn't have to worry about that now; they might not even offer me the job.

It looked like I was flying into LaGuardia around noon. Sweet — they were putting me up in a midtown hotel, which meant I'd be able to do a little shopping when I was done with the interview. But, yikes, I needed to start on my résumé right away so I could e-mail it to Lawrence before our meeting. I needed to pack too. And I wanted to spend some time praying about the *Out and About* opportunity. Whether or not this panned out, I was confident that God would work out the details. And who knows? Maybe soon I'd be on my way to New York for good. Hey, there were definitely worse things.

※　※　※

Monday night at Brit's Pub . . .

As Justin sat at Brit's Pub with a few of his friends from work, he didn't even bother to have a beer. He wasn't sure why, but he hadn't purchased one, and for once, he actually felt better sober. It was a strange phenomenon, for sure. He'd always enjoyed his alcohol; it was a great way to escape everything that bothered him. But the more he thought about what Kristin had been saying about her life — and more specifically life in general — the things that used to crank his chain, like alcohol, just didn't as much.

Now, that didn't mean he was ready to embrace everything that Kristin had said, but he was thinking about giving her a call. It had been a week, he missed her, and he wondered what was new in her world.

* * *

Since Sam had left for Europe and everyone else I knew would be getting ready for work, I was forced to take a cab to the airport. At six a.m. the cab driver picked me up and—in what was essentially a preview for New York City—drove like a madman, nearly veering off the road three or four times. I was all about getting to the airport a little early, but that was ridiculous.

I felt relieved when I made it there in one piece. Once I got to the airport and checked my bag, I grabbed a bagel at Bruegger's and perused the *Minneapolis Star Tribune*. For the first time in several years, I decided to browse through the classifieds to see what kinds of positions were available these days. And it didn't take long for me to realize that not much had changed since I first moved to Minneapolis. The majority of the jobs that actually paid well were in telemarketing and health care, two fields I couldn't be less qualified to work in. A little depressed by what I found (or the lack thereof), I put the paper aside and started reading the new issue of *Vogue* to see if I could find out what Lucinda's new position was.

Well, look at that—she'd taken the managing editor position, meaning she would get to decide which writers she wanted to work with. Maybe I'd call her while I was in New York—the worst she could say was, "Why would I bother hiring *you* as a freelance writer," right? And that would be that. Or maybe she'd remember how I slaved for her and actually give me a shot. I'd never written for a fashion mag before. That could be really fun, or at least a change from the norm.

* * *

In a Brooklyn Park post office . . .

Kristin spent her lunch break standing in line at the post office; she wanted Justin to have her gift as soon as possible. As much as she tried to distract herself with other things, he was always on her mind. She thought of the night he made dinner for her and how sweet a gesture that was. And, of course, like any girl with a crush, she replayed their kiss in her head about a thousand times. She knew it wasn't the healthiest behavior, pining over Justin the way she did. But she saw great potential in him, and frankly, more than anything, she just enjoyed his company. He made her laugh with his dry—and often sarcastic—sense of humor. She liked his self-deprecating nature, a quality they shared. But mostly she wanted to cheer him up, make him dinner, and go on dates with him again. Now that she and Sydney had worked everything out, she could date him freely without feeling guilty.

But until he called, she couldn't do a thing. But she did pray—a lot.

* * *

The last time I was in New York for work I saw so many Broadway shows for a story that I didn't have time for anything else. Not that I'm complaining, of course. That was a great gig for someone who enjoys plays and musicals as much as I do. But this time around

I hoped to walk around Manhattan, or at least a section of it, exploring as many nooks and crannies as I could. Plus, I just had to go to Serendipity 3 for one of their famous frozen hot chocolates.

But the first order of business was my three o'clock appointment at the *Out and About* office. Once I was in my hotel room, I unpacked my clothes and a steamer. Not sure what their dress code was, I thought I'd better step it up a notch, just in case. I didn't want to get ridiculed (think Andy Sachs in *The Devil Wears Prada*) at my initial job interview. Since New Yorkers always look so chic in black, I opted for a black two-button suit with a baby pink collared shirt and a great pair of black Marc Jacobs heels. (Okay, they are my only Marc Jacobs heels, but every time I wear them, I feel like a million bucks.) Sticking to the professional look, I purposely kept my jewelry and perfume to a minimum and flatironed my naturally wavy hair poker-straight. I put a few copies of my résumé in my black leather briefcase and was ready to go. Now I just had to wow them.

It had been a few years since I'd had a job interview. Frankly, I'm not a big fan of answering questions like "Tell me about your weaknesses" or "Where do you see yourself in five years?" But it's part of the process, and I knew I'd just have to wing it, silly questions and all.

I said a quick prayer as I headed to the sixty-second floor of a building I'd only walked past a handful of times. I didn't even know the name of it, but surely I wasn't going to be quizzed on that, right?

They were expecting me, apparently: As I walked into the lobby, the receptionist spoke to me as she picked up her phone. "Sydney?" she said. "Welcome to *Out and About*. I'll let Lawrence know you're here."

"Thank you," I said. Let the games begin.

Lawrence bustled out, shook my hand, and escorted me back to a conference room, where we sat across from each other at the largest, shiniest walnut table I'd ever seen in my life.

We talked a little about my flight and New York and the sudden demise of *Get Away*. He didn't once ask about my weaknesses, but I could tell he was sizing me up. And then Lawrence leaned forward across the table and got right to the point. "Sydney, I'm going to make this easy for you. I've called your references and spoken to your former boss, Lucinda, over at *Vogue*. You are very well thought of." He paused, and I smiled, not sure what to say. "I could sit here for hours and ask you all the usual questions. But I think you're the right person for the job, and I'd like you to come to work for us."

"Really?" I asked. "Just like that?"

"Yes," he said with a grin. "Just like that. We'd start you out at seventy thousand a year, and trust me, you'll earn every penny of it. It may sound like a lot given your Minneapolis salary, but New York's an expensive place to live."

"I don't know what to say." I hadn't expected it to be this easy.

"Say yes. I have an employment contract right here."

I laughed, but it was an uneasy laugh. Something about him gave me the creeps. "May I have some time to think about it please?"

"Of course. I can give you twenty-four hours." He began to fidget with the papers he'd brought with him and handed me an offer letter. "I'd rather know today. But your return flight is tomorrow night. That gives you some time to explore our little town and come to a decision." His smile was tight. "You'll see on the offer that there's a generous signing bonus, and moving expenses will be covered too."

"Thanks, Lawrence," I said, trying to seem cool in the face of an offer that basically amounted to my dream job. We're talkin' New York here! "I'll let you know before I leave."

"Very well," he said. "Think about it, Sydney. This is the opportunity of a lifetime."

And with that said, I had a lot to think about—and fast.

❋ ❋ ❋

In a small town in the Swiss Alps . . .

As Samantha looked out her window, she couldn't believe the view. Here she was, living amid the Alps, in all their snowy splendor. Even though she missed home and the people she'd left behind (especially Eli), she was thankful for such a once-in-a-lifetime experience like this. Adjusting had been a little easier than she expected, especially since she'd met Alexa, who was also completing her internship. Coincidentally, Alexa went to school at Northwestern College in Roseville, only a few miles from Bethel University, where Samantha went. Like long-lost sisters, they'd connected instantly. And after a while, Samantha finally realized why. It was because Alexa was a lot like Sydney—creative, a good listener, and always cracking jokes.

Sam was writing a postcard to Sydney later that afternoon when Alexa arrived with one of her friends. "Sam, I'd like you to meet Adam," she said as the two of them joined her in the dining hall. "Adam's interested in doing missions work in the Sudan when he graduates, so I thought you two would have lots in common."

"Perfect," Samantha said, putting her pen back in her purse. "Adam, it's great to meet you."

"The pleasure's all mine," he said. "Alexa has talked a lot about you."

"Not too much, I hope," Samantha said. "That would be embarrassing."

"Nah," he continued. "I can tell a beautiful heart when I see one."

"C'mon, you've got to be kidding me," Samantha said, and then realized she'd said out loud what she was thinking.

"What do you mean?" Adam said. "Oh, you thought I was trying to pick you up, didn't you?" Beside him, Alexa laughed nervously.

"I've definitely heard worse pick-up lines, if that helps," Samantha said with a grin.

"Well, frankly, you're not my type," Adam said testily. "And I wasn't trying to pick you up anyway."

"When I'm crying in my pillow tonight, I'll keep that in mind," Samantha said. And with that, she got up and went back to her room, wondering how her conversation with Adam had gone sour in such a hurry.

❋ ❋ ❋

Back in Minneapolis . . .

Pumping iron. Eli had been doing a lot of it ever since Samantha had left for Europe. As long as it had taken for them to finally start a relationship, he couldn't believe she was gone already (even if he did know she'd be back). He missed her more than he ever imagined he would. He'd sent her several e-mails, but it wasn't the same. So while she was away, he took his frustration out in the gym. And it seemed to be working. He'd noticed visible changes in his body—his arms were bigger and more toned, and he'd gained about ten pounds of muscle, which made his shirts fit a little tighter. He wondered what Samantha would think of the transformation, but unexpectedly, someone else gave him feedback instead.

"Eli, is that you?"

Eli put the free weights down and looked at the speaker. It was Aidan. "Hi. Yeah, it's me."

"How are you doing?" Aidan asked.

They'd never been friends; Eli had always suspected that Aidan knew he'd disapproved of the relationship with Samantha, although he couldn't say for sure. "I'm great," he answered, wondering where this was leading.

"Cool, dude," Aidan said. "You're looking pretty ripped."

"Ah, thanks," Eli said, feeling a blush rise up his face. "So . . . what's up with you?"

"I was wondering if you'd talked to Samantha recently," Aidan asked. "I haven't seen her around, and there's something I want to tell her."

"She's in Europe for an internship," Eli said. "We talk when we can. And e-mail."

"Could you pass a message along for me in your next e-mail?" Aidan asked. "I'm getting ready to go to India for six months with Searching for Justice and wanted to thank her for encouraging me to do that."

"No problem—but why don't you e-mail her yourself?" Eli said. "I'm sure she'd rather hear it from you directly."

"You think she would?"

"Yeah, man, e-mail her," Eli said.

"Thanks," Aidan said. "It was great seein' you."

"Take care."

The old Eli would've felt a little threatened by Aidan wanting to contact Samantha, but the new Eli was secure about what he had with her. And he knew that Sam would be excited that Aidan was actually going to do something meaningful with his life.

＊　＊　＊

Did I want to leave Minneapolis and move to New York? With Liam really, truly out of the picture, was it the right time to start over in a new city? There were so many questions to consider. And that signing bonus made the decision-making process all the more unclear. When you're unemployed, it's easier to put a higher priority on money than you normally would. After all, there were bills to pay and no guarantee that I'd get a job that was better than the one Lawrence was offering.

But as tempting as it was to take it immediately, I had an overwhelming feeling of ickiness as I left the *Out and About* offices. No matter how many times I tried to talk myself into taking the job, I just didn't feel peace about it. But I still hadn't made my final decision. Maybe some of the sinfully delicious treats at Serendipity 3 would give me inspiration.

An hour and one incredible frozen hot chocolate later, I decided to peruse the "street shops" in search of bargains. Somehow it helped distract me from the fact that I had twenty-four hours to decide if I wanted to take what seemed like a great opportunity. As I walked down Broadway, I decided it might be fun to add a knock-off Louis Vuitton bag to my already considerable purse collection, which helped narrow my sidewalk search—although the jewelry was pretty tempting too. (But wait—I'm unemployed at the moment.) As I looked at all the fake Kate Spades, Burberrys, and Dooney & Bourkes, I finally spotted one of this season's Louis Vuitton bags for a mere thirty-five dollars (the real thing would be several hundred dollars), and it was a darn good copy too. You've got to be careful when you buy from these street vendors, but sometimes a really good fake is a great souvenir.

By the time sunset arrived I was exhausted, so I hailed a cab and made my way back to my hotel, the Edison Towers Times Square. Even though it's in a section of the city known as a tourist's paradise, I love everything about this particular location. And I am a tourist, after all.

I remember my first visit like it was yesterday. On a whim, my friend Adrienne and I road-tripped to New York for New Year's Eve when we were in college. Like millions of other people who do the same thing, we wanted to see the ball drop at midnight. Adrienne had already been there countless times, so she wasn't particularly impressed. But I remember my reaction the first time we stepped off the subway and walked around. I was in awe of all the lights, the energy . . . everything about it. And now that I've been here a few times—some for business, others for pleasure—I still feel that childlike enthusiasm. But did I want to live here? That was a question I couldn't answer with any amount of certainty at the moment.

As I settled in my room and flipped on the television, I mentally made my list of pros and cons. And then I switched off the TV and prayed for God to give me wisdom, realizing I should've done that before I made the list. But I knew he wouldn't mind; at least

I eventually got it right by lifting my concerns to him.

Of course, like many decisions we make on a daily basis, God didn't announce the correct answer in bright, flashing lights in the sky. Unlike for Moses, he didn't suddenly give me a burning-bush sign. But after a few minutes of really examining my motives, I knew what was best for me. And when I resolved to do what I believed was right, I felt the quiet but powerful peace that helped me know with certainty there was something better for me if I waited a little longer.

Besides, even without Liam, I am in love with Minneapolis. It's my home. My friends are there, my family lives close by, and, despite the less-than-stellar winters, I can't imagine living anywhere else. At least for now.

* * *

After eight hours of sleep, a real New York bagel with cream cheese, and a leisurely morning with the *Times*, I called Lawrence. No point in prolonging the inevitable. "Good morning, Sydney," he began. "I trust you've made the right decision."

"I believe I have," I replied. "As generous as your offer is, I'm going to have to decline. But thank you for your confidence and the interview. You've helped me more than you know."

I think he was a little shocked by my answer. There was a pause, and then he said, "Only you know what's best for you. Give me a call if you're ever interested in freelancing."

"I will," I replied. *Well, that went well*, I thought. And since I was in the heart of the theater district anyway, I decided to treat myself to an afternoon showing of Monty Python's *Spamalot* before I had to catch my seven thirty flight back to Minneapolis. As I walked up to the box office to buy a ticket, my cell phone rang. From the area code, I could tell it was someone in New York.

"Sydney?" It was a familiar but not-yet-recognizable voice.

"Yes?" I handed the cashier my Visa card.

"I see you've forgotten me already," she said with a laugh.

I knew that cackle—all too well. It was Lucinda.

"Hello, Lucinda," I said, a little embarrassed. "How are things at *Vogue*?"

"Marvelous, darling," she said. From years of experience, I knew she was tapping her acrylic nails on the desk as she talked. Didn't she know that was bad for them? "But what's the deal with you? Lawrence over at *Out and About* just called to tell me that you turned down the job he offered you there. Seriously, what *were* you thinking? I spent a half hour giving you a fabulous recommendation."

"I guess I just wanted to keep my options open," I said, not really sure where *that* came from.

"Oh, like full-time freelance?" she asked. "I think you'd do really well with that."

"You do?" I asked in slight disbelief. "You think I could get enough work to stay afloat?"

"I know you could," Lucinda said. "You're a fantastic writer, and you turn stories around fast. You'd be terrific."

"Wow, thanks," I said. "I'm definitely going to consider it."

"Let me go one better," she said. "Would you have an interest in writing for *Vogue*? I'm looking for fresh voices. You don't have fashion experience, but I know you're into it. And I know you can write."

"I'd love that," I said. "Got any assignments available now?"

"Yeah, actually I do," she said. "I'm just getting ready to

assign our new issue. Why don't I give you the feature on Mandy Moore's new T-shirt collection?"

"I'd love that," I said. "I'm standing on the street, so can you e-mail me with the details?"

"I'll do that," she said. "And one last thing: I'm glad you're branching out. Lawrence needs you a lot more than you need him. And you can still get work from him."

It's weird how people can throw you for a loop sometimes. Here I always thought Lucinda hated me. And now she was going to pay me to write for *Vogue* and just offered me some of my best career advice yet. This was definitely a turning point.

CHAPTER 17

A CHANGE OF BIBLICAL PROPORTIONS

Maybe it is our imperfections which make us so perfect for
one another.

— MR. KNIGHTLEY (JEREMY NORTHAM) IN *EMMA*, 1996

Meanwhile, at the local PBS affiliate in Minneapolis . . .

AT EXACTLY 10:09, THE mailman walked over to Justin's
desk. "Your last name Stanley?" he asked as he handed him a
medium-sized box that was surprisingly heavy.

"Yep, that's me, man," Justin said. "Thanks."

Wondering who in the world could've sent him something at
work—considering he hardly ever received packages at work, or
even home, for that matter—his curiosity got the best of him.
So rather than open it neatly, he tore into it enthusiastically, like
a kid on Christmas morning. After removing all the extraneous
packing, he looked at the box. *What is* The Message? he thought
as he pulled out the soft leather book with his name on it. When
he opened it up, however, he quickly figured it out. Someone had
mailed him a Bible.

And since he knew only two people on the planet who might
have mailed him a Bible, and he wasn't exactly on speaking terms

with one of them, he guessed it was from Kristin. "So what did you get?" Simon asked nosily as he passed by Justin's office.

"Oh, I'm not sure," Justin said off-handedly. He wasn't about to have Simon say . . .

"Dude, that's a Bible," Simon said before Justin had a chance to finish his thought. "You are getting soft for this girl, aren't you? But that's actually kind of sweet."

Kind of sweet? That's the last thing Justin wanted to hear from Simon. But when he opened the Bible and read Kristin's inscription, he couldn't be angry with her, and he certainly didn't want to ignore her gesture, so he picked up his cell phone and asked her to dinner.

* * *

Before I left for the airport, I had two stops I wanted to make: the massive H&M store on Broadway and Thirty-Fourth and a bookstore to pick up reading material for the way home. H&M ended up being a great call. I picked up three pairs of black dress pants (one striped, one wide-legged, and one that was tapered at the ankles), two pairs of earrings, an army green jacket, and two knee-length skirts—all for around two hundred dollars. Even though I really shouldn't have been spending money since I was out of a job, I needed cute clothes for job interviews or meetings with potential freelance clients, right?

A block down from H&M, there was a merchant selling knock-off Chanel sunglasses. While some replicas are definitely better than others, I found a pair of Chanel aviators that looked identical to the three-hundred-fifty-dollar shades I'd tried on at the Minneapolis Bloomingdale's five or six times. "How about ten dollars?" I asked the man in charge, knowing I was shooting low.

"For you darling, sure," he said, handing me the glasses after wrapping them in tissue paper.

It was probably a good thing I wasn't going to be living here. Think of all the shopping opportunities I wouldn't be able to pass up on my lunch break.

As I walked toward Barnes & Noble, I couldn't help but consider what Lucinda had said about freelance writing full-time. Sure, it made sense in theory, given all the contacts I'd made at *Get Away*. And now that Lucinda planned to hire me to write for *Vogue*, who's to say that couldn't lead to even more clients? So as I picked up a copy of *Us Weekly* and the latest *Budget Travel*, I also grabbed *The Well-Fed Writer*, a book I'd heard plenty about but had never read because I'd never thought to become a full-time freelancer until now. Who knows? Maybe if I structured my schedule just right, I could devote an hour or two a day to my novel, which would be more than I had been doing.

✳ ✳ ✳

In the kitchen with the world's best view. . .

Samantha was staring out the window at the mountains as she snacked on a sandwich made of thick slabs of homemade bread and a wonderful local cheese. Adam walked up behind her and tapped her on the shoulder.

"I think I owe you an apology," he said. "I didn't mean for us to get off on the wrong foot."

"So what was that about, anyway?" she asked, not sure she was willing to let him off the hook that easily. "Here we are getting to know each other, and I make one joke—only one joke—and you spaz out?"

"I know, I was out of line. I guess it just hit a little too close to home—your comment, that is," he said with a bashful expression.

"How's that?" Samantha asked. She silently offered him the other half of her sandwich, but he shook his head no.

"You sure you want to know?" Adam asked. "It's a pretty painful story."

"If you feel comfortable enough to share it," she said, "I'll listen."

"Okay," he said. "But you have to promise not to laugh."

"I'll try my best," she offered earnestly.

Adam went on to tell Samantha how he'd dated a girl in college for three and a half years. Her name was Sadie. They'd met at a scavenger hunt during a Tuesday night singles service at Bethlehem Baptist Church. Unlike a lot of girls he'd dated in the past, Sadie was everything he'd dreamed about, right down to her shoulder-length, wavy blonde hair. She loved God with all her heart. She was smart, funny, athletic, and shared his passion for missions. And whatever they did together, no matter how lavish or inconsequential, they always had the best time. So right before graduation, he knew he wanted to ask her to marry him. He'd saved enough money to buy her a ring and two plane tickets to Paris and planned an elaborate proposal at the top of the Eiffel Tower. He even wrote a new song for her on his guitar called "Sadie, You're the One," with the last two lines serving as the official proposal:

Sadie, Sadie, I've loved you all my life
Would you make me the happiest man and be my wife?

But despite his plans for a long life together with Sadie, they never made it to Paris. When Adam told her he had a surprise for her, she quickly interjected, "Adam, we need to talk." Her tone had struck fear into his heart.

She'd said, "You know how much I love you. But I've been thinking about it, and the truth is, I can't end up with you—you're my *college* sweetheart. There are so many guys out there in the world, and I'm just not sure if I can settle down. You've been talking about settling down a lot lately. But I have to see who else is out there."

And just like that she was out of Adam's life. "So as you can imagine, my confidence hit an all-time low after that," Adam said. "I completely lost my dating mojo, and every time I met a pretty girl, I'd—for lack of a better word—freak out, thinking she'd want to hurt me too, just like Sadie. Which is no excuse for how I treated you," he said. "But you *are* pretty, so that's . . ."

"Thanks, Adam," Samantha said with a reassuring smile. "What Sadie did was awful, but that doesn't mean that all girls would treat you the same way. You have to give us another chance."

"That's why I'm here," he said. "Would you give me another chance and go out to dinner with me tonight?"

❋ ❋ ❋

Things were happening on all fronts . . .

Kristin wasn't sure how Justin would respond to her gift, but what she *was* sure of was that she wouldn't hear from him for a while. So when he called to ask her to dinner, she was pleasantly surprised. They agreed to meet at Potbelly, one of Kristin's favorite sandwich shops, at six o'clock.

To say she was distracted as she taught her fourth graders about prepositional phrases would be a huge understatement. She was downright giddy whenever she thought about seeing him. So much so that Brandon Meyers raised his hand.

"Yes, Brandon?" Kristin said, noticing a huge smile on his face.

"Miss Brown, are you in love?"

The entire class erupted into laughter.

Kristin *was* in love and hoped that one day Justin would feel the same way about her.

* * *

In the room with the magnificent view . . .

After he'd shared something so personally devastating, there was no way Samantha could turn down a dinner date with Adam. "I'd love to," she said. "What time were you thinking?"

They agreed to meet at the village pub at eight o'clock, then went their separate ways. Samantha knew she'd have to tell him about Eli sooner rather than later.

* * *

At another dinner date, over four thousand miles away . . .

At exactly six o'clock Justin pulled into the parking lot. Watching him get out of his car from inside the restaurant (Kristin was always ten minutes early to everything), her heart started beating faster and faster. She even felt a little sweaty as he walked up and gave her a hug. After ordering, they sat down in a corner booth. Without wasting any time, Justin said, "Thanks for the Bible, Kristin. I got it today at work."

"You did?" she asked, acting surprised. "I'm glad to hear it arrived."

"Yeah, I haven't had a chance to read it yet," he said. "But I will sometime, I promise. I never realized it was such a long book."

Sometime. Well, that was certainly more promising than never.

"How have you been, Justin?" she said. "I've missed you."

"I've been thinking about a lot of things lately, that's for sure," Justin said. "I don't think my brain's been this active since college."

Kristin laughed, thinking how incredibly cute he was. That was the love talking, of course.

"That's probably good," Kristin replied. "You know what they say about an idle mind. . . ."

"I do," he said. "And I've been thinking about us a lot too, Kristin."

"You have?" she asked softly.

"All the time," he said with a smile. "There's no way around it: I want to date you. For real."

CHAPTER 18

VIVA NASHVEGAS!

This is so bad it's gone past good and back to bad again.

— ENID (THORA BIRCH) IN *GHOST WORLD*, 2001

IT'S FUNNY, SOMETIMES, HOW quickly I can make up my mind about something and how quickly I can waver after the fact. When I flew back to Minneapolis, I was ready to begin my career as a freelance writer. I'd read a lot of *The Well-Fed Writer* on the plane and written down a bunch of business strategies I'd brainstormed. I had formed a plan for which clients I'd pursue first, considered the verbiage for how I'd describe the services I would offer on my personal website, and even dreamed up a catchy slogan for my letterhead and business cards. But one voice mail put all those thoughts on hold.

While I'd been out of town, a friend of mine living in Nashville had called to tell me there was a position open at *Songwriter's Monthly* magazine. A managing editor position. I should call Hilary Daniels right away. Wow, two leads in two days! I was curious to see what the job was all about; they featured many of my favorite artists in their publication, and it sounded like an excellent opportunity to branch out from what I'd been doing before.

If I'd been smart, I would've stuck to my original plan and

pursued my freelance writing immediately.

But I called Hilary the next morning and set up our interview for Monday so I'd have a couple of days to refuel back in Minneapolis before jumping on yet another plane. I honestly don't know how frequent fliers keep from going insane. I love traveling, but after as many trips as I'd been on lately, I was exhausted—physically, emotionally, and even spiritually. My body ached in places I didn't know existed from sitting in the airplanes' cramped seats. I hadn't done laundry in a couple of weeks and was tired of living out of a suitcase. I missed my church and the girls from my prayer group. In a nutshell, I was a mess, and now—if everything worked out with *Songwriter's Monthly*—I might be moving to Nashville in a matter of weeks.

In my rather fragile state, I called to see if Kristin was available to hang out after she got off work, and she was. I think she could hear my desperation because she said she'd leave as soon as the bell rang, instead of hanging around to straighten up the classroom like she normally would. She came to my place, and we walked to a nearby Cold Stone Creamery to drown our sorrows (or my sorrows, since she was in a really good mood for reasons I wasn't sure of) in ice cream. Sure, it probably wasn't the best remedy for my sorry state of affairs, but it was much better than, say, a round of cosmopolitans at the local bar. At least that's how I rationalized it as I indulged.

"So what's up, Syd?" Kristin asked as I stuffed my mouth full of ice cream. "I haven't seen you like this since Liam."

Strangely comforted by the fact that the Liam situation had been resolved once and for all, I said, "I don't know . . . do you ever get the idea that your whole life is tearing apart at the seams?" I said. "First it's my job. And then I always seem to be going out with someone who's completely wrong for me. I mean no offense to Justin, but how twisted is that—that he was going out with you when we were seeing each other?"

"I wouldn't have been too happy about that either," Kristin said empathetically. "If it had been me, I would've been mad too."

"Well, that's the thing: I'm not mad. I'm just really discouraged at the moment," I said. "It just doesn't seem like *anything* is going right. And to add insult to injury, I haven't filled myself up with anything good in so long that I'm completely running on empty."

Like a good friend, Kristin let me vent without trying to offer me any cheesy pat answers in return. But before I got too carried away with my rant, she asked if she could pray for me. So after we finished our ice cream, we walked back to my place, hopped in her car, and drove to Minnehaha Park along the river, where we sat on a small wooden park bench and prayed for each other. She prayed for everything I had mentioned earlier, and I prayed for her and even for her relationship with Justin.

A couple of hours later, feeling much better than I had before, I opened my Bible and read a few verses before hitting the hay early. I had a lot to do before I flew down to Nashville, after all, and I needed my sleep.

* * *

Meanwhile, stuck in crosstown traffic . . .

After leaving Sydney's place, Kristin gave Justin a call on her way home. Since Sydney had been in such a blue mood, Kristin hadn't really felt right about sharing that she and Justin were planning to start dating for real. In fact, Justin was actually coming to church with her on Sunday. And although she hadn't shown it much when she was with Sydney, she'd been on cloud nine ever since.

In fact, Justin had sent Kristin flowers at work just today—a gorgeous bouquet of red roses, greenery, and baby's breath—that had gotten everyone talking, including her students. "Somebody must looooove you, Miss Brown," Tabitha McPhee had said in the middle of the social studies discussion. "Yeah, what's his name?" Connor Clark had asked afterward. It was getting a little out of control, but Kristin didn't mind. She was in love, and there was nothing that could get her down at the moment.

*　*　*

The weekend passed quickly, and before I knew it, it was time to head to Nashville. Because I'd managed to chill, I felt far more prepared than I would've had I gone when I got back from New York. I'd managed to spend time with my best friend, get some decent sleep in my own bed, go to my Pilates class twice, and go to church on Sunday. Oh, and I'd done all my laundry too. And instead of loading up on comfort food (well, except for my ice cream binge), I ate healthfully and made sure to drink lots of water. Funny how well your body responds when you treat it nicely.

And soon I'd have the answer about the position at *Songwriter's Monthly*. I had a preliminary interview over the phone before I boarded the plane, just to make sure we were on the same page salary-wise before I flew to Nashville. While the figure paled in comparison to what I'd been offered in New York, the cost of living in Nashville was also significantly less, making the salary range attractive enough to get me on the plane.

But honestly, the paycheck was actually secondary in my mind.

I really wanted a job that challenged and inspired me, one that would provide an opportunity for career advancement and personal growth. In a managing editor position, I wouldn't be writing as much. Instead, I'd shape other people's work, learn the nuts and bolts of dealing with freelancers, beef up my copyediting skills, and have new experiences in the publishing field that would ultimately make my résumé more diverse. It would be a big change for me.

Those wouldn't be the only changes either. I was a little nervous about the possibility of starting over in a new office. I would be the new girl, which is analogous to being the new kid in school. You know how it is: Everyone's nice on the first day. If you're lucky your boss and a few coworkers may even take you to lunch. But after the first day you're pretty much on your own until someone accepts you into his or her clique. And trust me, office cliques are just as bad as high school cliques. They're exclusive, catty, and on the prowl for any dirt they can uncover about you. Until you find a friend or two, the workday can be pretty miserable; there's nothing worse than sitting in your office for eight-plus hours with no one to talk to, while all around you people are laughing at inside jokes you're not privy to.

If those thoughts weren't enough to keep my head spinning, the idea of moving back to Nashville had my emotions in a whirl. I'd loved the city that summer I interned at *7 Ball*, the same summer I'd met Liam. There's plenty that's great about Nashville. First off, there's definitely a reason they call it Music City. I've never seen so many amazing live shows as I have in Nashville. Almost any night of the week at small clubs like the Exit/In or 3rd & Lindsley or at legendary haunts like the Ryman Auditorium and the Grand Ole Opry, there's someone worth seeing. Some nights there are so many great options that you actually have to pick and choose. In fact, one memorable night that summer, I had my choice between Ryan Adams, Patty Griffin, and David Gray. (I eventually opted for the Ryan Adams show, but only after a lot of dithering.)

Nashville has plenty of great restaurants too. I've always loved Calypso Café for their enormous black bean salad and fruit tea, and the scrumptious tomato basil soup and homemade cranberry walnut bread at Bread & Company are to die for.

Frankly, Nashville is a city that feels more like a small town, and I've always loved that. Even while I interned, I would run into someone I knew almost everywhere I went, whether it was to Fresh Market to pick up some groceries or Bongo Java for coffee and a bagel. Somehow all the familiar faces were reassuring, even if sometimes I wished I hadn't run out for a breakfast burrito without putting my makeup on.

But the downside of this rosy Nashville picture is that it will always remind me of Liam and what he's all about, no matter how much time passes. The city exists to feed the music industry, and in certain circles, music, and more specifically making it in "the biz," is almost always the first topic of conversation. If you're out to lunch, there's a good chance your waiter or waitress is jonesing for a record deal. Ditto for the worship leader at your church, the barista at Starbucks, or the guy selling you T-shirts at the Gap. Even karaoke, something my friends roped me into on occasion, is an audition for a record deal rather than a chance to be silly and let off steam. Wannabe singers frequent the karaoke establishments, hoping their performance of a lifetime will be noticed by label execs who might happen to be in the neighborhood. Let's just say if you're hoping for a girl-power night when you can belt out Gloria Gaynor's "I Will Survive" with your other single girlfriends, Nashville isn't the place to do it. If your singing is less than stellar (and mine definitely falls into that category), the stares from those hoping to make it big can be hard to ignore.

Okay, I'll be honest: Even though I told myself I was truly over Liam, the whole choosing-his-music-over-me scenario still stung a little. Especially when I was on my way to the scene of the crime, the place he chose to move rather than choosing us. In fact, the more I thought about it, the more I wondered why I was going.

But there I was, plane ticket in hand, waiting to board at gate A19.

Two hours after landing in Nashville, I was waiting in the reception area at *Songwriter's Monthly*. Unlike the swanky New York office of *Out and About*, the atmosphere at *Songwriter's Monthly* is far more utilitarian. Everything is open to view, separated only by a glass wall. The wooden desks are old and chipped; the fluorescent track lighting is harsh and unflattering. The staff's oversized Mac desktops are at least five years old. But no one seemed to care. They were all hard at work. In the lobby they were displaying a recent issue, apparently the one that had been used at this year's South by Southwest in Austin. Patty Griffin was on the cover.

The receptionist made a quick call, and I watched a guy near the back of the large room rise and make his way toward me. When he got to the waiting area, he paused dramatically in front of the cover on display.

"Doesn't Patty look absolutely *gorgeous*?" he asked me.

"Um, I can't say that I've ever really kept up with whether Patty looks good or not," I said with a smile. "But I've always loved her music. Her songs cut straight to your heart."

"I like this girl, she has taste," the guy said to the receptionist. "I'm Patrick Delaney, by the way," he said as he extended his hand.

"And if I'm not mistaken, you're Sydney, right?"

"I am," I replied. "I'm here for an interview with Hilary Daniels."

"Actually, Hilary called in sick today. I just found out I'll be doing your interview," Patrick said. His eyes held mine just a little too long for comfort. "Lucky me."

Ew. Was he really that smarmy, or was he just a smart aleck? I couldn't tell for sure.

"Apparently you're only going to be in town for a brief spell, right?"

"Just overnight," I said.

"Well, I don't know about you, but I'm pretty hungry. Would you mind if we head over to J. Alexander's and do our interview over lunch?" he asked.

I hadn't had one of their delicious salads in ages. "Sure, that sounds great."

"Good, good," he said in his distinct Southern drawl. "Give me five minutes to wind up something at my desk, and then we'll head out."

Twenty minutes later we walked out to the adjoining parking garage and squeezed into his red Mazda Miata. "Sorry about the small car," he said. "I had to borrow my sister's today since my car is in the shop."

"Oh, I'm sorry to hear that," I said. "Car troubles are never fun."

"You're telling me," Patrick said. "This repair is fixin' to set me back a lot of money. Let's just say a Hummer isn't exactly cheap when it's been sick."

The "fixin' to" expression has always cracked me up. When I'd first arrived in Nashville for my summer internship, I'd never heard anyone say "fixin' to" before. In fact, the first time I heard it just after I'd moved into my apartment complex, a neighbor said she was fixin' to go to the supermarket, and I'd politely but oh-so-wrongly asked her, "What are you fixing?"

And I still remember her response to this day. She'd laughed and said, "Honey, if you're gonna live here in the South, you've gotta know two things. First, if you're about to do something, you're fixin' to do it. Second, anything's better when it's fried—especially Thanksgiving turkey."

I wanted to take her word for it, but I couldn't ever bring myself to say "fixin' to." And fried turkey? That's just wrong. My mother would have had a stroke if I'd so much as suggested it. I won't even get into the whole cornbread stuffing issue. I was born in the Midwest, 'nuff said.

Patrick was rambling on and on about his car. "Yeah, gas ain't cheap either," he said. "It's getting more and more expensive to fill up Bobbie."

Now I'd heard everything. "Bobbie?" I asked. "Your car actually has a name?"

"Yeah, doesn't yours?" he retorted. Honestly, this guy was a piece of work. "I find that if your car has a name, it tends to treat you better."

"That's a great theory, but how do you explain Bobbie's current trip to the mechanic?" I asked.

"Well, if you were my wife, you'd still have to go to the doctor from time to time, right?" he asked.

"I suppose so," I said. "So does that mean you're married to Bobbie?"

"Not exactly, although she's definitely caused me fewer problems than any woman has."

I sighed. This was shaping up to be a Nick and Nora kind of conversation, and I wasn't sure if I was up to it. I began to wonder if our interview was going to be equally as interesting. As it turns out, I didn't know the half of it.

"So I'm going to cut to the chase," Patrick said, menu in hand. "Are you seeing anyone at the moment?"

"What?" I sputtered. "Did you *really* just say, 'Are you seeing anyone at the moment?'"

"I did," he replied, smiling. "It's relevant." He saw the look on my face but kept on. "It is!"

"How's that?" I asked, raising my eyebrows.

"I'm sensing that you're not," he said with a laugh. "Am I right?"

"I'm currently unattached," I said primly. "But I still don't see how that's *your* business."

"Feisty, aren't we?" he said. "I like that!"

I was getting angrier by the moment. Honestly, this good ol' boy shtick wasn't what I'd had in mind when I'd shown up for an interview. "I don't know what's going on here, but I hardly see how my relationship status has anything to do with whether I'm qualified for this job or not. From my résumé, you can see—"

"Okay, okay, I'll tell you why I asked."

This should be good, I thought as I glanced at the menu. At that point I couldn't bear to make eye contact with him, even if he was really cute. *No, no, no, did I just think that? He's not cute, he's annoying. We've been here for twenty minutes, and we haven't discussed the job yet. Grrrrr!*

"Folks who are single just work so hard," he said, grinning. "In at dawn, always staying late, working on the weekends . . ."

Was this guy for real?

"Once there's a significant other, though, they just want to work 'regular hours.'" He made little quotation marks in the air with his fingers. "Suddenly they want to come in at nine thirty and leave at five because they've got to, you know, have a life. We're looking for slaves." And with that he burst out laughing.

Ah, that's the game we're playing, huh? I rolled my eyes.

"So are you saying that *you* don't pursue relationships because it could potentially cause productivity issues at work?" I asked. "I'm dying to know how you've managed."

"Well, if that's not the best pick-up line I've ever heard!" Patrick kept grinning. "I manage just fine. But maybe we'll have to go out sometime to see."

In your dreams, I thought. "Are we actually going to have a job interview, or were you just inviting me out to test my nerves?" I said, my cheeks hot with frustration. "Because if it's the latter, I wasted a lot of time and money to be here."

"Oh, calm down," Patrick said. "I'm having fun, aren't you?"

"Fun? You call this *fun*?" I asked. "I'd hate to see your idea of sheer agony."

Before another verbal attack could begin, our waitress arrived.

CHAPTER 19

THE LAST HURRAH

People wait their whole lives to see an ex when things are going really good. It never happens. You could make relationship history!

— ALEX FLETCHER (HUGH GRANT) IN *MUSIC AND LYRICS*, 2007

Later that evening in Minneapolis . . .

SO HOW IS IT that your apartment is always clean?" Justin asked Kristin as they sat down at her dining room table for dinner. "No matter how hard I try, my place is always a mess. There's a spill here. A bunch of clothes over there. Dishes everywhere. But your place is always spotless."

"Guess it's a special talent I have," Kristin said as she passed the butter for the buttermilk biscuits to Justin.

"You're the perfect woman," Justin said. "Even these biscuits are homemade."

"Well, I don't know about perfect," Kristin said. "But my mama raised me right, I guess. She was always passing on little tips about cooking and cleaning for when I met the right man."

"And I'm reaping the benefits," Justin said. "These are delicious."

"Thank you," Kristin said. "It's fun cooking—especially for you."

Over the last three days, Kristin and Justin had slipped into a comfortable routine of cooking for each other. She didn't know many guys who cooked, let alone as well as Justin did.

And while cooking and eating together was definitely a joy, she loved that he helped her clear the table and do the dishes afterward. Most of the time they stayed on task, and the job was completed in ten minutes or so. But last night he spontaneously decided that a dish soap fight was in order. And by the time it was all said and done, he'd ended up throwing so many bubbles at her that the floor was soaking wet—not that either of them minded.

Even though Justin had always hoped he'd experience domestic bliss at some point in his life, he never imagined that it would actually happen. Or be so much fun. And as they finished their homemade beef stew and buttermilk biscuits, Justin knew he wanted to do whatever it took to make Kristin happy for a lifetime.

❁   ❁   ❁

"Sheer agony, huh?" Patrick said. "It appears that our potential managing editor has a penchant for hyperbole."

"Ah, I see that I'm still a candidate," I replied.

"Yeah, I haven't disqualified you just yet," he said. "So why do you want to be a managing editor, anyway? Your portfolio shows that you're a pretty talented writer. But you know, that's not what managing editors do. They manage."

"Um, yes, I know. But every once in a while a person needs a change, professionally speaking," I began. "After working at *Get Away* for so long as a writer, I thought it would be challenging to try the flip side of the coin. I feel like I could offer writers a lot of encouragement and support since that's my background. Who better to work with freelance writers than a fellow writer?"

Patrick nodded. "Yeah, I can see how that would work, but would you be willing to settle for shaping someone else's work in his or her voice rather than creating something in your own?" he asked.

"Yes, I would. And as someone who's written so much, I'd have the utmost respect for maintaining a writer's point of view," I said.

"Well, I'm not buying it, Syd. Can I call you Syd?" he said. He was back in the *Thin Man* routine again, so I decided to play along.

"Hmmm, you've known me for what? Two hours? Syd is usually reserved for those closer to me," I said. "But, hey, whatever floats your boat."

"I'm not a boat owner, sorry," he quipped. "All right, bad joke. What I'm saying, Syd, is that I've read your work, and it's far too good for you to even consider becoming an editor. You need to be writing. Have you considered starting your own freelance writing business? You could even write for us."

"It's funny you should bring it up," I said. "I've been considering doing that. Then I got the call about this position and decided to go for it."

"I honestly think you should keep writing," Patrick said. "And to show my appreciation for your talent, I'll give you next month's cover story on Keane. We can pay you a nominal fee plus expenses, since we're looking for an in-person interview with them in England."

"Wow," I said. "Thank you." I was so surprised I'd temporarily lost my ability to channel Nora Charles.

"Welcome to *Songwriter's Monthly*."

Maybe Patrick isn't sooo bad, I thought to myself as he paid the check.

"How would you like to celebrate our new partnership by checking out Josh Rouse at the Belcourt tonight?" Patrick asked. "It's a sold-out show, but I've got two tickets."

"The perks of the job, huh?" I asked.

"Yeah, there're lots of cool freebies," he said. "So I know we got off to a bad start and all, but what do you think? Wanna see Josh Rouse?"

I really enjoy Josh Rouse's music. Every time he's been in the Twin Cities area, his show has been sold out, so I haven't been able to see him yet. And since I was stuck in Nashville, I had to do *something* fun, right?

"Sure," I said. "I'll give you another chance. But only because you have tickets to Josh Rouse."

"Hey, if you're just *using* me, that's fine," Patrick said. "It's your conscience." He smiled.

"Yeah, well, I'll get over it," I said with a laugh as we walked toward his borrowed Miata.

The concert was at the Belcourt Theatre in Hillsboro Village, a hip section of town I hadn't visited in ages. After grabbing a Pink Poodle (that's a raspberry latte piled high with whipped cream) at Fido, Patrick and I walked around the neighborhood, since the concert didn't start for another hour. Patrick had given up his sarcastic, rapid-fire delivery in favor of a more normal conversation. What a relief.

"Did you hang out in the Village much when you lived here?" he asked as he sipped his chai tea latte.

"Yeah, I did actually," I said. "I loved shopping at Posh and having breakfast at the Pancake Pantry. Their Caribbean pancakes were my favorite."

"Caribbean, huh?" he said. "I'm definitely partial to the Georgia peach variety."

"Ooooh, those are really good too," I said. "The blueberry ones aren't bad either."

"Agreed," he said as we crossed the street and I talked him into looking around in Pangaea.

"I love everything in here," I said. "They have the best jewelry, fun skirts . . ."

"What, exactly, makes a skirt fun?" he said. "I'll be the first to admit that I'm not exactly a fashionista."

"Really? I wouldn't have guessed that," I said as I checked out a brown silk skirt with butterflies embroidered on it. "If you even know the word *fashionista*, then you must have some interest in how you look. Or maybe you've just read too many of your sister's issues of *Vogue*. Since you don't date, you must have learned the word from somewhere," I said.

"Aren't you just Ms. Detective?" he asked with a laugh. "You should get that skirt. I think it would look great on you."

"Thanks," I said. "I think I have to get it. What do you think of these earrings with it?"

"Seems like they'd work," he said.

"Well, Mr. I-don't-know-anything-about-fashion, I'll take your word for it," I said as I paid for my purchases.

"Ready to be wowed by the Rouse?" Patrick asked.

"Wowed by the Rouse, huh?" I questioned. "Yeah, I'm ready."

As we found our seats in the fifth row, I realized I'd forgotten how cool the Belcourt is. I'd only been there a couple of times that summer so long ago (or so it seemed now). It's the only place in town that shows independent films, and I was the sort of college kid who fancied herself an intellectual, so I'd gone to see a couple of documentaries there. I don't remember much about the films, but I do remember how tasty the popcorn was. But since this was a rock show, I skipped the popcorn.

"These are great seats," I told Patrick. "Thanks again for inviting me."

"Oh, so we're friends now?" he cracked.

"Yeah, I guess so, but don't push your luck," I joked.

The first few songs were nothing short of incredible. I was really enjoying myself, and I could tell that Patrick was too. Everything was going perfectly until I noticed Liam and some new blonde girl sitting two rows in front of Patrick and me. At first I tried to play it cool. Maybe Liam and whoever she was wouldn't even look over. It was dark, after all, so that was a possibility. But after Josh played "Winter in the Hamptons," Liam looked over his shoulder for some reason, and we made eye contact.

It was only for a second, but it felt like an eternity, and suddenly I felt sick to my stomach. I whispered in Patrick's ear that I was "off to the ladies' room" and hurried out of the theater. But rather than let me be, Liam soon followed.

"Sydney, *Sydney*, is that you?" he asked, knowing full well it was.

"Hi, Liam," I offered without much expression. "You must be in town for work, huh?"

"Yeah, we're recording a new album at Blackbird Studio," Liam said proudly. "It's coming out next year, and I'm so excited. It's our first for Atlantic Records. We ended up nailing that showcase in LA. You know, the one you didn't end up seeing."

As if I cared.

"That's cool," I said, wondering if he was even going to bother to ask how I was doing or why I was in Nashville.

"So is that your boyfriend in there?" Liam asked.

"I don't see how that's any of your business," I said.

"Hey, I'm just making conversation," Liam said. "No need to get mad."

"I'm not mad," I replied. "If anything, I'm a little surprised to see you, that's all. I'm here for a job interview at *Songwriter's Monthly*, and one of the editors asked if I'd like to see Josh Rouse with him. I mean, it's Josh Rouse; how could I turn that down?"

"I know, I was thrilled when the record label gave me tickets too," he said.

"Yeah, and here we are missing the show," I said.

"Well, I saw you there, so I thought I'd say hello. I do feel bad about everything that happened with us, you know," he said.

"Oh, don't start with that," I said. "You always feel bad about what happened, but you never want to change. In case you wondered, that's why we're not dating at the moment and you're with whoever she is."

"Whoever she is? She's my *wife*, Sydney," Liam said. "I met her in Los Angeles — Stan actually introduced us after the showcase. It was love at first sight, and we got married a week later. She's signed with Atlantic too."

"How fantastic for both of you," I said as I felt the tears start coming. "If you're married, then why don't you have your ring on?"

"Well, Stan says it's better for people not to know whether an artist is married or not. Keeps the mystique alive," he said.

"Wow, that's great, Liam," I said. "Just like usual, your music always comes first. I hope the two of you are happy together. Or better yet, the *three* of you."

"Ha, ha, ha, you think you're so smart," he said angrily. "I finally found someone who understands me and how important my music is. I guess that's why it never worked with us."

"I guess so," I said softly as tears streamed down my face. "I'd better get back in there. I'd say it was nice to see you, but that wouldn't be completely honest."

With that said, I made my way back into the dark theater, feeling completely shattered emotionally.

Patrick could sense that something had changed. "Hey, Syd, what's up? I actually started worrying about you because you were gone for so long."

"Thanks, I'm fine," I said. "Just ran into an old boyfriend unexpectedly, and as it turns out, he's married now. So that's that."

"Do you need to talk about it?" he asked. "We can leave right now."

"Nah, I wouldn't want you to miss the show," I said. "It's Josh, after all."

"No, I think we need to go now," he said. "You could use some cheering up."

He was right, I *could* use some cheering up. But it was a little strange being cheered up by someone I barely knew. Then after another song, I didn't even care. I just needed to leave the Belcourt fast.

We drove to Patrick's downtown apartment in silence as I replayed the entire scenario in my head. *Why, of all people, did Liam have to be there?* I thought to myself. Every time I'd successfully gotten over him, he seemed to reappear at the most inconvenient and unexpected times. And now he was married.

It wasn't that I even wanted to be married to Liam. Okay, at one point I did, but after the trip to LA, that fantasy was over for good. But seeing him again and finding out he was married hurt in ways I never imagined it would, which is exactly what I told Patrick later that evening.

"Of course it does," he said. "If you hadn't really loved him before, it wouldn't have mattered. Unfortunately love isn't something you can turn on and off like a light switch. If it was, it wouldn't be so spectacular."

"Did you hear that on *Oprah* or something?" I said with a laugh.

"I see your sarcasm has managed to surface," he quipped. "Okay, what's your poison? I've got vodka, Baileys, scotch, and lots of beer. Anything you want."

"Thanks," I said. "But I don't really drink that much. And I'm not sure it would make me feel better right now."

"Well," he said, "I've got ice cream."

"Now, that poison works for me," I said. "What kind do you have?"

"I've got Häagen Dazs, Ben & Jerry's, and Maggie Moo's," he said. "More specifically, that's dulce de leche, chocolate chip cookie dough, and vanilla."

"Gotta go with the dulce de leche," I said. "That's hard to refuse."

Two scoops later I was feeling much better as Patrick and I sat on the couch and talked. I told him the Liam story from the beginning. "That was the first problem," he said. "You're not supposed to fall in your love with your interview subject. What sort of journalist are you, anyway?"

"A very naive one," I said. "I figured it would be okay, just that one time."

"That's understandable, I guess," he said. "He was charming, self-assured, and he pursued you."

"Oh, don't I know this," I said. "I fell for him instantly and carried that torch for a long, long time."

"Women." Patrick shook his head.

"Then when we really got together, he knew he had me wrapped around his finger."

"At least you didn't say, 'He had me at hello,'" he said with a smirk. "I was getting nervous there for a second."

"That's almost how it was." I sighed. "He just couldn't ever prioritize our relationship ahead of his music, though. He tried and tried, but his career always won out. And then there was his evil manager, pushing Liam away from me however he could. I just . . ."

Before I could continue, the tears came again in full force. "Just cry it out," Patrick said, putting his arm around my shoulder. It seemed like he was really trying to be nice. "It's all going to be okay, Sydney, it really is."

"How do you know?" I asked, my nose all snotty, my face streaky from the combination of tears and foundation.

"Everything works itself out," Patrick said. "When it's the right time, someone new will come along, and you'll forget all about silly ol' Liam. I know exactly what you need," he said.

"What's that?" I asked.

And before I could say another word, he kissed me, which was exactly what I *didn't* need — more confusion.

CHAPTER 20

THE DAY THE WORLD STOOD STILL

God was showing off when he made you.

— RABBI JAKE SCHRAM (BEN STILLER) IN *KEEPING THE FAITH*, 2000

I SNAPPED MY PHONE SHUT and scribbled down my most recent freelance writing deadline in my trusty dayplanner (no matter how hard I've tried, I haven't been able to get excited about upgrading to a PDA). As I did, I realized it's been exactly six months since my last day at *Get Away*. In some ways it feels like it was only yesterday that I cleaned out my cute corner office for good. But in other ways it feels like it's been much longer because so many things have significantly changed in my life.

By now you've probably guessed that I didn't become a personal dog-walker to the stars—or any of the other exciting ventures that Kristin jokingly suggested. Instead, I started my own freelance writing business, just as Lucinda had recommended when I was in New York. I still don't have a name for it, but my motto is *Stylish Copy on a Deadline*, which I think sums up what I do pretty well. With all of the contacts I had in the travel industry, it was a no-brainer to continue writing about that. In fact, in the past few months I've crossed off two more destinations on my Places I Absolutely, Positively Must Visit Before I Die list. First

I visited Samantha in Prague in July. (The verdict? Absolutely breathtaking.) Later I went to Hawaii on business for a story on "Ten Cliché-Free Ways to Enjoy All the Aloha State Has to Offer." Even without pig roasts, a brightly colored lei around my neck, or hula dancing, I had a blast, especially because I tag-teamed that assignment with one from *Vogue* (thanks Lucinda!) in which I got to hang out with the cast from *Lost*. Not only did I learn Evangeline Lilly's beauty secrets, the focus of the article for *Vogue*, but I got to learn a lot about the mysterious features of the show. Of course, I can't tell you about any of them.

In addition to travel, I've also expanded my repertoire considerably. I write for a few national music publications (I've even done one short article for *Rolling Stone*—wow!) and review movies for a few local newspapers, which is one of my favorite new gigs. But what's been far more exciting than not having to worry about what I wear to work or how long a lunch I take is that I've *finally* started writing my novel in my spare time. I've always talked about it, but now I'm actually doing it. And no surprises here, I'm sure, but it's about relationships. Back in high school, my English teacher said the key to being a successful writer is to write about what you know. And after all I've been through, I feel qualified to shed a little insight from my less-than-stellar track record.

Speaking of which, probably the most intentional change in my life has to do with relationships—or, rather, my approach to those of a romantic nature. Believe it or not, this serial dater has officially resigned from her post. That night with Patrick when I blubbered over Liam—and Patrick kissed me—was actually my last date. And, no, I'm not kidding.

It's not because I'm bitter that things didn't work out with

Liam or that I'm necessarily kissing dating good-bye. Rather, it's more of a deliberate attempt to focus on other aspects of my life. I don't know about you, but by devoting all that energy to dating, I was nearly sapped of my resources. Burned out. Especially spiritually. And I just needed to get that back somehow.

Not that I don't think about dating from time to time, of course. There's such an exciting rush that accompanies first dates, first kisses, everything that comes with the territory. But along with saving things like my favorite movie, *Roman Holiday*, for someone I really care about and who cares about me in return, I've decided I also need to be more protective of my heart. I've given it out much too easily before to guys like Liam who didn't necessarily deserve it.

I've even started praying some pretty radical prayers, like *Lord, you know the desires of my heart, but I only want to be with someone in your perfect timing* and *Lord, you know I really want to share my life with someone, but if you don't have that person for me, then I'll happily serve you no matter what.*

Now, those prayers may not sound strange or even particularly revolutionary to you, but I'd never prayed that way before. I'd only thought of what I wanted, what I needed—not what God had in mind for me—and my prayers were always a reflection of that selfish thinking. Little did I know what he had in store and how quickly it would arrive once I'd given up worrying about dating and just gone about my usual activities.

You know how everyone always tells you that "it'll happen when you least expect it"? I always hated when people said that. After all, how could you *not* expect it when it was all you could think about sometimes? And why did not expecting it all of a sudden become the contingency factor for something good happening? Seriously, it's silly thinking, but I can't tell you how many times I've been told that over the years.

Occasionally in my frustration, I'd yell out (only in the comfort of my condo, of course, so people wouldn't point and say, "There's that crazy Sydney again, barking at God because she hasn't met her soul mate"), "Okay, God, here's me *not expecting it*," hoping my good intentions would somehow cancel out my anxious tendencies and I'd be blessed. But did anything happen as a result? No, nope, nada, zilch, zero.

But as my college literature professor said ad nauseam, "Clichés are clichés for a reason, and maybe that's because some element about them is true." It took awhile, but I finally figured out what she was talking about one cloudy Saturday afternoon at Moose & Sadie's, this great little coffeehouse not far from my place. As I sipped my favorite caramelly drink, I tried to solve the daily Scrabble puzzle in the Minneapolis *Star Tribune*.

And then it happened when I least expected it.

As much press as crossword puzzles have gotten recently in movies like *Wordplay*, I've never had the skill or the desire to be a novice, let alone an expert. For whatever reason, my brain doesn't connect with the clues, and I hate it when you miss one because it throws off the entire puzzle. But Scrabble puzzles? I love those. And I can even complete them in pen. But that day's puzzle, especially the third word in the series, was giving me grief. Just as I was about to give up, someone spoke up. "Try dwam, " I heard a deep male voice say behind me.

Dwam? Is that even a word?

"I know what you're thinking," he said as he walked closer. "That can't possibly be a word. But it's actually a rather nice one. It means a daydream."

"Well, there you go; now I've learned something new today, thanks to you," I said. "By the way, I'm Sydney."

"I'm Gavin."

As I looked deeply into his gorgeous brown eyes that were accentuated with flecks of green, I suddenly got this feeling that I'd seen Gavin somewhere before. But I guess when you travel for a living that could simply be a by-product of the job. *No, wait a minute*, I thought to myself, *I do remember where I've seen him before . . . could he be . . . Mr. Hottie?*

"Hey, I know this may sound insane, but is there any chance you went to London this past year?" I asked, hoping he wouldn't think I was some kind of psychopath.

"As a matter of fact, I did," he answered. "How did you know that?"

"I think we were on the same flight back to Minneapolis," I said. "If I remember correctly, your Martin guitar was actually in the seat next to you."

"You're right," he said. "That's so funny that you remembered that. Did you find it strange that I had my guitar right beside me?"

"Well, strange wasn't exactly the word that came to mind. But it did make me wonder if you were so wealthy that you could actually afford to purchase a seat just for your guitar," I said with a grin. "Or if you were a rock star in the making."

"Neither of your theories are correct," Gavin said with a sly smile. "I've had a couple of bad experiences with checking my guitar in the past, so when I found out it wasn't a full flight, I decided to carry it on. Of course, there's hardly any room in those overhead storage compartments," he continued. "So I thought, 'Why not put it right next to me?'"

"I see," I said. "So you're not a rock star?"

"No, just a humble singer/songwriter," he laughed. "I was in London for a couple of gigs. They didn't pay much, but it was fun to play in front of a new crowd. At most of the places I perform in Minneapolis, it's just the same people over and over again, so I guess I was looking for a change of scenery."

Three hours and who knows how many cups of coffee later, our unexpected run-in casually evolved into our first date. "So what are you doing tonight?" Gavin asked as the coffee shop started to get crowded.

"I was going to catch a movie, but I'm sure I could be convinced otherwise if the offer was right," I said.

"Oh, is that so?" he replied. "What if I offered to take you to dinner?"

"Oooh, dinner is always a great idea," I said. "What did you have in mind?"

After talking about our likes and dislikes regarding food (he likes almost anything but pimento cheese, while I'm a little more particular, especially in the meat department, where I'm not too fond of anything aside from chicken), we decided that a good greasy pizza sounded perfect.

* * *

Merrily we roll along . . .

Justin couldn't believe how quickly his words had come out the day he told Kristin he wanted to date her. But being with her somehow makes him want to be a better man, and he's glad she's so patient with him in the process. And if all goes well, he can't wait to marry her and start a new life.

In the meantime, they've agreed to take it slow. As happy as Kristin is, she isn't willing to risk everything for someone who doesn't share her beliefs—still the most important part of her life. But she has high hopes for Justin. He's been coming to church with her fairly regularly now for almost six months, and she's certain that God is reaching Justin's heart.

* * *

Even though it was technically my first date with Gavin, it sure didn't feel like a first date. Our conversation was so natural and effortless that it felt like we'd know each other for years. Whether we talked about the basics like where we grew up (Dallas for him, small-town Wisconsin for me) or deeper issues, like our thoughts on politics and war, it was all copacetic. As a pastor's son, Gavin also had plenty of intriguing stories about growing up in the church and all that entailed. But unlike a lot of pastors' sons, Gavin said he never went through the classic rebellious phase in high school or college. Instead, he poured that energy into learning Russian because from a young age he felt God's call to serve there. Although it was not the easiest language to learn, Gavin spent countless hours studying so he could be his best for what ended up being a two-year stint as a missionary in Rostov-on-Don after college.

Interestingly enough, it was his time in Russia that inspired him to pick up a guitar once he moved back to the States. Since he didn't keep a journal, songwriting ultimately became his creative and emotional outlet. In a couple of weeks, he penned eight or nine songs, and after he started playing them for people, a new career direction was realized. "So would you play something for me sometime?" I asked as we finished our last slice of pizza.

"I will if you promise to be nice," Gavin said.

"I'll be on my best behavior," I replied.

"Come to think of it," Gavin said, "I might actually have one of my CDs in the car. If you'd like a preview now, we could check it out."

"I'd like that," I said as I followed him to his beat-up black '57 Chevy. Now, when I say his car was beat-up, I'm not saying it was a clunker by any means. In fact, it was very cool in the vintage sense—a collector's item he just happened to drive on a daily basis. As I joined him in the front seat, he said he needed to grab something quick from the trunk. Of course, my curiosity got the best of me, wondering what he was retrieving, but I didn't look back. When he returned, he brought his beloved Martin. "You still want to hear something?" he asked.

"Of course," I said. "What are you going to play for me?"

"A Gavin Williams original," he said. But as soon as he started playing, I immediately recognized the song as U2's 'All I Want Is You.'"

"Original?" I asked him. "Does Bono know you're stealing his songs?"

"Ah, a U2 fan, huh? I was just testing your prowess as a music critic," Gavin said. "I'm happy to say you've passed the test. Now here's an actual Gavin Williams original called 'Talk to Me.'" And he sang:

> When the sidewalk seems superficial
> and you blink at the concrete and can't see your feet
> and your shoelaces are untied and you wonder who's

> born and who's died
> come talk to me, I've found an answer, and I don't
> think that you don't care.

I liked how he sang and played—it was an unfussy acoustic sound that reminded me a little of Nick Drake with hints of Damien Rice and Ryan Adams. And while it seemed like so many artists were content to borrow heavily from their influences, Gavin clearly had his own thing going. And did I mention how adorable he looked when he sang?

When he finished the song, I clapped enthusiastically. "I love your sound," I said, trying to show my approval without going over the top. After all, I didn't want it to be *too* obvious that I was into him. He could've sung the alphabet, the phone book, or "Hey Jude" in pig latin and I wouldn't have minded.

"Have you ever tried pitching that song to anyone? That sounds like a number one Christian radio hit to me," I said.

"Not really," he said. "But, hey, if you know anybody who'd be up for recording it, just let me know."

"I'll be sure to keep that in mind," I said.

He went on to play a few more songs, including my favorite, a worshipful song called "Ten Thousand Ways." I thought the words couldn't be more appropriate for the moment:

> Lord, you're good to me
> Oh, so good to me.
> Lord, you're good to me.
> Oh, so good to me.
> You've got ten thousand ways to bless me.

After he put his Martin back in the trunk, we walked around downtown Minneapolis, noting how there were so many more bars than churches. Then, while passing one of the particularly sketchy sections of Hennepin Avenue, he grabbed my hand until we had completely passed through. "It's my obligation to keep you safe," he said with a laugh.

"Okay," I said. "So far you're doing a respectable job."

I liked how his hand felt—a little rough in spots from playing guitar but also warm and protective, since my hand was slightly smaller than his.

As we passed the movie theater on Block E, he asked me, "the resident movie critic," if there was anything worth seeing. "Oh, I'd be game for just about anything," I said. "Okay, let me revise that—anything but the one about the pack of serial killers. I'm not a big fan of gory movies or horror flicks."

"Me either, actually," he said. "But if worse came to worse, you know I'd protect you from them," he said with a grin.

"That's good to know," I said. "I might have to take you up on that—I have some pretty scary clients, after all."

"Hey, I never said I'd protect you from scary clients," he said. "I have to draw the line somewhere."

"Fair enough," I said as I perused our movie options. "Nothing really looks that good to me, but I have an idea. There's a theater in Uptown that plays old movies, and they're showing *Casablanca* tonight," I said. "What do you think about that?"

"I'm definitely game," Gavin said enthusiastically. "*Casablanca* is one of my all-time favorites."

As if I needed another reason to like the guy, apparently Gavin had good taste in movies too. Now, I don't want to sound like a crusty fuddy-duddy or a traitor to my generation, but they just don't make movies like *Casablanca* anymore. No matter how many times I've seen it, I never get tired of it. The dialogue is brilliant and witty. The chemistry between Rick and Ilsa is palpable, and the ending is delightfully bittersweet, unlike romantic comedies today, where you see the happy ending coming from a mile away.

And with Gavin, the *Casablanca* experience was greatly, greatly enhanced. We shared a bucket of buttered popcorn and discovered we have yet another unusual thing in common—we both like mixing in plain M&M'S with our movie popcorn for the perfect sweet/salty experience. How weird is that?

❀　❀　❀

Meanwhile, in Arden Hills . . .

Samantha was showing Eli the rest of her pictures from Europe. She'd taken somewhere around seven hundred pictures on her trip, and it had taken her two months to put them all in a scrapbook, but Eli patiently looked at each one as Samantha explained where she was and what was going on in each shot.

He'd never missed someone as much as he'd missed Samantha when she was away. But despite his occasional bouts of sadness, he'd managed to catch up on his reading for school and worked *a lot*. After landing a job as a rock-climbing instructor at the YMCA, he finally said good-bye to his jeans-folding days at the Gap, much to his boss's chagrin. Apparently, Chelsea had had a huge crush on him (even if she had a strange way of showing it). In fact, on his last day, she had asked him out for drinks, and he was forced to let her down gently. "Chelsea, I'm sorry," Eli began.

"I'm dating someone else I love very much. But even if I wasn't, I would've felt weird dating my former boss."

Surprisingly enough, she took the news well and immediately started flirting with the new hire, Marcus.

For Samantha, her time away from Eli gave her clarity. After going out for a couple of disastrous dinners with Adam because she couldn't bear to say no, she realized again how good Eli was for her. Their foundation of friendship had made a romantic relationship so much richer—and far easier—than she could've expected. It was everything she'd hoped for—for so long.

❋　❋　❋

As we watched the World War II story unfold, Gavin played with the ends of my hair and put his arm around me. I loved his touch and secretly hoped this would be the first of many, many dates for us. From the start, there was something different about spending time with him. For starters, he was five years older than me, which definitely helped in the oh-so-crucial maturity department. But aside from that, I got the sense that he'd already lived a lot of life in his thirty-two years. Even though he was a musician, he didn't have the same wanderlust that so many guys in their twenties have, which was a refreshing change from the norm (or to get specific, Daniel or Liam). He'd already been there, done that, and gotten the proverbial T-shirt. Instead of focusing on how many places he could go, he simply wanted to serve God however he could with his music.

And unlike a lot of the guys I'd gone out with, he actually talked about his faith in an engaging way—and frequently— which was a *very* attractive quality. Not in a superspiritual, overbearing manner, but in a way that genuinely reflected how important his relationship with Jesus was to him. Before the movie we talked about the importance of prayer and our struggles with keeping a daily Bible-reading schedule. In college he was a Bible major, and it definitely showed as we talked about favorite books of the Old and New Testament. Mine were Psalms and Philippians because they were personally encouraging. His were Jeremiah and the Gospels because they were so "rich" in truth. I'd never heard someone describe particular books of the Bible as "rich" before, and somehow, the way he explained it inspired me to go back and read them again.

After the movie we walked around Uptown, a prime section of town for people-watching, something we both enjoy. As we circled Calhoun Square, we started up another conversation. This time the subject was past relationships, something that's usually a no-no on a first date. But as naturally as we'd talked about everything else, we shared a little about our respective histories. We both had dated a lot—and learned a lot from the relationships that didn't work out—and hoped that one day, in God's perfect timing, we'd meet the one we were meant to spend the rest of our life with.

And as crazy as it sounds, I was pretty sure I'd just met him.

Eventually, as I glanced at my watch for the first time all night, I realized it was almost two in the morning. "Need to get going?" Gavin asked.

"I definitely don't want to get going, but I probably should," I said. "I have to get up early for church in the morning."

"You just want to get rid of me," Gavin said playfully.

"Yeah, you must have read my mind," I said. "I've been trying to get away all night, but couldn't seem to find a way."

"Okay, miss smarty pants, let me walk you to your car," Gavin said.

But as we walked past where Gavin's car had been parked, we discovered it was gone—it had been towed. After asking the parking attendant where his vehicle had been towed to, he asked me if he could have a ride home.

"I hope my guitar's okay," Gavin said.

Turns out Gavin lives only fifteen minutes away from my place. To save money on rent, which is hefty in this particular section of Minneapolis, he shares a huge three-bedroom apartment with a guy who goes to school at Bethel University. "All he ever does is study," Gavin said. "Makes me glad I'm not still in school."

"Yeah, I'm glad my studying days are over too," I said. "Although I'll admit I didn't do that much when I was in college. Well, except for my journalism classes. Those were the ones that really mattered to me."

"I can't wait to read some of your stuff," Gavin said. "I've always loved to write too. I really hope to get a novel published someday."

"I'm working on that myself," I said, thankful we had a few extra minutes in the car. "And if you're lucky, you just might be in it."

"I'd like that," Gavin said. "Depending, of course, on whether I got to be the hero or the villain."

As he finished his thought, I pulled into the long, winding driveway at his apartment complex. "For the record, I had an amazing time tonight, Sydney," Gavin said. "I'll give you a call this week."

"I'll look forward to it," I said, scribbling my number down on the back of a client's business card. "Thanks for dinner and for such an incredible night out."

"You're welcome," he said. And then he leaned over and softly kissed me on the cheek and said good night.

Even after he left, I could still faintly smell his cologne and feel his kiss on my cheek. I'd never been so deliriously happy after a date in my entire life.

CHAPTER 21

IT'S A WONDERFUL COURTSHIP

Did I tell you how divinely and utterly happy I am?

— HOLLY GOLIGHTLY (AUDREY HEPBURN) IN *BREAKFAST AT TIFFANY'S*, 1961

WHEN GAVIN SAID HE'D give me a call, he actually followed through. I know that probably doesn't sound all that signifi-cant, but it officially marked a new chapter in my dating experi-ence. Suffice it to say, everything about dating Gavin was different from what I was accustomed to.

Unlike in past relationships, I didn't obsess over the details of our conversations, analyzing them with a fine-toothed comb with my girlfriends later on to decode their hidden meaning. I didn't have to. I didn't worry about when (or if) he'd call next. He always did. I didn't feel like we needed a DTR every two weeks, because I knew exactly where I stood with him. I didn't even have to play coy and pick up on the third ring when he called just so he'd think I wasn't waiting around for him. I could completely be myself, which, frankly, was liberating.

Even my closest friends noticed a new spring in my step with each date we'd go on. And the happier I was, the more forgetful I became. On my way to an interview for a magazine article I was writing one particular morning, I made a quick pit stop at

Caribou for a latte, only to lock my keys in my running car. Another morning I drove twenty minutes to downtown St. Paul to work on an assignment for an advertising firm, only to realize I'd forgotten my laptop, not to mention my research, at home. With each month that we dated, my list of mishaps only grew longer. But if that was the worst thing about being in a stable relationship, well, I think I could deal.

For five months Gavin and I went on a seemingly endless string of dates. On our second date we went to his church together for the first time. It was an experience we'd never forget as thirty married couples renewed their vows in front of the congregation. Despite my incessant teasing once the service ended, Gavin promised that he wasn't trying to send me a message by bringing me along for the ride. Not that I would've minded, of course.

Our third date marked yet another milestone when I cooked him dinner for the first time at my place (three-cheese tortellini with our family-recipe red sauce and homemade German chocolate cake for dessert) and showed him *Roman Holiday*. (By the way, I'm glad I'd never shared my movie with anyone other than him; it's still my favorite viewing to date.) On our fourth date it was his turn to impress me with one of his all-time favorite movies. We watched *The Godfather* as we ate takeout from P. F. Chang's on plastic plates with plastic utensils (he is the consummate bachelor, after all).

To be honest, I knew nothing about *The Godfather*, other than it had something to do with gangsters, and there were a couple of references to it in *You've Got Mail*. And while I'm still a little disturbed by the scene with the horse head (I'll spare you any further details), I'll never forget *The Godfather* for one very important reason. About halfway through, Gavin kissed me for the first time.

It was the kind of kiss that's usually reserved for the end of a romantic comedy—the kiss that comes after boy meets girl, boy falls in love with girl, boy loses girl, and boy wins girl back. But in the love story of Sydney and Gavin, we skipped the last two steps and went straight to happily ever after. It was a predictable story, but it certainly won rave reviews from our family and friends, not to mention the protagonists.

We loved being together, no matter what we did. There were nights we got all dressed up and went out for a night on the town. But we were just as happy playing Scrabble at a nearby Starbucks. Or going for a long walk. Or better yet, listening to music together for hours during a long road trip, whether it was to Dallas to meet his family or to Chicago for a U2 show. He introduced me to The Replacements. I introduced him to Death Cab for Cutie. Our musical education was now complete.

Our first trip to LA together was also one of my favorite moments. I was in town for a movie junket, but there was still plenty of time to explore the city. We had gourmet omelets and orange juice at Mel's Diner on the Sunset Strip and late-night coffee and dessert at the Chateau Marmont. While walking around Hollywood and basking in the sun, we talked about starting a magazine together, discussed what we'd name our future children (he even initiated the discussion, not me), and contemplated how much it would cost to live by the beach in California.

Then, in a completely spontaneous moment after my work was done, we rented a car and drove up Highway 101 (which is something everyone should do once, in my humble opinion), eventually ending up in San Francisco after stopping in Santa Barbara and Carmel. We did all the touristy things—Alcatraz, a ride on the cable cars, a trip to Fisherman's Wharf. But my favorite moment was one sunny afternoon when we packed a picnic lunch and spread out a blanket in Golden Gate Park. After eating our pasta salad, plenty of San Francisco's signature sourdough bread, and Ghirardelli mint chocolate brownies for dessert, we read books and played Scrabble and snapped plenty of digital pics.

After San Francisco, we flew back to Minneapolis, never happier. It felt so amazing to be in love with someone I knew I was going to share my life with. And although we'd talked about getting married fairly early on in our relationship, I was still shocked when Gavin proposed on the five-month anniversary of our first date. Even back in my high school journals I remember writing how I wanted to be surprised whenever I was proposed to. So, unlike my friends who shopped for rings at the mall with their boyfriends and planned to get engaged on a specific holiday like Thanksgiving or Christmas, Gavin opted for the unconventional: an ordinary Thursday night that later became extraordinary.

We were watching *The Office* and waiting for our pizza to arrive when I heard a knock on the door. "Do you mind getting that, Syd?" Gavin asked. "My back's been sore all day."

"Sweetie, how come you didn't tell me about your back sooner?" I asked as I walked toward the door. "I could've picked up some Advil and Icy Hot at the pharmacy."

As I handed the delivery guy a twenty-dollar bill, he insisted, "This one is on the house" and couldn't stop smiling, sort of akin to Will Ferrell's character in *Elf*—you know, the Christmas movie where he sports the awful yellow tights and says, "Smiling's my favorite."

Not one to argue about a free pizza, I tipped the slightly creepy, smiling pizza guy, and he was on his way. "Mind bringing that over here?" Gavin asked as he got situated on the couch.

"Sure," I said. "Why do you suppose the delivery guy gave us our pizza for free?"

"Maybe there's something wrong with it," Gavin said.

"Like what?" I asked. "Forgetting your pepperoni?"

"Why don't you check?" he said.

"Okay," I said. Gavin seemed to be acting a little odd too.

I quickly figured out why. In addition to the pizza, there was a small white box from Kay Jewelers. With trembling fingers I opened it and found the most gorgeous hemp-free engagement ring inside.

And before I could say anything, Gavin got down on one knee and asked me to be his wife.

Simply put, it was one of the happiest moments of my life.

CHAPTER 22

HERE COME THE BRIDES

Mawage. Mawage is wot bwings us togeder tooday. Mawage, that bwessed awangment, that dweam wifin a dweam.

— THE IMPRESSIVE CLERGYMAN (PETER COOK) IN *THE PRINCESS BRIDE*, 1987

GAVIN'S PROPOSAL CAME ONE day before Rain's big day, and I wasn't about to tell her we'd gotten engaged until after she and Stinky Nate said "I do." As I've learned from countless girlfriends who've gotten married over the years, a bridesmaid should *never* steal a bride's thunder. That particular rule wasn't, however, on the "informative two-page memo" (her words, not mine) that Rain e-mailed all her bridesmaids to let us know how we could best serve her. While it was all pretty much common sense, it did provide me with a laugh or two. Only Rain could get away with sending something like that out. Other brides behaving the same way would be labeled Bridezilla, but since Rain had actually crocheted our bridesmaid dresses by hand and only charged us ten dollars each because that's all she'd ever want to pay for a bridesmaid dress, it was hard to get too angry with her. Even if my dress wasn't exactly flattering in any way, shape, or form and made me itch as badly as when I had the chicken pox in second grade.

But despite my Pepto-Bismol pink dress and the wilted daisies woven into my hair, Gavin maintained that I was "cute as can be," even though I still was convinced he was humoring me. He was definitely a good sport about coming to the wedding, especially since he didn't know Rain and Nate very well. But to make up for the lack of face time, I'd told him quite a few stories beforehand, which actually made him look forward to the blessed affair.

"Do you think Stinky Nate might actually shower for his own wedding?" Gavin asked as he made a perfect Windsor knot in his pink silk tie.

"I'm going with no," I said as I stared at the atrocity of a dress in my floor-length mirror. "He's very committed to his principles."

"Aren't you glad I don't share the same convictions?" Gavin asked.

"You don't even know the half of it unless you've actually come within three feet of him," I said. "Seriously, give him a hug, and you won't smell the same until *your* next shower."

＊　＊　＊

The festivities began promptly at ten o'clock with a bridal brunch. Surprisingly enough, the flaxseed pancakes and tropical fruit weren't horrible. But as much as Rain tried to convince me of their tastiness, I just couldn't bring myself to try the vegetarian bacon or tofu sausage. Something about them just wasn't right, and I wasn't about to find out what. Since Rain was such a huge fan of juicing (her personal favorite was carrot papaya with a splash of mango), she also had on hand several professional "juiceperts" (again, her words, not mine) who could supposedly anticipate what vitamins we needed just by looking at our hands. While I wasn't necessarily buying the science of it, the strawberry-apricot smoothie they made for me was delicious.

After brunch we were treated to complimentary "organic" mani-pedis from a local spa, which was nice, except that I wasn't exactly sure what made them organic. Everything they did seemed pretty much the same as always. But the neck massage as my nails dried felt so amazing that I quickly forgot about the semantics or the supposed organic experience in a hurry. It was just heavenly.

Normally after the bridesmaids have been beautified, they help the bride get ready. But as stated emphatically in our memo, Rain didn't want our help with that. She wanted to get ready by herself so her grand entrance would be a surprise for all. In the meantime, we were told to check in with the band to make sure they had the right sheet music—Billy Joel's "River of Dreams" for when she walked in and Etta James' "At Last" for the recessional. Once the band was set, we were asked to "explain to the flower girls exactly what they were supposed to do."

Neither of those tasks took very long, so I went and found Gavin and gave him a kiss before the ceremony began. He always looks hot in my humble opinion, but I must say his black Hugo Boss suit took it to a whole new level. He looked like he'd stepped right off the pages of *GQ*. I still couldn't believe we were actually getting married—that God would see fit for me to spend my entire life with such an incredible man (who also happened to be a snappy dresser).

"You look gorgeous," Gavin said as he wrapped his arms around me. "Now go and make Rain proud," he said with a laugh.

As the guests were being seated, I noticed Kristin walk in with Justin. They were holding hands and couldn't stop smiling.

Honestly, I'd never seen either of them look as happy as they did right then. Kristin was glowing in a light pink A-line dress with thin spaghetti straps and lace trim around the bottom hem, while Justin was wearing a sharp dark gray suit with a pink tie that matched Kristin's dress perfectly. I never thought I'd see Justin in a suit, let alone a suit with a pink tie, but it looked good on him. They were a really cute couple, and I was happy for them.

Spotting me, they walked over and said hello. "Why, Syd, that's a very interesting dress you have on there," Kristin said with a laugh. "I'm glad Rain and I aren't that close."

"Well, if you can believe it, she crocheted it herself," I replied. "At least I won't feel bad about burning it once the wedding is over."

"That's definitely a plus," Kristin said. "I have a closet full of ugly satin dresses in every color imaginable."

"Yeah, I remember a few of those," I said. "Emerald green for Maria Elizondo's wedding. Canary yellow for Lizzy Captain's—oh, and the worst was pumpkin orange for Tara Birch's fall extravaganza."

"Yeah, when you have to call your wedding an extravaganza, that's probably the first clue that it's not going to be a real classy affair," Kristin added.

"Justin," I said, smiling, "you look so dapper."

He smiled back. "Dapper, huh?" he asked. "Coming from you, that's quite a compliment. By the way, I hear congratulations are in order," he said as he straightened his tie. "I hope I get to meet the lucky guy."

"You're coming to the reception, right?" I asked.

"We're planning on it," he said, looking over at Kristin for approval.

"Yep, we'll be there," Kristin said. "Let me see your ring."

Justin let out a sigh.

"Oh, I know, Justin," I said sympathetically. "All this ring talk is super boring."

"Boring and quite terrifying, to be honest," Justin said. "Girls just make such a big fuss. It's only a ring."

"But it's *the* ring," Kristin interjected. "It's the one we have to wear forever."

"Yeah, I suppose," Justin said. "Guess I better start saving, huh? What is it, three months' salary?"

Kristin and I looked at each other and grinned. Clearly, Justin was crazy about her and thinking about their future together.

CHAPTER 23

YOU MAY KISS THE BRIDE

When you realize you want to spend the rest of your life with
somebody, you want the rest of your life to start as soon as
possible.

— HARRY BURNS (BILLY CRYSTAL) IN *WHEN HARRY MET SALLY*, 1989

As EVERYONE TOOK THEIR places in the staging area, the
bridesmaids lined up. Each of us was wearing a different
pastel-colored dress—Rain's younger sister, River, wore baby
blue, while her older sister, Lake, wore pale yellow. Stinky Nate's
only sister, Natalie, wore mint green, and I, of course, was wearing the aforementioned Pepto-Bismol pink. The groomsmen lined
up behind us, not next to us. Per Rain's orders, the bridesmaids
would walk in without the groomsmen to symbolize our individ-
uality—whatever *that* was supposed to mean. Then the groomsmen would follow a few seconds later, each wearing a pastel tie
that perfectly matched our homemade dresses. We were all ready.
The only one left unaccounted for was Stinky Nate.

After five minutes had passed, I started to worry. What if he'd
suddenly decided that he wasn't going to show—that getting
married wasn't what he wanted? When another five minutes had
crept by, I asked the minister to give us a moment. I snuck a peek

at the wedding guests, and they looked a bit restive. Oh boy. I looked everywhere for Nate, to no avail. Finally, I knocked on the door of the bride's hideout. "Rain, can I come in?"

"Sure," she replied. "C'mon back, Nate's here too."

When I saw her, it was immediately evident that she'd been crying. "What's wrong?" I asked, suddenly worried.

"Rain just had a small case of prewedding jitters," Nate reported, as if it were as common as the flu. "But she's doing fine now. She was worried that getting married would risk her independence. But I assured her that being together for a lifetime would only make us more sure of ourselves."

Not completely buying into the psychology of what he was saying, I simply nodded. "Well, I'm glad that you're feeling better, Rain. Are you ready now?"

She nodded and smiled shakily.

❋　❋　❋

Even though I'd never been in a wedding party before, I always thought I had a rough idea of how things worked. But not with Rain. She had so many amendments to the usual wedding procedures that all of us were confused at one point or another. "All you have to do is read the memo," Rain would say whenever someone would ask a question. After a while we used her stock response for any wedding-related matter because we'd heard her say it so much over the past six months.

"What's left to buy on Rain and Nate's wedding registry?"

"All you have to do is read the memo."

"Is there going to be a deejay or a live band at the reception?"

"All you have to do is read the memo."

"What are the names of Rain's parents again?"

"All you have to do is read the memo."

Okay, so it was probably a little funnier to us than it is to you. But this whole crazy experience has seriously made me consider what kind of wedding I want to have. Unlike a lot of girls who envisioned their dream weddings while playing with their Barbie dolls, I never really gave it much thought. I was more concerned about meeting the right guy and figured the rest would all fall neatly into place.

But now that I've been engaged for nearly twenty-four hours, questions about our big day have already been coming in at record speed.

"Have you set the date yet?"

"Will you be having a big or a small wedding?"

"Who are you going to get to do the flowers? I know someone who can help you get a discount."

"Where do you think you'll get your dress? David's Bridal is having a huge sale."

Whew—I can't imagine what'll happen once we've been engaged for a full week. But in the meantime, Gavin and I are trying to keep our ideas to ourselves. But we do have them. About ten of them, to be exact. One is to get married in the church I attend in downtown Minneapolis. Two is to get married in Gavin's dad's church in Dallas. Three is to get married on a beach in Aruba, and four is to elope to Paris. Five involves a flight to London. And so on. Once we got started, imagining creative ways to formalize our commitment was fun—really fun.

Oh, yes, Rain's wedding. "River of Dreams" had just started playing, and Rain was walking down the aisle. Surprising everyone, she wasn't wearing her normal Rain-like attire. Instead of wide-leg jeans, a smock top, and pigtails, she looked absolutely stunning in a white, off-the-shoulder gown that was cinched at the waist and full and flowing in the back. Her dirty blonde hair was pinned up in a modern updo, and she was wearing a vintage silk veil and simple pearl earrings. At closer glance, I saw she was actually wearing makeup too. Her cheeks had a slight flush, her eyes were defined with a soft gray liner, and her skin was just glowing. Who knew that Stinky Nate could make a girl so happy?

After we sang "Holy, Holy, Holy" and "Amazing Grace," the pastor made a few remarks about the sanctity of marriage. Unlike the rest of us, he was dressed in very low-key attire: taupe linen pants, a white button-up shirt (no tie), and Birkenstocks, which would normally fit well with Rain and Nate's vibe. But today they looked so elegant that one would think he'd shown up at the wrong service.

But as the dressed-down pastor read the familiar passage from 1 Corinthians 13 — about what love is and what it's not — even Rain, who I've never seen shed a tear before, was visibly moved. And when she read her vows to Nate, vows she'd written herself, she was full-on crying. They were so sweet, even with some strict feminist ideals like "even though we'll be coequals in everything we do, I promise to cook for you on special occasions" and "when we decide to have children, I will select names from nature for them." You gotta love Rain.

Another funny moment came as they were pronounced husband and wife. Stinky Nate was apparently so excited by the declaration that he actually started jumping up and down. Repeatedly. I tried to see if I could make eye contact with Gavin to see his response, but unfortunately he was watching Nate too.

Before the reception started, Rain changed out of her wedding dress and opted for a pale yellow sundress that was the picture of simple elegance with its clean lines and regal embroidery adding a little color to the back. As I helped her hang up her wedding dress, she immediately noticed my engagement ring. "Sydney, do I see what I think I see on your ring finger?" she asked excitedly.

"If you think it's an engagement ring, you're right," I replied. "I didn't want to spoil your big day with my news, so I thought I'd tell you later on."

"What are you talking about spoiling my day? Sydney, that's *amazing* news!"

"I know," I nearly shrieked. Oh no, I was becoming one of *those* girls . . . the ones who freak out whenever they talk about being engaged. Oh well, I'm over it. I was much too happy not to be excited.

So I told Rain how Gavin had unexpectedly proposed, and she started crying. "Wow, I don't think I've ever seen you cry until today," I said with a laugh. "And now *twice*. What's going on?"

"I'm just so incredibly happy, Syd, and you will be too. Today was the best day of my entire life."

"That's so great to hear," I said. "Would you like me to touch up your makeup for you?"

"All you have to do is . . ." she began. And then she grinned. "Just kidding. Go ahead and touch up away, Syd."

About thirty minutes later Rain and I finally made it to the reception. The room had been magically transformed into a ballroom of *Great Gatsby* standards, continuing the unexpectedly upscale décor of the ceremony. There was a big band in one corner of the room playing classics of the thirties and forties. A selection of fine wines and cheeses were set out on every table, along with beautiful vintage glassware for the punch and champagne. The gorgeous crystal chandelier in the center of the ceiling really gave the room the feel of old Hollywood.

"May I have this dance?" Gavin asked as he snuck up behind me and gave me a hug.

"Why, certainly," I said as he twirled me around and then dipped me dramatically.

"Can you believe this is going to be us someday very soon, dancing at our wedding?" he asked.

"I actually can," I said with a grin. "I just wish it could be tonight."

"Well, who says it can't be?" Gavin asked. "There's a pastor here already. All we'd need is a marriage license. Unless you had something a little more glamorous in mind."

"What are you suggesting, Mr. Williams?" I asked.

"I think you know exactly what I'm suggesting, Miss Alexander," he said. "I'm thinking maybe number four could work really well if you're up for a covert operation."

"Excellent thinking," I said. "In that case, we'd better say good-bye to Rain and Nate, don't you think?"

As the band finished playing the Sinatra favorite "I Get a Kick Out of You," Gavin and I walked over to the happy couple and congratulated them on their marriage.

"Wait a minute, aren't you going to stay around and watch me toss my bouquet?" Rain asked.

"Oh, I'm already getting married," I said with a wink. "Best to let someone single catch it."

"Yeah, you're probably right," Rain said. "I promise to call you when we get back from our honeymoon."

"*Au revoir*," I said as I grabbed Gavin's left hand, kissed him on the cheek, and daydreamed about our exciting journey ahead (passport required).

etc.

bonus content includes:

▶ Reader's Guide

▶ Sydney's Recommendations for Life's Little
  Circumstances

▶ Sydney's Itinerary for the Best Girlfriend
  Weekend Ever — in Minneapolis

▶ About the Author

READER'S GUIDE

1. Given her lackluster track record, why do you think Sydney keeps on dating? If you were Sydney, would you be inclined to give up?

2. What do you think about Sam's theory about birth order and relationships? Do you think there's validity to it, or is it nothing more than psychobabble?

3. It's often been said that in love relationships, opposites attract — and the same goes for friendships. Despite the obvious differences between Sydney and Rain, why do you think Sydney allows Rain to set her up with Justin?

4. It's evident early on that Eli wants to date Samantha. From the list he's made, what do you think is his most compelling reason for not doing so?

5. Have you ever made a list of places you absolutely, positively must visit before you die? If so, what destination is on the top of the list? Why?

6. Do you think Sydney's decision to move to Minneapolis in hopes of seeing Liam again was crazy or romantic? Would you have done the same?

7. When you discover that Liam is engaged to Anneka, are you panicked or relieved for Sydney?

8. If you were Samantha, at what point would you have decided that Aidan wasn't right for you? Was his Ferrari/Honda comparison really the clincher in your opinion?

9. Even though they seem to have a nice time together, why do you think Sydney shuts down Gareth's advances so quickly in London?

10. When Liam invites Sydney to go to LA with him, it seems like he wants to commit by letting her be a part of his major business decisions. But when it's all said and done, he still chooses potential success over a long-term relationship with her. Why do you think it's so difficult for him to stand by Sydney when she'd do anything for him?

11. How do you feel when Justin eventually chooses to be with Kristin rather than Sydney? Do they seem like a good match? Why or why not?

12. Based on his obvious respect for Kristin and her beliefs, do you think Justin will eventually convert to Christianity? Why or why not?

13. When Sydney is offered the job in New York, she turns it down pretty quickly. Would you have accepted it? How about the position in Nashville? Why do you think Sydney declines these great opportunities?

14. At Rain's wedding, Sydney and Gavin leave abruptly. Where do you think they're going?

etc.

SYDNEY'S
RECOMMENDATIONS
FOR LIFE'S LITTLE CIRCUMSTANCES

SYDNEY'S TOP TEN BREAKUP MOVIES

If you need a good cry, nothing beats these flicks for generating the waterworks!

1. *The Notebook* (2004)
2. *Four Weddings and a Funeral* (1994)
3. *Love Actually* (2003)
4. *Eternal Sunshine of the Spotless Mind* (2004)
5. *An Affair to Remember* (1957)
6. *My Best Friend's Wedding* (1997)
7. *Say Anything* (1989)
8. *As Good As It Gets* (1997)
9. *Sleepless in Seattle* (1993)
10. *The Holiday* (2006)

SYDNEY'S TOP FIVE BOY-FRIENDLY
ROMANTIC COMEDIES

If you find yourself at Blockbuster with a guy you kind of like, rent one of these!

1. *Two Weeks Notice* (2002)
2. *How to Lose a Guy in 10 Days* (2003)
3. *Keeping the Faith* (2000)
4. *Notting Hill* (1999)
5. *Jerry Maguire* (1996)

SYDNEY'S ITINERARY FOR
THE BEST GIRLFRIEND WEEKEND EVER—
IN MINNEAPOLIS

Grab a gaggle of girlfriends and head to the Twin Cities for an inexpensive getaway. (Okay, it depends on how much you spend at the mall!)

FRIDAY

6:00 p.m.—Fly into the Minneapolis/St. Paul International airport.

7:00—Celebrate the sweet deal you got on a posh hotel room in downtown Minneapolis by jumping on the bed. If that seems too childish, a simple but convincing "woo-hoo" at the top of your lungs will do.

7:05—As soon as you've given the room a proper once-over, peruse your wardrobe options. If nothing strikes your fancy, borrow something stylish from one of your friends. (After all, what are friends for?)

7:30—Now that you're looking gorgeous, grab some appetizers and drinks at one of the nearby pubs. If you're feeling like something a bit fancier, take a taxi to Block E, where everything's available: Tex-Mex, Thai, Italian, you name it.

8:40 — Hope you wore comfortable shoes because it's time to get your groove on at any of Minneapolis's way cool dance clubs.

10:00 — Okay, your feet are probably hurting — especially if you're debuting your new stilettos. So rest for a few (fifteen minutes tops) because the best shows are just getting started at First Avenue.

11:30 — Properly exhausted, head back to the hotel to veg and discuss all the cute guys you spotted earlier.

SATURDAY

10:00 a.m. — Good morning, sunshine! Hope you enjoyed sleeping in because you've got a big day ahead.

11:00 — Now that you've showered and gotten ready (make sure you're wearing comfy shoes), grab a bagel at Bruegger's before heading to the Aveda Institute for some major pampering!

11:30 — Mani-pedi.

12:30 — Hot stone massage.

1:00 — Pay up and hail a taxi. Destination: Mall of America.

1:30 — Gasp at the sheer hugeness of this mall!

1:31 — Head to Urban Outfitters to check out the cute accessories.

1:45 — Starbucks break. (Can you make it this long before a coffee buzz?)

1:55 — Begin shopping till you drop!

3:30 — Starving. Must have sustenance.

4:30 — Check out makeup at Sephora!

5:00 — Resume shopping.

7:00 — As a tribute to your youth, ride The Mighty Axe at The Park at MOA.

7:15 — Leave the mall, walk across the street to IKEA, and browse away.

8:00 — Hail a cab and head back to the hotel.

8:20 — After showing each other all the things you picked up today (preferably on sale!), change into your cute pj's.

8:40 — Order room service (a decadent dessert to share, perhaps?).

8:45 — Hop online and see what church services are available downtown.

8:46 — Give your feet a rest after all the walking you did today. See what's on HBO and relax (guilt-free) for the rest of the night.

SUNDAY

8:30 a.m. — Pick up the *Star Tribune* to see what's playing at the Guthrie Theater later in the afternoon. Read while you have an omelet and coffee at Keys Café.

9:40 — Walk down to Nicollet Mall and check out the Mary Tyler Moore statue. Peek in all the store windows.

11:00 — Check out a church service at any of the great downtown Minneapolis churches.

1:00 — See some great off-Broadway entertainment at the Guthrie — preferably a musical!

3:00 — Now that you've recovered from breakfast, grab

something quick to eat before you rush back to the hotel to pack and check out.

4:00 — Hail a cab for the airport and head back home after a fab weekend of fun!

ABOUT THE AUTHOR

CHRISTA ANN BANISTER has worked as a respected music critic and freelance writer for various Christian publications, including *CCM Magazine*, Crosswalk.com, *Christian Single*, and ChristianityToday.com, not to mention kick-starting the inaugural Christian music blog for MTV's Urge.com. While *Around the World in 80 Dates* isn't strictly autobiographical, many of the situations were unfortunately inspired by actual events. Christa lives in St. Paul, Minnesota, with her husband, Will. They love to play Scrabble and throw darts on a map and dream about someday going wherever the darts land. And until her book hits the *New York Times* best seller list, Christa is happily employed as a freelance writer for her many, many clients.

CHECK OUT THESE OTHER GREAT TITLES FROM THE NAVPRESS FICTION LINE!

The Reluctant Journey of David Connors

Don Locke
978-1-60006-152-3
1-60006-152-4

Family man David Connors is standing on the brink of suicide. In his darkest moment, he finds an old and mysterious carpetbag buried under a snowy ledge. Soon, what seems like coincidence draws him closer to understanding and healing. As David reaches his journey's conclusion, he gains freedom from a devastating childhood event.

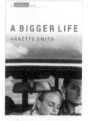

A Bigger Life

Annette Smith
978-1-57683-995-9
1-57683-995-8

Joel Carpenter's life was never supposed to turn out this way. After making a careless choice that permanently shattered his marriage, he now finds himself estranged from his ex-wife, Kari, and sharing custody of their son. And just when Joel thinks the worst is behind him, Kari receives tragic news that threatens to forever alter their lives.

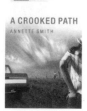

A Crooked Path

Annette Smith
978-1-57683-996-6
1-57683-996-6

Manny Ortega works on an Eden Plain cattle ranch for cranky, prejudiced Owen Green. Over time Owen and Manny forge a close friendship, but the arrival of Owen's daughter, Chaney, strains their relationship as she and Manny fall in love. Owen's deeply hidden issues involving race and class are revealed, while a tragic accident threatens to shatter any hope of reconciliation.

To order copies, visit your local Christian bookstore,
call NavPress at 1-800-366-7788, or log on to www.navpress.com.

To locate a Christian bookstore near you, call 1-800-991-7747.